Macdougal Alley

Macdougal Alley

A NOVEL BY
TATHEENA ROBERTS

alyson books
los angeles | new york

MANUFACTURED IN THE UNITED STATES OF AMERICA.

THIS TRADE PAPERBACK ORIGINAL IS PUBLISHED BY ALYSON PUBLICATIONS,
P.O. BOX 4371, LOS ANGELES, CA 90078-4371.
DISTRIBUTION IN THE UNITED KINGDOM BY
TURNAROUND PUBLISHER SERVICES LTD.,
UNIT 3, OLYMPIA TRADING ESTATE, COBURG ROAD, WOOD GREEN,
LONDON N22 6TZ ENGLAND.

FIRST EDITION: FEBRUARY 2001

01 02 03 04 05 ⬛ 10 9 8 7 6 5 4 3 2 1

ISBN: 1-55583-540-6

LIBRARY OF CONGRESS CATALOGING-IN-PUBLICATION DATA
   ROBERTS, TATHEENA.
     MACDOUGAL ALLEY : A NOVEL / BY TATHEENA ROBERTS.—1ST ED.
     ISBN 1-55583-540-6
     1. GREENWICH VILLAGE (NEW YORK, N.Y.)—FICTION. I. TITLE.
   PS3568.O24745 M38 2001
   813'.6—DC21   00-045399

CREDITS
COVER PHOTOGRAPHY BY PHOTODISC INC.
COVER DESIGN BY B. ZINDA.

FOR MY GRANDDAUGHTERS,
KRISTEN AND MARY

1

July's sun made Mina's head throb, and the pain in her stomach grew unbearable as she stood with her Aunt Wilhelmina and the other mourners at her mother's graveside. As the sun sweltered, Father O'Bryan droned on, his brogue thickening. His white surplice was caught for a moment by a gust of sultry air as he solemnly shook holy water over the casket.

When Mina crossed herself, the starched collar of her blouse chafed the back of her neck. She felt a warm wetness run down the inside of her right thigh. Now she was sure she was going to be sick. With a terrible swiftness the gravestones and the people started to whirl around her. As the first shovelful of dirt hit the lid of the wooden coffin, she looked frantically for a way to escape, but the next moment someone pushed a shovel into her hands. She tried to fight back the terror as she realized what was expected of her.

Gripping the rough handle, she lurched toward the open grave, but her knees gave way, and in a half-faint she melted to the ground. Just as she thought she would disappear completely, hands reached for her and the shovel fell into the pit, hitting the lid of the coffin with a hollow sound. Then someone was pulling her back from the darkness—darkness that rushed at her from the gaping hole.

Aunt Wilhelmina Frome gathered Mina against her ample body and whispered endearments in German. Her

1

dark eyes behind her veil were full of loathing as she glared at her dry-eyed brother-in-law, Gustave Arenholt, standing across the open grave, shoulder to shoulder with Father O'Bryan. He had neither acknowledged Mina's distress nor made any effort to come to her aid. One more incident that reinforced her dislike for her dead sister's husband, and further proof that the man cared little for his stepdaughter, Mina Arenholt.

Returning from the Holy Cross Cemetery in a limousine, Mina kneaded a soggy handkerchief with stubby, nail-bitten fingers, trying to hold back her tears. Her straight red hair, parted down the middle, lay in two limp braids against the starched white collar of her midi blouse. A leggy 13-year-old, her freckled face was pale and expressionless now. She slumped gratefully against her aunt, her head rocking gently on the old woman's shoulder with the motion of the car as they headed homeward toward Jackson Heights. Her abdominal pains easing, she felt sleepy and safe with Aunt Willie's arm around her.

Gustave, stony-faced and silent, sat staring at the passing parade of storefronts along Roosevelt Avenue. His coarse features gave no clue as to what was turning in his mind after witnessing his wife's cancer-ravaged body lowered into its final resting place.

Late afternoon traffic was heavy. The elevated trains roared and shook the pavement as they passed overhead. Breaking the uncomfortable silence in the car, Wilhelmina threw back her dark veil and turned to the silent man beside her.

"I brought my things, Gus." She motioned to the black overnight case at her feet. "I'll be staying a few days." Her voice was sharp. "I'll put Gretchen's clothes in order and see that they are disposed of as she would wish. The studio gave me a week off, so I can stay until Sunday. If you and Mina need me longer, I'm sure I can get a few more days."

Nodding briefly, Gus continued to stare out the window.

Mina meant the world to Wilhelmina, widowed and childless. She had hoped Mina would come to live with her in Astoria, but that was before Gretchen had made her daughter promise to keep house for Gus after she was gone. Wilhelmina felt uneasy about the child taking on such responsibility. She remembered her sister's words from a few days before: "Gus has been the only father you've ever known, Mina. Be good to him and see to his needs when I'm gone. Remember, I'm counting on you. Promise you'll do as I ask."

Wilhelmina remembered the look of despair she'd seen on Mina's face. "I will, Mama, I promise, but don't go, Mama. Please don't die." Tears streamed down the girl's cheeks, and sobs shook her as she buried her head against the frail body on the bed.

It was wrong for Gretchen to demand so much from one so young, Wilhelmina thought, but in the last few years Gretchen had been blind to the fact there was no love between her husband and Mina. Lately she had seen fear in Mina's eyes when Gus was near her, and that look haunted her. She decided she must keep a watchful eye on the situation, promising herself at the right opportunity she would have a heart-to-heart talk with her niece. She had to find out why Mina was so afraid of Gus.

When they got back to the house, Mina dashed upstairs without a word. Wilhelmina heard the bathroom door slam as she put her things away in the spare room at the end of the hall. Below, Gus went straight to the kitchen for a bottle of beer. The screen door banged behind him as he stepped onto the back porch.

The house had been closed up all day and was unbearably stuffy. The air in the guest room smelled especially stale. Wilhelmina struggled with the window. Finally, she persuaded the reluctant sash, and the late afternoon breeze rushed into the hot little room.

Her window faced its counterpart next door; all the houses on the street were identical except for color. From 86th to 89th, the pristine replication reached all the way to Northern Boulevard. Built in the early '20s, they offered a modicum of affluence to middle-class working people. Each stoop had the same number of steps descending abruptly to the sidewalk. Wilhelmina wondered if the owners ever became confused on foggy nights as to which house was theirs. She preferred her apartment building in Astoria with its ancient elevator and the ever-present cooking aromas in the halls. It was safe and comfortable to have neighbors just a wall away, friendly people to share gossip with in the vestibule on cold winter mornings.

She sat down heavily on the edge of the painted iron bed and took out the pins that held her veil. Removing her hat, she let it fall in her lap. Her head ached. Perhaps she could find a bottle of aspirin in the bathroom. Easing her swollen feet out of black pumps, she let her toes absorb the coolness of the bare floor. She got up wearily and padded down the hall in her stocking feet.

The bathroom door was closed. She knocked, but there was no answer. She tried the handle. The door was locked. "Are you in there, Mina?" No answer.

Gus was downstairs, so she was sure he wasn't in there.

She called once more, then put her ear to the door, but heard nothing.

"I know you're in there, Mina. Please answer. If you're not feeling well, maybe I can help. Come now, *Liebchen*, open the door. That's a good girl."

After a few seconds the lock clicked and the door opened. Mina leaned against the door frame. Her eyes were puffy and red.

On the way back from the cemetery, Wilhelmina had thought Mina was feeling better. Perhaps she had been letting her grief have its way with her in the privacy of the bathroom. Still, she couldn't be sure.

"Oh, Aunt Willie, I think I'm dying," she sobbed. "I must have cancer like Mama!"

"Now, now, what's this about cancer and dying, *Liebchen*? A young person like you has a long life to live before she has to worry about dying. Come, let's put some cold water on those red eyes of yours, then you can tell me all about it."

Wilhelmina took a towel from the rack and went to the wash stand. What she saw answered all her questions. In the basin were Mina's underpants soiled with dark red stains. A faint smile quivered at the corners of the older woman's mouth as she gathered her niece in her arms. In a soft voice she murmured, "Dear one, you are most certainly not going to die, not for a very long time." She held Mina close and whispered, "But I'm certain of one thing. From this day on you will be a woman, not a little girl anymore." Lord, she thought, hadn't Gretchen talked to the child about getting her period? "It's all right, you're just fine. Now stop crying. It's perfectly natural. You aren't sick, Mina. Didn't Mama talk to you about menstruation?"

"Oh, no, is that what it is?" She pulled away from her aunt's embrace. "No, Mama never..." she hesitated. The tears were gone, and her eyes brightened. "But Katy did. Katy's sister Maureen got it last year just before confirmation. Katy told me about how Maureen wasn't allowed to take a bath for a whole week!" She was breathless with excitement. "Katy doesn't have it yet. Oh, I can't wait to tell her. She'll be positively livid with envy that I got it first." Mina's eyes sparkled at the prospect of sharing the news with her best friend. Then her exuberance evaporated as quickly as it had appeared. "But Aunt Willie, I didn't think it would happen like this, the pain and the mess and everything."

"This is just the way it happens, Mina," Wilhelmina smiled. "Now, just dash some cold water on those eyes and leave your panties in the basin to soak. We'll look around in Mama's things. There must be a box of Kotex tucked away somewhere." She opened the medicine cabinet and found a bottle of aspirin, then sighed with relief. Thank Mary and Joseph for small miracles! Two of these and a short nap before she had to fix supper was just what she needed. Holy Mother, it had been a long, sad day, but certainly one to be remembered.

2

MINA ARENHOLT

When Aunt Willie returned to Astoria, life settled into a regular routine. Gus usually got home from the bakery at about quarter of 6, giving him time to open a beer, light up a cigar, and get comfortable in his Morris chair before *Amos 'n' Andy* came on. After the second beer, Lowell Thomas and the news drifted through a cloud of blue smoke, and I tried to get things on the table by the time he signed off with, "So long until tomorrow."

We sat at the oak table, Gus in his regular place, his back to the kitchen door. I sat in Mama's chair, which he said was only fitting because I was the woman of the house now. I didn't like the way he said that. It made me feel full of shame. Gus never really talked to me except to ask how school was going. I knew he didn't care all that much, but I guess he felt he had to say something. So I usually answered "fine" and let it go at that. Mostly we ate our meals in silence unless he'd had a bad day at the bakery.

Then he'd blow off steam with something like, "That goddamn nigger let the goddamn oven get too hot again, and the *vorterbrod* burned all to hell! Had to throw out four dozen loaves and make new batter. What a waste! I should fire the black son of a bitch."

Of course, he never did fire Lionel because he knew he'd never find another helper who would put up with his bad temper.

It was always the same, though; the two of us had nothing much to say to each other. I just listened to him over the sauerbraten and watched the veins in his neck bulge. Then I cleared the table, and after the dishes were done I went to my room to do homework while Gus opened his third beer and settled in his chair with the *Post*.

Alone in my room, I missed Mama something terrible. She had been confined to her bed most of last year, and I had to help her to the bathroom those last few months before she went to the hospital. I never stayed after school or went to Katy's because Mama needed me. I fixed breakfast for her every morning before I went to school. She couldn't make it downstairs, so I would make her a sandwich and leave it on her bedside table with a thermos of milk.

After school I fixed her bed, gave her a sponge bath, and changed her nightie before I brought supper up to her. At the very last she was too weak to talk much, but I knew how grateful she was and how frightened she was of dying. During that time there was so much love in her eyes. I knew it was for me, and I wanted to tell her not to be afraid, but I couldn't find the right words.

I never told her about Gus.

And I'm sure she never heard him sneak down the hall to my room at night. Her sleeping pill kept her unaware of anything till morning.

When I think about it now, there are times I'm almost happy she's dead. Maybe it's a mortal sin to think that way, but I know Mama's loving me in heaven. If she were here, she'd find out for sure about Gus...and never love me again.

It started shortly after Mama was confined to her room for good. One night I was dreaming I was Eleanor Powell dancing in top hat and long black stockings, tapping away with cameras rolling and music all around. Suddenly the lights and music vanished, but I still heard the tapping. I realized neither I nor the sound was in the dream anymore. The tapping was coming from the other side of my bedroom door. Something was wrong. *Maybe Mama's worse*, I thought, my heart pounding.

"What is it?" My voice shook. Suddenly I felt afraid and small. There was no answer.

The knob turned and with barely a sound the door opened. A dim figure slipped into the room. The door closed without a sound. I could hear the beating of my heart and held my breath.

It was him. He stood motionless, his back to the door. I saw the outline of his white nightshirt in the blackness of the room. He didn't speak. I heard his breathing, and for what seemed a very long time he didn't move; neither did I. My body was frozen, but I managed to stammer, "Is Mama all right? Does she need me?"

His bare feet made no sound as he moved toward the bed. "Shush! Don't talk." He sat on the edge of my bed, the springs groaning under his weight. His body smelled sour, and his stale beer breath was hot in my face. "Just be quiet." His hands fumbled with the blanket. Then, with a terrible swiftness, he pulled the covers back and heaved his body against me.

"No!" I screamed.

"Shut up, Mina," his voice rasped close to my ear. Then the bed began to shake as he struggled with his nightshirt. Swearing under his breath, he pulled it over his head and flung it across the room. It made a muffled thud as it hit the dresser.

Pulling my knees tight to my chest, I rolled to the other side of the bed, desperately trying to make myself small. Facing the dark wall, I was trapped. His naked body came at me, all sweaty.

"Just relax, goddamn it. You'll like it." The stubble on his jaw scraped my neck, and spit from his mouth oozed over my cheek. He gripped my shoulders, and his fingers dug into my flesh.

Wincing, I buried my head deep into my pillow, but he pulled at my nightgown, twisting and bunching it around my waist.

"No, don't!" The pillow stifled my cry. He pushed something warm and hard between my buttocks. I tried with all my might to squirm away. I had to be free of that awful thing, but the more I struggled the tighter he held me and the harder he pushed.

"Goddamn it, lie still!"

"No! Let me go." I found my voice at last as I realized what was between my legs. "Stop. Don't!" I screamed at the top of my lungs.

"Be quiet, you little bitch."

My sobs choked me, and my body was shaking out of control. One of his arms was across my stomach, pressing me hard against his undulating hips. His other hand grabbed my breast. It hurt so much that I thought I was going to faint. One after another, rasping spasms exploded from his lungs as his jerking grew more violent.

A strange feeling came over me. This wasn't happening to me, but to someone else. I'd wake up in the morning safe in my bed, fix breakfast for Mama, and go to school like always. I closed my eyes tight and told myself that when I opened them it would be morning, and I'd be back in my bed, waking from a terrible dream. To see if it worked, I opened my eyes. Gus still had me pinned down. This was real. I was trapped, I was losing myself. He was making me into someone I would despise forever. I couldn't escape, and I knew with dreadful certainty I would never be free of him.

"Oh, you bitch, you bitch," he gasped, and with each thrust I felt that awful thing rubbing between my legs. His hips pushed faster, harder and harder against me. He was biting my ear, and just when I was sure he would rip it from my head, his whole body convulsed. An animal sound burst from him, and his grip relaxed. His body went limp as he fell across me. His breathing came hard, like a winded runner.

Realizing this was my chance, I leaped from the bed, landing hard on the floor. Tripping over my long nightgown, I made a dash for the door, and ran stumbling down the dark hall. When I reached the safety of the bathroom, I slumped to the tile floor, my back against the door. I listened for sounds from the hall, but the house was quiet. All I heard was the sound of my own heart.

Curled on the floor, I felt a cold wetness in my lap. My nightie lay sticky and heavy against my thighs. I looked down at myself and what I saw made me retch. Making it to the toilet just in time, I fell on my knees, and with my arms hugging the bowl, vomited until there was nothing left to throw up. When my heaves stopped, I didn't dare go back to my room, so I spent the rest of the night lying on the bath mat next to the tub. Shivering, I covered myself with Mama's old yellow chenille robe that hung on the door. I had no hope of sleep. I just lay there waiting for the window over the sink to show light while thoughts churned in my head.

The worst of those thoughts was that I was responsible for what Gus had done to me. He'd never acted like a real father, but still there had never been any truly bad feelings between us. He'd say, "Do what your mama says. She knows best." He always left things concerning me pretty much up to her.

A long time ago Mama told me about my real father who had been a brakeman on the Long Island railroad. He got crushed between two cars in an accident in Bayside one stormy winter night. Mama married Gus a year later, and he gave me his name. Mama never said anything to me about her not being married to my father, but I overheard her talking to Aunt Willie about it on several occasions.

Aunt Willie hadn't approved of him from the start. She has very strong opinions, and Mama's marriage to Gus was a source of many bitter arguments between them. Aunt Willie hated Gus and made no bones about how she felt: "*Ach*, that baker from Roosevelt Avenue!" Her German accent grew pronounced, almost guttural, when she got angry, and she was always angry when she spoke about Gus.

Why did he come to my room like that? Why did he do that awful thing to me? The questions whirled. Did it have something to do with Mama being sick for so long? He had been irritable and angry a lot lately, especially over the doctor bills that were piling up. Sometimes he said things that sounded like he blamed her for being sick all the time, like she was being that way just to spite him.

I didn't see Gus the next morning, and I was glad because I was sure I'd never be able to face him again. He left for work before I was dressed. When I got down to the kitchen to fix Mama's breakfast, I noticed he hadn't eaten anything. He usually had coffee and *wienerbrod* before he left the house to walk the four blocks to Northern Boulevard. There was no dirty cup or plate in the sink.

I remember how awful I felt when I took Mama's tray to her that morning. I couldn't bring my eyes to meet hers for fear I'd burst into tears. Then she would want to know what was the matter with me. As I fluffed her pillow and fussed with her bedclothes I made a solemn vow never to let her know what had happened.

Every day the guilty feelings grew. Each time she looked at me I was sure she saw the dirtiness inside me.

But now, with Aunt Willie back home in Astoria, there was just Gus and me in the house, and it was worse than I could have imagined. While she was here he mostly left me alone, except for one time when I was cleaning up after supper.

Aunt Willie had gone upstairs and I was scraping a plate over the garbage pail with one foot on the treadle that flips the lid open. He came behind me, reached over and put his hand down the front of my dress. The lid of the pail banged shut as I spun around to face him. "Don't do that, Gus. Stay away from me," I hissed, afraid Aunt Willie might hear and come rushing downstairs.

"What's the matter, little lady? All of a sudden you're too good for your old man? Come on, she can't hear anything. It's been a long time. Be a good girl now." He grabbed at my waist and tried to put his arms around me. I pushed him away real hard.

"Keep away from me, Gus."

"OK, Mina, you win. I'll wait till the old woman's gone," he said with a wink. "Don't worry, our secret is safe." His eyes were hard as he laughed softly. Turning, he disappeared through the swinging door to the dining room.

As I stood by the sink, hot tears flooded my eyes. I let them roll down my cheeks and into the dirty dishwater.

3

1938—THE EXTORTION

Kathleen Frances Conklin ducked her head behind the book she had propped on her desk. Behind *Algebra II* she carefully unfolded Mina's note. In familiar, precise penmanship it said: *Meet me after school. I'll wait for you on the steps. M.* She folded the note into a small square and tucked it in the back of her book, safe from Sister Bernadette's penetrating blue eyes.

Sister paced the aisles between the desks, her black habit whispering softly about her ankles. Study hall was quiet, save for an occasional cough and the faint squeak of Sister's high-laced shoes. The regulator clock on the wall above the oak-framed litho of the Sacred Heart clunked the minutes away. That picture always had a strange effect on Katy. The flaming heart, exposed in an open hole in Jesus' chest, sent a shudder through her. That particular feeling, her mother once told her, was caused by someone walking over your grave.

After turning in her seat and catching Mina's eye, Katy resumed her halfhearted attack on her algebra assignment. Finally, the 3 o'clock bell rang, and the room exploded with the sounds of 30 young girls rushing to their lockers.

Mina was waiting on the front steps of the turn-of-the-century brick building that housed the girls' classes at Sacred Heart Academy. Her eyes danced with excitement as she greeted her friend. "Katy, wait till you hear what I'm going to do. You'll never believe it, not in a million years!"

They fell into step and walked toward 89th Street. The air was damp and cold. The late afternoon sun glazed the bay windows of the row houses, but did little to warm the wind gusting out of the west. Katy blew on her fingers; she had forgotten her gloves. "Come on, Mina, don't be so mysterious. Tell me what it is you think I won't believe."

Shifting her books, Mina linked her free arm with Katy's. "It's a dream come true. I never thought it would happen. Mama always wanted me to, but Gus said he had better ways to spend his money. Anyway, the other night I asked him again, and this time he said I could."

"You could what? Mina, get to the point, for heaven's sake. The suspense is killing me."

"Gus said he'd pay for my ballet lessons. Can you believe it? I start next Tuesday afternoon. I enrolled yesterday. That's why I couldn't walk home with you. I went straight up to Northern Boulevard and filled out my application at the Hill House Dance Studio. It's only one class a week to start with, but if I get good enough, I know I can talk him into letting me take it twice a week." Mina was breathless, her usually pale cheeks flushed pink.

"Wow! How did you do it? That sure doesn't sound like your stepfather. You're always telling me what a skinflint he is."

"Well…" Mina paused, trying to pick the right words, "he's a lot more reasonable lately. That's how come I asked him again, and this time it worked. He said yes." Never would she be able to tell Katy what really changed her stepfather's mind.

It had been so easy, and she wondered why she hadn't thought of it before. She wasn't sure how she'd gathered the courage, but the desire had been so strong for such a long time. Perhaps that had fed her boldness at the dinner table two nights ago. She remembered how strong and grown-up she felt facing him across the table. "If you won't let me have lessons, I'll tell Aunt Willie everything. Then what will you do?"

He was just about to take a swallow of his beer when the words struck him. For an awful moment she thought he was going to hurl the glass at her. His face turned red and the veins bulged on either side of his neck.

"You what? You wouldn't dare. What do you suppose she would think of her precious niece?" He laughed, and his lips curled back to show the gold fillings in his teeth. "Oh, no, little lady, I don't think you'd risk it, because she'd see you for the little whore you are."

Hardly recognizing her own voice, she screamed back, "I don't care. I'll tell her if you won't let me take lessons." Up went her chin, and her eyes never wavered.

His chair almost fell backward as he leapt to his feet. He stood for a moment, breathing hard. Then, like air leaking from a pricked balloon, the fury suddenly went out of him. "OK." His shoulders sagged. "You can have the goddamn lessons." He threw his napkin down and stomped out of the room. His footsteps scraped on the stairs, and after a few seconds his bedroom door banged shut, reverberating loudly through the house.

He didn't bother her that night, and the next morning he left for the bakery before she came down for breakfast. On the table she found two crisp $10 bills propped against the sugar bowl. That night, after a wordless dinner, he finally spoke. "Was $20 enough to start your lessons?" His voice was the closest to caring she could remember.

As Mina spoke to Katy, her words grew dreamy. "Mama used to tell me about Anna Pavlova. She saw her dance at the Hippodrome in Boston a long time ago. Mama always wanted to be a dancer, but her parents wouldn't hear of it. They told her it was just a foolish dream; she'd get over it, and besides, they couldn't afford such luxuries.

"They never let her have her dream. I don't think she ever got over the disappointment, because she kept a scrapbook of clippings from papers and magazines. They were all pictures and articles about famous dancers."

"How sad," Katy sighed. "Maybe someday you can fulfill her dream for her."

"Mama's favorite was Pavlova," Mina went on. "I remember one picture of her in a slim yellow gown. She was wearing a large-brimmed bonnet of the same color, and she was holding the hem of her skirt in her outstretched hand. Her head was tilted back and her eyes were very dark. Under the picture it said: IN HER FAREWELL PERFORMANCE PAVLOVA DANCES THE GAVOTTE FOR HER ADORING PUBLIC. That was Mama's favorite picture. I remember tears filled her eyes when she showed it to me.

"Katy, maybe I'll be famous like that someday. This is my chance. I'm not going to let anything spoil it. I've dreamed of being a ballerina ever since Mama took you and me to Radio City Music Hall on my tenth birthday. Remember? They danced *Swan Lake* and the corps de ballet were all in white with little feathered caps on their heads.

"It was so beautiful! I knew then I wanted to be just like that. I hope it's not too late. I should have started years ago."

Many times Katy had heard her friend talk of her ambition, but never with such passion. Caught by Mina's enthusiasm, she hugged her. "You will be a dancer. I know you will. I think it's just wonderful. And it's never too late to catch your dream."

As the girls reached 86th Street, the sun slipped behind the canyons of Manhattan and became lost in a violet haze.

"You're really lucky to be taking lessons. Maybe your stepfather isn't as much of a tightwad as you thought." Katy squeezed Mina's hand. "It's getting dark, and I'm freezing. Can you stay over Saturday night? Ask your stepfather while he's still in a good mood. See you first period tomorrow. Bye." With a quick wave she dashed across the street.

Mina stood for a moment watching Katy grow smaller as she hurried toward The Tower Apartments on 82nd Street. In a rush, the all-too-familiar feeling of loneliness overwhelmed her. It seemed to start somewhere between her chest and stomach, like the dull pain of an aching tooth, and it always settled in the place where her heart should be. Her feet felt like blocks of stone as she started the walk home.

4

1937—CROWN HEIGHTS, BROOKLYN

"How is it by you, Chana Dubovitch? You have a list from your Mama? I should fill the order, *nu?*" Moishe Goldstein's eyebrows, two bushy crescents, rose over horn-rimmed glasses. A broad smile sketched fine lines at the corners of his blue eyes. Pushing his black felt hat to the back of his head, he leaned over the counter and beamed at the pale girl with the empty string bag.

"*Shalom*, Mr. Goldstein. Here's Mama's list," she answered in a small voice. He held the slip of paper close to his nose for a moment as he adjusted his glasses. "Mama says for you to be sure the cans of Season sardines are stamped with a "U." Last week I bought some for her at Rosen's and she made me take them back because there was no mark. She was very angry." Chana's voice was breathless. "Please be sure the milk is Pasedick, and Mama wants the big package of noodles and the large jars of Rakeach gefilte fish." Her fist crushed the new $5 bill her mother had put in the pocket of her navy-blue sweater.

Paying no heed to Chana's discomfort, he turned away from the counter, all the while clucking his tongue. "That Rosen, you should not do business in such a store. If you want kosher, do business by me; I keep a strict *yiddishikiet* establishment. Never you mind Rosen with his *goyishe* brands."

Moishe's red beard was still quivering with indignation

as he returned with the milk and gefilte fish. Licking the stub of a pencil retrieved from behind his ear, he proceeded to add up the bill. "That comes to $3.50. Anyone can tell your Mama's no *shiksa*. She keeps a kosher household and is particular about observing the *mitzvahs*. A good daughter can learn from such a pious woman."

Chana handed him the crumpled five, and the cash register bell rang. He offered back a $1 bill and a 50-cent piece which she dropped into her pocket. She felt more at ease now as she watched him arrange her purchases in her old market bag. A trace of a smile softened the tenseness about her mouth. "Thanks, Mr. Goldstein. Have a happy Passover."

"A joyous *Pesach* to the family of Rov Dubovitch. Go in health and return in health, Chana." A wide grin parted his beard, revealing one shiny gold tooth.

Anxious to be on her way, she lifted the heavy bag from the counter. It was already almost 5, and the bakery would be closed if she didn't hurry. The bell on the door jingled behind her. She was glad to be out of the stuffy shop. The cold air felt good on her cheeks as a light drizzle wet the sidewalk. Shifting the bag to a more comfortable position, she headed up the block toward Frankel's bakery.

Kingston Avenue was crowded with last-minute shoppers. Bearded men in dark coats and black hats filled the sidewalk. Women, kerchiefed against the dampness, hurried by, eyes cast down, their shopping bags heavy with purchases for the holidays. Schoolboys in *yarmulkes* and side curls darted in and out among the shoppers, ritual fringes flopping beneath their black jackets. The press of *Hasidim* on the avenue always made Chana feel like a stranger in a foreign land. Sometimes she was actually afraid and imagined that when they looked at her they could tell she didn't belong.

She had more than enough money for the *matzo*. It smelled a little like burnt cardboard, but the warm paper bag felt good. The air was colder now and the rain was coming down hard. She crossed the street by the subway entrance and hurried up President Street. Three long blocks to go before she'd be home. The sidewalk was deserted and rain dripped from the bare branches of the old linden trees arching over her head. Passing cars made hissing sounds, splashing water into the gutters, their headlights glaring off the slick black asphalt.

Mama would be cross because she had been gone so long. Chana suddenly realized water had seeped through the soles of her shoes. Her short, dark curls clung wet against her cheeks and the wool sweater was scratchy and cold on her neck. Hunching her shoulders, she started to run. When she reached her front stoop she was drenched and out of breath. Balancing the shopping bag with one arm, she managed to find the lock with her key. The heavy oak door banged shut behind her.

The street lamp outside shone dimly through the glass panels of the door, making the only light in the dark vestibule. A thin streak of yellow showed under the kitchen door at the far end of the hall. Chana leaned against the door for a minute to catch her breath. The faint aroma of roasted chicken reminded her she was hungry. The house was quiet. Her stepfather and Yudel would be in the library on the second floor.

Every evening, the hour before supper, Mendel Dubovitch heard his youngest son Yudel read his *Gemara*. The frail 13-year-old was gentle and of a serious nature, and Mendel made no secret of favoring the boychick over his grown sons Yakov and David. The older offspring had never exhibited the promise of becoming a Talmud *chachem*. Yudel would be that *chachem*; the scholar of scholars every father longed for.

"Is that you, Chanala?" Her grandmother's voice was warm and reassuring. The light in the kitchen was almost blinding after the darkness in the hall. Chana squinted and sniffed the delicious orders coming from the stove.

"Yes, Bubbe, I got everything Mama had on the list." The glow of the room and the small but plump figure of her grandmother made for such an exquisite feeling of security that Chana forgot for a moment how uncomfortable she was. The stove's friendly heat soothed her cold limbs and warmed her heart.

Chana's grandmother, Sarah Blumenthal, a bird of a woman in her early sixties, stood by the range, a basting spoon in her hand. She motioned Chana to put the groceries on the counter by the sink.

"Look at you, you'll catch your death wet like that! Chanala, darling, go upstairs and get out of your soggy things. We eat in half an hour. Hurry now, before you should start sneezing already."

As she sat on her bed pulling off her wet socks, she heard a knock at the door. "Chana, may I come in?" Miriam Dubovitch, dressed in a prim blue *shalley* and wearing a new blond wig, awkwardly entered the room. Her words held the slight edge of impatience that had become her habit these past months. "Did you get everything I put on the list?" Chana remembered Bubbe's explanation: "You have to understand your mother's condition, Chanala."

"Yes, Mama, I got everything you wanted." She wriggled

out of her damp skirt, letting it fall on the floor about her ankles.

"There was change, yes?" Miriam's hand fluttered wearily to her distended abdomen, a gesture she affected often of late due to her advanced pregnancy.

"Yes, Mama, there was a dollar. I left it on the kitchen counter." Chana pulled her slip over her head and tossed it on the bed.

"Well, best you hurry now. Get into dry clothes and put your wet things in the hamper. Don't leave them all over the room. Come down as soon as you can and set the table. I'll be helping Bubbe dish up. Your father and Yudel will be finishing the lesson directly, so don't dawdle."

It was now more than two years since they had moved to Crown Heights, yet every time her mother referred to her husband as "your father" Chana felt the pain of no longer living in Manhattan. A large brownstone on President Street in Brooklyn was home now. She missed the old gray building on Riverside Drive with the friendly doorman and the rattling elevator that wheezed its way to their sixth floor apartment. Gone was the big window seat in the living room where she sat watching the boats on the river while the sun sank, red and hazy, behind the Jersey side. She missed the twinkling lights on Henry Hudson Drive when night fell over the city. Never again would she smell the sweet fragrance of Papa's pipe or the faint scent of turpentine that always clung to his rough tweed jacket. The world of the *Hasid*, the world her mother embraced so lovingly as a *boalot teshewa* (a convert), was her home now.

Mendel Dubovitch had married Harry Stern's widow, and it was taken for granted by everyone in the neighborhood that her young daughter, Chana, was a convert also.

Not wanting to bring unhappiness to her mother, she said nothing and tried hard to fit in. Still, she was sure the real Chana was gone forever. She was a Dubovitch for better or worse, and there was nothing she could do about it. Chana Stern was lost back there in the city. Sometimes she wondered if she would ever find her again. Bubbe was the only one who understood how she felt.

They would never make Sarah Blumenthal into a Hasidic woman. No one could change her. Bubbe always referred to her granddaughter as Chana Stern, which made Miriam angry, but Bubbe didn't pay any mind. It was her stubborn way of preserving her granddaughter's identity.

Chana pulled a clean blouse over her head, ran a quick comb through her damp curls, and hurried down to the dining room.

5

CHANA STERN

I remember the times Papa and I went to Central Park together. We'd sit on a bench near the lake with our sketch pads. He taught me how to catch the children at play with a minimum of pencil strokes. We drew the people rowing on the sunlit water and the ducks foraging among the weeds along the shore. I knew then I wanted to be an artist more than anything else in the world, and one day I told him so.

"You will be, my little Chanala, you will be," he said with a smile.

I loved our trips together because he made me feel so special.

On Saturday mornings Papa and I used to take the subway to the Natural History Museum to see his latest work. When we arrived at the old castlelike building I'd stop for a moment at the black meteorite in the entrance hall. I loved to fit my fingers into the little holes on its cool, smooth surface. Enjoying a delicious shiver, I'd remind myself I was touching something from outer space. Then we'd mount the marble stairs under the belly of the great gray whale that hung suspended over our heads, its mouth open and dark.

On Saturday mornings the lobby was always crowded with groups of children herded by teachers or parents. The sound of scuffling feet and the echoes of excited voices bounced off the stone walls, making a riot of sound. I wanted to shout to everyone we passed, "Never mind the dinosaurs, first see Harry Stern's paintings upstairs. Go see the wonderful dioramas my father has painted."

On the third floor, behind glass windows, exotic wild animals stood motionless on grassy plains or by the edges of marshes. On a tree limb a tiger crouched, his glass eyes fixed on some distant prey. In frozen flight, birds soared before the grandeur of the High Sierras. Each window along the winding corridor was a glimpse of nature made real by the magic of Papa's brush. He could trick the eye and bring all of the outdoors into those small scenes. As Papa and I stood in front of his work, I would tell whoever was standing near us, "See, that's my father's painting in the background. Isn't it beautiful?"

Just as the old Chana Stern was lost, so were those wonderful times when Papa was with us and we were all happy in the city. Sometimes at night when I was waiting for sleep I would go back to Riverside Drive. Behind closed lids I'd relive the laughter and the pain again:

I'm there eating supper on that stormy night. I hear the shrill ring of the telephone that ripped our lives apart. It's like a movie in slow motion. With her back to Bubbe and me, Mama stands in the glare of the kitchen light, the phone to her ear.

"Yes, this is Miriam Stern." She catches her breath with a sort of gasp. There are no more words. Then she slowly returns the receiver to its hook. Her hand is shaking, and the phone almost topples over. For what seems a terribly long time, she stands with her back to us. She's quiet, and the stillness in the room makes my heart stop.

Bubbe's frightened voice breaks the silence. "What is it, Miriam?"

Mama doesn't move or answer. Suddenly, I can't swallow the food in my mouth.

As she leaps from her chair, Bubbe's fork falls onto her plate, making a sharp clatter in the silence. Then Bubbe is standing with her arms around Mama. "What is it? Tell me what's wrong." But Mama still doesn't answer. In that moment I know nothing will ever be the same in our lives and a horrible thing has just happened to us all.

As Papa crossed the street after coming up from the subway a block away, he was struck by a taxi speeding on the icy street. Although it happened almost directly in front of the apartment, we never heard anything; no sirens, nothing until that phone call. We were eating our supper, and Papa's dish was covered and kept warm for him in the oven.

The three of us went to the hospital that night, but he had already slipped away and we never got a chance to say good-bye. The policemen, who came to talk to Mama the next morning, said that because of the ice on his windshield, the taxi driver never saw Papa.

When Rabbi Steinmetz spoke at the memorial service at Congregation Emanuel, he called Papa's death a tragedy for his small family, and a great loss to the art world. The whole congregation delivered the *Kaddish* because there was no son to say it for him. I remember it was then that the tears finally overwhelmed me.

There was a picture and a whole column in the obituary section of *The New York Times*. The picture was taken years before when Papa taught at Columbia, and he didn't have his mustache and his elegantly clipped beard. I never knew him like that, so young.

The rest of the winter, life took on an unreal quality.

Mama hardly left her room. Bubbe said it would take time for the grieving, but after several weeks she was still not eating with us. Chanukah was a sad time that year. Bubbe lit the candles because Mama would have nothing to do with the holiday. She never left the apartment and refused to see any of her friends. At mealtimes Bubbe would take a tray to Mama's room. Most of the time it came back to the kitchen barely touched. She was so far away from us. Her brown eyes had deep violet shadows under them, and when I tried to talk to her, they'd look past me as if I weren't there. She was like a prisoner locked away in a world of despair. She lost weight daily and made little effort at grooming. Her slender body faded before our eyes.

By April, just before Passover, Bubbe had become so alarmed at the state of affairs that she called our old friend Dr. Solomon to come to the apartment. He and his wife Rose were Mama's and Papa's closest friends. David Solomon was head of the psychology department at Columbia.

They all met years ago when Papa taught at the university and Mama was a student at Barnard. Rose was in Mama's class at Barnard, and they'd been close friends as long as I could remember. Every year they worked together at the bazaar organized by the Temple to raise money for the children's ward at Mount Sinai Hospital.

Rose came with her husband that night hoping she could help. At first Mama refused to see them, and for a while it looked like they would have to count their visit a failure. But Bubbe pleaded with Mama until she finally gave in. Dr. Solomon spent several hours alone with Mama in her bedroom. Bubbe served coffee and *rugelah* in the living room while we waited for the outcome of his talk with Mama.

I don't know exactly what Dr. Solomon said to her, but the next week Mama left for a three-month stay at a sanitarium in the Catskills. It was lonely in the apartment with just Bubbe and me. That June I was particularly sad because Bubbe was the only one who came to my eighth-grade graduation; Mama was still at the sanitarium.

Bubbe bought me a white silk dress at Bloomingdale's and ordered a large bouquet of pink carnations that matched the trim on the dress. Tears filled her eyes as she put the bouquet in my arms after the ceremony. I remember tears had burned hot against my own eyelids as I searched the auditorium to find her sitting small and alone in the audience. I wished with all my heart that Mama were there too. I remember saying to myself, "This is what it's like to be an orphan." But then I assured myself that I really wasn't because Bubbe was there for me. I missed Papa most awfully that night.

&a   &a   &a

Mama came home in July. It was terribly hot in the city. I didn't go to Camp Mudjekeewis as I usually did. I didn't mind not going because Bubbe would have been left alone in the apartment and I really wanted to be home when Mama returned from the sanitarium. When she got home there was color in her cheeks and she had put on some weight. But the best part was she seemed almost her old self again, except every once in a while she'd become quiet and her eyes would look past me.

That summer she spent a lot of time at Temple, which was odd because she had never gone much in the past, except on the High Holy Days. She started making a special effort to keep a kosher household. Bubbe tried her best to keep up with Mama's newfound piety, but every so often I

30

noticed her looking at Mama as if she were a total stranger. By the end of summer it was evident Mama was trying to make a completely new life for herself.

She no longer went to B'nai B'rith with Rose Solomon, and she left Congregation Emanuel to go to an Orthodox temple downtown. I went with her several times and tried hard to understand her need to plunge into religion, but I didn't like having to sit in the balcony during the service. Sitting there behind the lattice screen made me feel hot and uncomfortable, crowded in with all those perspiring women.

One morning as I was tidying up Mama's room, I noticed a black book on her bedside table. It caught my eye because of the large gold Star of David on the cover. Under the star, in bold letters fashioned to resemble Hebrew characters, it said DAUGHTERS OF ZION and under that in smaller letters, INSTRUCTION ON THE MITZVAHS. I had heard the word *mitzvah* once or twice, but it was strange to me, so later that morning I asked her to explain its meaning.

"*Mitzvah* is the Hebrew word for commandments, Chana."

"But why do people use old Hebrew words instead of English?" I asked.

She looked at me with her beautiful brown eyes, which seemed so large lately. Her voice was barely audible. "Chanala, we have so much to learn about where we came from and who we really are." The intensity of her words sent a chill through me as I realized I barely knew this person my mother had become.

She started using Yiddish and Hebrew words regularly. To me they sounded foreign and outlandish, but she was patient and always explained their meaning. She started attending classes every Tuesday evening at the temple downtown. After the meetings she would return to the apartment with her arms full of books, and every night after supper she'd take them to her room and close the door.

I overheard her talking to Bubbe late one night. They were sitting at the table in the kitchen, and she had a book before her. I couldn't hear everything they said, but I caught the words *Hasid* and *Lubavitcher*. I had never heard either of the words before, but it wasn't long before she started talking to us over supper about her class and what she was learning. Her eyes flashed and her breath came fast as the words tumbled from her lips. She told us we had only been half-Jews; to become whole we had to embrace the commandments. She said the only way to be a whole Jew was to become Orthodox. Bubbe said very little when Mama talked that way, but I could tell she disagreed.

One night as we sat talking after supper, Bubbe put her napkin down and shook her head. "Miriam, why should we go back to what made life so hard for us? By becoming so different again, all that we have gained over the years will be thrown away. Life will become difficult once more. For me, I'm Jewish enough already—no need to overdo. You should do what is right for you, but remember, Bubeleh, it won't be easy for Chana if you bring so much change into her life."

It all started when Mama decided to become a convert, a *boalot teshewa*, but that was just the beginning of many changes in our lives. The biggest of all, however, was her arranged marriage to Mendel Dubovitch, the leader of her Tuesday class. "The meaning of the Hebrew words *boalot teshewa* is 'one who has returned,'" she explained.

Mama spoke softly that night. She told me she had decided to become a *Hasid*. I could hardly believe what I was hearing, but her eyes shone with joy and she hugged me, so for the time being my dismay turned to happiness for her. Her voice trembled with emotion. "Chanala," she said, "remember at *Yom Kippur* the dark man with the beard and the odd fur hat? He was dressed in a black silk caftan and stood on the cantor's right before the Ark holding the scroll of the Torah. He and the man on the cantor's left declared three times permission of the congregation to pray before the singing of the *Kol Nidre*. That is the man who has been teaching us on Tuesday nights; that is Rov Mendel Dubovitch from Brooklyn. He is very close to the Rebbe in Crown Heights. He goes all over the state lecturing and bringing converts to the *Lubavitcher* Court."

Her words were hushed, and there was a tenderness in her voice I remembered hearing when she spoke to Papa. It was then I knew for certain she was in love with Rov Dubovitch. Still, I had no comprehension of the changes to come. I didn't realize the world as I knew it would be lost to me forever.

6

PASSOVER

Miriam bent her head over the flame. Her dark eyes reflected the brilliance of the candles as she watched them for a moment before blowing out the taper. She stood in silence as she gave one last look to see that everything was perfect before the family entered the dining room. The flames grew steady and tall, bathing the linen-covered table, the polished silverware, and the special Passover dishes in a warm brilliance. Miriam checked the *seder* plate Bubbe had brought to the table. Everything was as it should be.

She sighed. Her back hurt and her legs ached. She had worked hard for weeks preparing the house and seeing that all was *peysakhidk*, untainted. Now everything was ready and done in strict accordance with the *mitzvahs*. All the laws had been kept, and this was her day. She hoped she had not forgotten anything, since the family would surely notice if she had made any errors. Elijah's cup sparkled in the candlelight as it waited for his invisible spirit to join the celebrants. With trembling hands she caressed the Moroccan-bound *Haggadah* that lay at her husband's place. Then turning to her mother, a faint smile erasing the tired lines around her mouth, she whispered, "All right, Bubbe, you can call them now."

When Bubbe pulled the sliding doors back, Chana caught her breath at what was spread before her in the soft light. Wearing a white linen *kittel* with knotted silk cord around his waist, Mendel Dubovitch led them into the dining room. He wore the traditional broad-brimmed fur hat. It sat like a crown above his black beard, which rested majestically on the snowy folds of his *kittel*. He eased his large frame among the cushions arranged on his ornately carved bench at the head of the table.

Yakov, the eldest son, took the chair at his father's right. Behind thick glasses, Yakov's moist eyes surveyed the scene, his expression critical. Miriam watched him, feeling as usual the weight of his disapproval. Somehow with that look, the glow she had felt as she lit the candles earlier faded. She was aware again of the ache in her back and the heaviness of her distended belly. She glanced quickly at her husband for reassurance, but Mendel seemed unaware of her anxiety.

Sallow and thin, Yakov wore his black fedora pulled low about his ears. A white collarless shirt was buttoned tight against his protruding Adam's apple. Chana had been told he favored his dead mother in looks as well as temperament. If that were true, she was sure she would not have liked the wife who died giving life to young Yudel on the family's sad journey from the Ukraine to Palestine.

David Dubovitch, affectionately known as Dov, sat on Mendel's left with his brother, Yudel. The young boy wore a velvet *yarmulke* and a short black jacket. His *payess* were freshly curled. Heavy horn-rimmed glasses made his nearsighted blue eyes seem rather large for his thin face.

Yudel's palms were sweaty and his mouth was dry. He had rehearsed for days how he would ask the "Four Questions" when it was time for him to stand before the family and speak. He loved the miraculous story of salvation at the Red Sea and Mount Sinai when the Torah was

given to the children of Israel. He was aware of the impor-
tance of his role in the coming ceremony. His heart pounded against his ribs as he waited for his time to speak.

Dov had his father's dark eyes and olive complexion,
but his resemblance to Mendel stopped there. Dov's black
hair curled loosely about his ears under the snap-brimmed
hat he wore at an impudent angle. Mischievous lines crinkled at the corners of his brown eyes. To the delight of
Pessie, his wife of half a year, he kept his black beard
clipped and trimmed. His concern for grooming brought
disapproving looks from his father, who reprimanded him
often with lectures on the sins of vanity and pride. Dov
always answered his father saying, "*Abba*, your wisdom is
great. I will mend my ways." But he continued to keep the
dark hairs on his handsome face stylishly tamed.

Chana felt at ease with Dov and Pessie, who were not
many years older than she. The vivacious Pessie was the
newest member of the family, and unabashedly in love with
her young husband. Hasidic custom forbade any outward
show of affection, but their lingering glances spoke elo-
quently of the deep passion between them. She was not
much taller than Chana, and in the last few months had
taken to wearing a charming new *shaytl* of short red curls
that framed her face, making her look younger than her 16
years. She had made Chana her confidante from the first
day they met. It was good to have a real friend, Chana
thought, as their eyes met across the table. She knew later
they would find time alone to talk and giggle over the
events of the day.

Rivke, Yakov's wife, settled her heavy body across the
table from her husband and proceeded to give attention to
her twin daughters, Gittel and Raizel, fidgeting in their

seats beside her. The seven-year-olds reflected their mother's German ancestry with pale eyes and straight red hair wound in tight braids above their freckled foreheads. Already both girls displayed a tendency toward obesity.

Bubbe set the crystal decanter of Mogen David wine at Mendel's place, then quietly took her seat between her daughter and granddaughter. As if by some unheard signal, all chatter subsided. A veil of silence fell over the room, snaring everyone's breath in its tenuous threads.

Miriam looked pale and anxious. Her hand fluttered to arrange an errant curl of her blond wig. Chana felt like squirming in her seat but didn't. Instead she kept her gaze on her stepfather's hand as he lifted the decanter to fill her wineglass.

Slowly, Mendel's head fell back until his beard pointed directly at the ceiling. He raised the silver tray with the three *matzos*. His voice rose as he delivered the ancient Aramaic prayer.

"*All who are hungry, let them eat. All who are needy, let them come and celebrate peace with us. Now we are here; next year may we be in Israel. Now we are slaves.*" His voice broke as his own experience brought personal meaning to the next words. "*In the year ahead may we be free men.*" Then he raised his wineglass, and his voice was strong again. "*Not only once have they risen to destroy us, but in every generation. Yet, the Holy One, blessed be He, always delivers us from their hands.*" After touching the glass to his lips he broke into a rousing Hasidic song.

Everyone at the table had held their breath as he intoned the ancient scripture. Now as one they began to breathe again. It was time to rejoice and enjoy. They raised their glasses and drank deeply of the sweet, strong wine.

One more time they filled their glasses as the men continued to sing the *Zimeras*.

When the singing ended, Mendel's gaze fell on his youngest son. "*Nu?*" He spoke quietly, nodding his head toward the eager boy.

Trembling, Yudel rose to his feet. In a high, reedlike voice he spoke in Yiddish. "Papa, I want to ask four questions." Then he changed to Hebrew as required. His voice was stronger now as he asked, "*Why is this night different from all other nights?*" He stood taller with each question. After the fourth, everyone answered in Hebrew, "*Slaves were we unto Pharaoh in Egypt.*" After Mendel finished reading from the *Haggadah*, he gave the signal that it was the right time for Yakov to spill the drops of wine that symbolized the ten plagues of Egypt. Mendel broke small pieces from each of the three *matzos*, wrapped them carefully in a napkin, and ceremoniously hid them among the pillows on his bench.

The distribution of the ritual foods on the *seder* plate came next. When that was done, Mendel announced in a loud, clear voice, "*Seelkham arukh* (the table is set). Now eat and drink and may it do you good."

He raised his glass, and the men burst into song again as Miriam and Bubbe brought the tureen of *matzo* ball soup and platters of roast chicken with *matzo* meal pancakes to the table. They passed the decanter around once more, and soon everyone was busy talking and eating. After several hours of song and wild dancing by the men, the flushed company welcomed the invisible prophet Elijah to the table, where his filled goblet awaited him.

Chana had been given the duty of seeing that the front door was left open so his spirit could enter at the right time.

All eyes turned toward the open door, and voices swelled with the old song, *"The prophet has arrived today; Messiah will come in the future!"*

So ended the first night of Passover.

Chana's head ached from too much wine, but Miriam's usually pale cheeks were flushed. She was filled with pride as everyone at the table complimented her. A faint smile softened the sober lines around Mendel's mouth as his eyes met hers, and she knew she had pleased him.

7

1939—THE OVERNIGHT

Mina got up early Saturday morning and put together a casserole, which she left in the icebox for Gus. She was sure he'd eat at Harry's Grill after he closed the bakery, and as usual spend the rest of the evening at the Knights of Columbus hall playing pinochle. She left a note on the kitchen table with instructions on warming up the tuna pie for Sunday dinner. The note ended with: *Going to spend the night at Katy's. Be back after supper Sunday.*

She hurried cleaning up the breakfast dishes and flew upstairs to pack her overnight bag, all the while feeling the familiar rush of excitement. She was going to be with Katy, free for a whole night and two wonderful days.

Katy's father, Patrick Conklin, was the super for the Tower Apartments. His family lived in the tiny flat in the basement next to the furnace room. Cooking odors constantly filled the windowless rooms, but Mina loved being in that crowded little apartment. When she was with the Conklins, they made her feel like one of the family—but most of all she just loved being close to Katy. Tonight they would snuggle in bed and probably not get a wink of sleep. Like always, they'd talk and giggle the night away till it was time to get up for Sunday mass.

It was just the four of them for supper that night because Maureen, Katy's older sister, was staying the weekend with a girlfriend in Flushing.

Cheeks rosy from the heat, Mary Conklin, her plump body wrapped in a faded gingham apron, stood by the stove. Her gray Irish eyes danced with merriment as Patrick retold the familiar story of their courtship in Dublin. He never tired of exaggerating and embellishing his youthful exploits. Mary always nodded at each telling as if it were the first time she had heard the story.

Across the oilcloth-covered table they watched Patrick slice the steaming meat on the platter before him as the pungent aroma of corned beef and cabbage filled the little kitchen. Mina felt a wave of happiness, and in the same moment realized she was terribly hungry. At home she seldom felt like eating. Facing Gus and the food she had to prepare for him, her appetite often deserted her. She usually forced herself to eat in those silences that frequently fell between them. How different it was to be with this jolly and voluble family, and how magnificent it was to be genuinely hungry. Relishing each bite, she ate ravenously as Mary kept replenishing her plate. Finally shaking her head, she pushed her chair back from the table.

"No more, please, Mrs. Conklin. I can't swallow another bite. Honest, I'll explode if I eat any more."

"Surely now, we wouldn't be wanting that to happen. An explosion in this small kitchen would be a disaster we could hardly cope with. And after all I went through to make an apple cobbler, I would hate to see you fly into a million pieces before you had a chance to enjoy it." Everyone laughed. Mary winked at her husband as she picked up his empty plate and took it to the sink. There was more laughter all around as Patrick finished his last story about times in the old country. As they ate the sweet and spicy dessert, the conversation turned to plans for the girls' graduation in June.

After the dishes were done they settled on the sagging mohair couch in the living room. Patrick fiddled with the radio dial until he got Gabriel Heatter with his familiar "Good news tonight..." which turned out to be bad news from Poland, and even worse news about the long lines of unemployed at the soup kitchens in the city. There was a promise, however, from President Roosevelt that things would be looking up since the CCC camps were providing work for more men.

After the news Patrick checked the furnaces for the night. When he came back, he and Mary went off to bed with an admonition to the girls not to stay up all hours talking. "Don't be late for early mass in the morning," Mary added when she kissed them good night.

Katy switched stations to get *The Shadow*, then turned out the lights. Kicking off their shoes they huddled together on the sofa. The faint glow from the radio dial made the darkness scary and intimate. They listened spellbound to the familiar nasal voice of Lamont Cranston: "Who knows what evil lurks in the hearts of men? The Shadow knows."

Katy sighed. "I wonder what the Shadow looks like. His voice sends goose bumps all over me." She giggled and enjoyed a delicious shiver.

"I'll bet his hair is wavy and black and he wears a mustache like Clark Gable," Mina whispered. They both laughed and huddled closer.

For a half hour they were transported to the tenuous world of mystery and intrigue that is *The Shadow*'s special domain. At 10:30, when the exotic adventures of *Chandu the Magician* came to an end somewhere in deepest Africa, they turned off the set and went to the kitchen for milk and cookies, which they carried down the hall to the small bedroom Katy shared with her older sister.

Wearing just slips and panties, they climbed into the big double bed. They snuggled in the warm darkness with covers pulled up to their chins.

Mina was fascinated by the dancing lights that marched in a steady procession across the ceiling. These phantom images, made by the lights of passing cars on the street above, crept through a narrow window high on the bedroom wall. After some minutes of silence the conversation turned to boys, which it always did when they were alone.

"Did you hear what Mary Alice said to Johnny Monahan when he called her a mouthy broad in study hall last week?"

"No, what did she say?" Mina tried her best to sound interested.

"Well, Mary Alice shot right back and called him 'shanty Irish.' Said he talked like he'd just gotten off the boat from the old country, with his brogue and all."

"That sounds just like Mary Alice," Mina murmured sleepily as she snuggled deeper under the covers. Katy loved to comment about what boy was paying attention to what girl, who carried whose books home after school, and who said this and that in the hall between classes.

Mina listened as she always did when Katy ran on about boys, but she herself never had much to say on the subject. It was just nice listening to Katy's voice in the intimacy of the darkened room.

Boys flocked around Katy, but for some reason they never seemed to notice Mina. She felt uncomfortable around them, although she never let on about that to Katy. So she always chimed in as if she were interested. It was sort of an act, pretending they were important to her. After all, she couldn't let Katy know how she really felt. Actually, she wasn't at all sure how she felt about boys.

"Have they decided on long or short skirts for graduation?" She interrupted Katy's next story about Mary Dee and Kenny Dority.

"What, Mina? Oh, I don't know. It will be up to Reverend Mother," she said. "Most everyone wants long, but with the Depression and all, Reverend Mother could insist we make do with short skirts this year. Mama wants to make my dress, but I'm trying to convince her to let me shop for one at Macy's or maybe Bonwit Teller if they're not too expensive."

Katy yawned. She was getting sleepy and had exhausted all her boy talk. She sighed and nestled close to Mina. Throwing her arm across the covers, her hand came to rest ever so lightly on Mina's breast. Katy's hair brushed against her cheek, sending an electric shock racing the full length of Mina's body. Blood rushed to her face, and she silently thanked the saints for the merciful darkness that hid her blushing. Holding her breath, she tried to keep her heart from doing a St. Vitas and leaping from her chest. Strange thoughts raced through her head. Was this what dying was like? Didn't people say "I'm so happy I could die?" Was she actually going to expire right there and make that saying come true? Maybe she would go directly to heaven from the very spot where she lay. The feelings were so delicious, she closed her eyes tight not to let them escape.

Suddenly everything seemed to be in slow motion, and she was, of all things, Heathcliff lying next to Cathy on Penniston Crag in *Wuthering Heights*. There were scudding clouds playing hide-and-seek with a full moon and frosty stars. The wind off the high moor lifted Cathy's hair, which smelled of heather, fanning it lightly against his cheek. Or was it her cheek?

She seemed to be watching this, and at the same time she was a part of it. An odd and blissful sensation filled her body. Then the cry of the wind in the cliffs above their heads began to fade and the rocks evaporated in the ground mist.

The roar died over Penniston Crag, and all that was left was the drumming of Mina's heart, loud in her ears.

Now she was back in the dark room with the moving lights dancing above her on the ceiling and Katy's warm body pressed close to hers. Not daring to move, she let tears of joy escape the corners of her eyes. They coursed down her cheeks, ending up in little puddles in her ears. It was so quiet. She wondered if she should say something, but her mouth felt like flannel. What was Katy thinking? What did she think of what had happened? Then she realized Katy really hadn't been there with her on the crag. Oh, it was all so confusing. There were so many questions crowding in on her, and a peculiar uneasiness lay in the pit of her stomach.

What had really happened? There wasn't any answer. Suddenly her thoughts were interrupted by a sound like a kitten purring. No, that wasn't it. She turned her head ever so carefully on the pillow. Holy Mother! It was just Katy snoring softly.

8

MINA ARENHOLT—BEYOND ABSOLUTION

The next morning it was hard for me to meet Katy's eyes as we dressed and got ready to leave the apartment for mass. Katy's parents had left earlier for the 7 o'clock. We overslept so we had to catch the 11 o'clock by ourselves.

My thigh brushed hers when we knelt for Communion and my cheeks burned crimson. I closed my eyes. All I could see behind my lids was Katy's face bending over me, her lips parted and close to mine. When the priest placed the wafer on my tongue, it almost went down the wrong way. I was afraid I was going to choke to death right there before God and the whole congregation, but I finally managed to get it down.

My rosary was burning the flesh of my clasped hands, and tears of shame and guilt scalded my eyes. I stumbled on the way back to our seats. Fortunately, Katy caught my arm just in time. I didn't dare look at her, but I knew she was staring at me like I was crazy or something.

"Are you OK, Mina? What's gotten into you? You've been acting funny all morning," she hissed as we settled in our seats. I couldn't bring my eyes to meet hers.

All that afternoon we just hung around the apartment trying to get down to our homework. We finally ended up lying on our stomachs on Katy's bed, quizzing each other for the Monday morning test in Sister Luke's class in Greco-Roman History. Patrick and Mary had gone over to

Jamaica on their Sunday duty visit to Patrick's mother, so we were alone.

When Katy asked me questions I should have known without a moment's hesitation, my mind pulled a blank as if I had mush between my ears instead of brains.

As we lay there with our books spread before us, her shoulder pressed mine. Raindrops began to lick the narrow window pane high above the bed, and the room grew dark for three in the afternoon. It was so quiet between questions that I could hear the ticking of the kitchen clock far down the hall. Suddenly Katy flopped over on her back, her pointy breasts swelling under her light blue sweater as she stretched one arm above her head. I felt like I couldn't breathe—there was a painful ache in my throat—and I was seized by a crazy desire to bury my head between those beautiful mounds. For a moment I thought I would go mad if I didn't do just that.

"I can't study. Let's just talk," Katy said. "We know all the answers anyway. Gee, it's beginning to rain, and you'll have to leave soon. Want to see if there's any corned beef left to make sandwiches?"

"No. I'm not hungry," I said, managing to steady my words by holding my face muscles tight. My voice sounded small in the silence that followed. Suddenly my resolve was gone, and my body fell over hers. Of all the stupid things, my head landed in the middle of her tummy. Right off she started to giggle and I felt foolish, but her arm came down to cradle me against her.

"Poor Mina," she murmured, rocking me back and forth like I was a baby. "Are you still feeling queasy? I thought you were going to faint at Communion. Maybe you're getting your period or coming down with something."

I wriggled in her embrace and found my face buried between those beautiful breasts. Lord, I was doing just what I had fantasized a moment ago. "I love you, Cathy." My voice was muffled by her sweater. I couldn't believe I'd said that, and called her Cathy too. I prayed to God she hadn't heard me.

"I love you too, Mina. I always will. But why did you call me Cathy?"

Laughing and not waiting for an answer she sat up abruptly. "How about seeing if there's any cobbler left? Honest, you'll feel better if you eat something."

She jumped off the bed, leaving me gasping like a fish out of water, my face burrowed in the rough chenille spread, and feeling more alone than I ever remembered.

I don't know how I ate the cobbler she cut for me. My heart was doing flip-flops all over the place, but I managed to collect my wits and sound casual. "Maybe I'd better start for home now before it gets really dark, what with the rain and all."

I managed a semblance of a smile and told her to thank her folks for me. I still couldn't look her in the eye when she asked me again why I called her Cathy. I fumbled, saying, "I don't know. Are you sure I did?"

"Well, it doesn't matter. It's a much prettier name than Katy anyway. Come on. I'll help you get your things together."

At the door she hugged me and said, "I love you, Mina. You're my best friend in all the world. You can call me Cathy any time you want."

She was holding me in her arms again! Oh, Mother of God, I couldn't stand it. I had to get out of there.

On the way home the thought struck me that I was

going out of my mind and probably to hell because of these feelings. *Sweet Jesus, is this another mortal sin I must add to the Gus one?* I asked myself, remembering I had never gathered the courage to tell the priest at confession about Gus's visits. *If this is a sin, I'm beyond absolution, to say nothing of having any hope of salvation.* The rain came down in sheets. The streets were dark and almost deserted. By the time I reached home I was soaked to the skin and thoroughly miserable.

9

MINA ARENHOLT—THE DIARY

For my 12th birthday, Mama gave me a green leather diary complete with a tiny brass key. I never got around to writing in it because I didn't have anything romantic or important enough to fill its creamy white pages. I picked it up today and wiped it off with one of my old gym socks to make the leather shine.

I lay on my bed, pen poised for the plunge. The little book was open in front of me, its blank pages ready at long last to receive my thoughts:

April 3, 1939

Dear Diary,

Maybe if I write down the words that fill my heart now I'll be able to read them later and understand who I am and what my life is about. I don't have the foggiest idea what is happening to me. Seeing my emotions put into words might clear my mind and bring some understanding to all of this.

When I run into Katy in study hall or when we are changing classes, I can hardly speak for the butterflies in my stomach. At night, as I'm waiting for sleep, there's such a sweetness all over my body when I remember how it was lying next to her—the warm moistness between my legs disturbed me greatly, and yet at the same time, it excited me.

Why do happiness and a nagging dose of guilt seem to be one and the same? How can that be? I've never been in such a dilemma. Somewhere, way back in my mind, a small voice keeps saying I shouldn't be feeling these things.

Holy Mary, Mother of God, pray for me, for I'm sure in need of your intervention.

April 4, 1939

Dearest Diary,

I'm certain my confusion is somehow entangled with my shame at what I let Gus do to me. It seems impossible that these feelings should be linked, but both have a frightening sameness about them.

Lord, when I read what I have written, the words almost leap from the page to eat me alive. My pen races along with a will of its own. Indeed, it seems to have just that, and I simply become the observer of what it writes.

Dear Diary, I'm going to put your key on a chain around my neck for safekeeping so these words will be locked away from prying eyes. To make doubly sure no one will read you, you'll be tucked between the mattress and box spring of my bed.

April 10, 1939

Dear Diary,

A week has gone by since you received the first scribblings from my troubled heart. However, my pen hasn't been idle. Of all things, it's taken to poetry. Yes, I've composed a ballad to my dearest one. It tells of my love with such passion. The words ignited me, and I was like a flame as I read it one more time before I slipped it into Katy's algebra book.

She was whispering something to Mary Alice and didn't notice me. It was just before the bell rang for study hall. I watched her with my breath held tight in my throat, and for the longest time I thought she would never open her book. She finally tore herself away from Mary Alice and opened Algebra II. My note glided to the floor like a paper airplane.

Sister Josephine was pacing the aisles between the desks, and it landed right at her feet. She spoke sharply. "Kathleen, I believe this dropped from your book. Please be more careful." Her dark Italian eyes snapped with disapproval.

Oh, God! I almost expired. She held my life in her pudgy hands and thrust it under Katy's nose. I prayed Katy would claim it.

She looked at Sister with a question mark as plain as day. Then she glanced in my direction. I gave her a quick nod. Right off she looked back at Sister with that beautiful smile she uses when she's reprimanded. She took the paper from Sister's hand and tucked it into the front of her book. Her eyes were on me. I felt the blood rush to my cheeks, but I managed a weak grin. Then, dropping my eyes back to my book, I melted with relief. The crisis was over.

I didn't get much studying done. All I could think of was what Katy would say after she read my words.

On the walk home from school she was quiet. It took all my courage to ask if she'd read my poem. So many questions buzzed in my head, and I began to panic. What in the world had I done? Would she think I was crazy? Would she stop being my friend?

Silence held my tongue hostage. Why didn't she say something?

Waiting for traffic on 84th Street, we stood side by side. Our shoulders touched, and she sewed her warm fingers to mine, whispering in a low voice, "Your poem is lovely,

Mina. I love it. Am I really like that to you?"

My heart almost leapt from my body. I could hardly believe what I was hearing. The word "love" hung in the air like a precious jewel. I couldn't find words to answer her. I just held her hand and blinked back tears of happiness.

Katy said she never knew I was into poetry and that her favorite poet was Walt Whitman. "Have you ever read Leaves of Grass? *Your poem is every bit as good, honest it is." She smiled, her face close to mine, and I fell into her eyes as the sidewalk melted under my feet. I didn't feel the earth again until I reached my own street. The rest of the way home the heaviness returned as it always does when I have to leave Katy.*

April 11, 1939

Dear Diary,

Wonder of wonders, Leaves of Grass *was at the library. I found a table by the window and sat down to read. I lost myself in Walt Whitman's magic. It's surprising that a person can express such love and warmth in words alone. I wonder what kind of man he was. Perhaps a long time ago there were such men. Anyway, I couldn't wait to read his work aloud with Katy. Walt Whitman is my favorite poet now.*

It was almost 2 o'clock when I finally closed the book and realized I was ravenous. I hadn't eaten anything since breakfast.

Last week Katy and I ate our lunch together on a playground bench. We exchanged sandwiches, and Katy said I reminded her of Isadora Duncan and someday I would be famous. Can you imagine? Since then I've started collecting scarves. I pose with them in front of my dresser mirror. I sway and turn, trying to catch what she sees in me that reminds her of that notorious dancer. I work harder than ever now in ballet class. I'm determined to fulfill Katy's prophecy. When I gaze into her blue eyes, I'm sure anything is possible.

10

MINA ARENHOLT—IN KATY'S ROOM

Saturday, a week before graduation, we were trying on our dresses in Katy's room. It was muggy and hot in the underground apartment. I found it difficult to pull the tight-fitting bodice over my clammy skin. The full skirt clung damply about my legs.

Katy's dress came from Macy's as she had hoped, but I had to make mine because Gus wouldn't hear of my going to an expensive store. I found a Butterick pattern and some white voile at Floyd's on Roosevelt Avenue. It came out pretty well, but I still felt self-conscious about it being homemade.

After checking how they fit, we wriggled our sticky bodies out of the billowy folds and hung them side by side in the closet. I was staying overnight. Katy had the room to herself now that Maureen was married and living in Bayside.

Patrick and Mary were off to a ball game in Brooklyn. The Dodgers were Patrick's passion, and he and Mary never missed a home game. Before they left the apartment, Mary instructed Katy on how to warm up the chicken leftovers for supper. After the game, they'd go for Chinese before catching the subway back to Jackson Heights.

It was so hot we didn't put our clothes back on. "Let's take a shower to cool off," Katy suggested as she wrestled with the hooks on her bra. She stepped out of her panties, threw them on the bed, and stood naked before the mirror. My eyes made a tour of her slim body. My cheeks burned and my heart pounded.

The shower was tepid. Little needles of water dappled my flesh with a marvelous deliciousness; I felt tingly all over. I turned my face to catch the spray, and with my eyes shut, I let the water drench and slick back my hair. We were facing each other. As I moved, our bodies touched. The shower was really only big enough for one. The close space behind the curtain was a magical place filled with the sound of drumming water.

Katy put a bar of soap in my hand. "Here, soap me, Mina."

Turning, she presented her back to me. I brushed my hair from my eyes. "OK, I'll do you, then you do me."

My hands slid slowly over her round shoulders, down the length of her slender torso, and stopped. I froze with the soap in my hand. The water kept pouring over us. *My God*, I thought, *is this really happening?*

"Come on, Mina, all over." She laughed and moved her hips slowly. "Legs too." Her voice echoed in the tiny shower. Coming back to my senses, I let my hands travel over slippery skin till they found the small dimple between her firm buttocks. Spreading her legs, she raised her arms to the spray. As I stroked her inner thighs, she threw back her head. With eyes closed and her lips parted, she murmured something, but with the rush of water I couldn't make it out. My senses were spinning, and joy flooded my body. Slowly she turned and faced me. Taking the bar from my trembling fingers, she stroked my neck and arms, then tenderly her hands traced the contour of my breasts. At her touch, my nipples tightened and blossomed. Katy leaned closer, and her own small nipples brushed mine. Paroxysms of delight like star bursts sent me reeling. Suddenly our bodies came together, and I felt every precious curve of her fit into mine.

There were no words, just the music of the water pelting us, running down our legs and gurgling as it found the drain under our feet.

"Let's get out of here," I gasped. I had to rescue myself from the abyss yawning before me. I had to escape being swallowed and lost forever.

Katy's hair was soapy in my mouth as I fumbled blindly to turn off the water. An awful silence hung between us when the torrent stopped. We were both breathing hard. Neither of us spoke as we made large business of scrubbing ourselves dry. Katy suddenly dropped her towel on the bath mat. Naked, she raced down the hall to her bedroom. I followed.

Throwing herself spread-eagled on the bed, she opened her arms to me. Panting, I fell on top of her into the warm, moist embrace. I knew I was lost as I heard my own voice begging her to kiss me. Her lips parted, and I covered her mouth and gave her the gift of my tongue. Like the Fourth of July, rockets burst behind my eyelids. Urgently she guided my hand to her breasts, and under my fingers her nipples rose like yeast. Opening my eyes, I watched my own nipples pucker. Then in a blinding moment, Katy's fingers found me and went inside. My hand was touching her there too, with the same rhythmical urgency. I was like a thief with arms full of booty, coming again and again for the prize. Drowning and dying all at the same time, the world was whirling away from me at breakneck speed. I felt myself disappearing with Katy's body pressed to mine.

"Goddamn it! What the hell?" Light flooded the room. Patrick Conklin's voice leapt from the open door and reverberated against the walls of the tiny room.

Terror seized me, and for a painful moment neither of us could move. Katy stiffened and gulped for air as if she were drowning.

Bursting from the doorway, Patrick moved with lightning speed. His powerful body loomed over us as he tore Katy from my arms. He shook her as a dog shakes a rabbit, her head flopping back and forth. The look in his eyes was terrifying, and I was afraid Katy's neck would snap. I clutched the bedspread to cover my nakedness and found myself staring into the gray face of Mary Conklin leaning weakly against the door.

"Stop it! Stop it!" she wailed. But Patrick kept on shaking Katy, his face all scarlet, the veins bulging dangerously on either side of his neck. He was gasping for breath. At Mary's frightened plea, the violence seemed to go out of him. He just stared at Katy as if she were a total stranger. In that moment, she broke free, and the force of her effort sent her spinning across the room to land against the wall, where she slid limply to the floor.

"Holy Mother of God! Have you lost your senses, Patrick Mark Conklin?" Mary shouted, her eyes darting from Katy, whimpering like a wounded puppy on the floor, to me, huddled under the pink chenille bedspread, then back again to her husband towering over the bed.

"Patrick," she shrieked, "do you hear me? What's going on? Have you gone stark raving mad?"

"You should be asking them what's going on." His finger shook as he pointed at me and then at Katy, still crumpled in a silent heap against the wall. He raised his arm, and

I was sure he was going to hit me. "You goddamn lesbian bitch!" He shook his fist in my face. "Put your clothes on and get out of my house. I never want to see your bitchen face around here again!"

The words exploded from his lips as bubbles of saliva formed at the corners of his mouth. "Damn you, Mina Arenholt. If you ever come near my daughter again, I'll kill you. I swear to God I will!" Shaking with rage, he turned his back on me, grabbed his wife by the arm and shoved her into the hall. Turning abruptly in the doorway, he glared at Katy on the floor. "Get your clothes on, girl. I'll deal with you later." He slammed the door. The silence in the room was suffocating.

Realizing I could breathe once more, I came to my senses and leapt from the bed. I stumbled about the room, frantically picking up my clothes, and yanked my gradua- tion dress out of the closet. All the while, Katy was mak- ing strange heaving noises like she was going to throw up. She staggered to her feet, grabbed her slip, and ran out of the room.

As I heard the bathroom door bang shut, I struggled with my skirt and blouse. The word *lesbian* spun in my head. By the sound of his voice and the way he spat the word at me I knew it meant something bad and dirty. I got my blouse on backward, but I didn't care. Nothing mattered.

I don't remember what was going through my mind on the way home. There was a numbness mixed with a fore- boding that pervaded every fiber of my being. I wanted des- perately to squirm out of the tangle of feelings strangling me. I didn't know how to cope with what was happening. Patrick called me a lesbian. What did that mean?

The house was dark and quiet when I reached home. I

guessed Gus was at the lodge hall as usual. I took the stairs two at a time up to my room, threw my things on the bed, switched on the bedside lamp and sat down with Mama's dictionary. There it was under "L" in bold black letters:

Lesbian (noun) 1. a native of the island of Lesbos.

I was beginning to remember. We studied that Greek island in ancient history class. It was inhabited only by women. I read on:

2. the ancient dialect of Lesbos.

Then I saw it:

3. a female homosexual.

My hands were trembling as I flipped the pages back to the "H's":

Homosexual (adj.) relating to, typical of, or displaying homosexuality. (noun) a homosexual person with sexual desires for others of one's own gender.

The printing began to swim and waver on the page. My God, there it was: *Sexual activity with a member of the same sex.* That was crazy! How could that refer to me? The only girl I loved was Katy, and our love for each other was special and pure. What we felt couldn't be sexual. Sexual was the dirty things Gus made me do in the dark when he came to my room. *That* was being sexual. It wasn't the same as loving Katy. No, it couldn't be the same, I told myself. Never would I believe it was the same, no matter what the dictionary said.

My thoughts spun out of control. I remembered hearing boys snicker about *homos*. They called them "queers" and "fairies."

Once at a slumber party, Mary Alice O'Connor said her mother told her those people were diseased and would surely go to hell for the nasty things they did to each other.

My hands were cold and sweaty as I turned to the "Q's":

Queer (adj.) 1. crooked, deviating from the norm. 2. strange. 3. homosexual slang.

There it was again, that hateful word. Oh, Mary, Mother of God! They have the same meaning, homo, queer, fairy, lesbian. There it was in black and white for all to see, and no one ever questioned Webster's, no matter what.

I felt sick at my stomach. Lord, maybe the disease was already swarming over my flesh like a mass of maggots.

I jumped from the bed and ran to the dresser mirror. Did it show? Could people tell? The face that stared back at me was the face I saw every day. Leaning closer, I studied my eyes. People say you can tell about a person by looking into their eyes. Mine looked all right. Or did they? They were bloodshot and full of fear, but they weren't shifty, like a pervert's. Still, I couldn't be sure. Maybe others would see something different.

What would a holy person like Sister Frances see when she looked at me? Would she notice my *queerness* when I sat in class? Oh, Lord! And what about Reverend Mother? Nothing escaped her. Would she ferret out my terrible secret?

Tearing off my clothes, I dove beneath the sheets, not bothering to put on my nightie. Sleep was a far-off thing for all the crazy thoughts tumbling in my head. The worst of these was the realization that I might never see Katy again. Just imagining it was almost more than I could bear. How could I survive such a calamity? It just couldn't happen. It was too horrible to even think about.

Staring wide-eyed into the darkness, I heard Gus unlock the front door and stumble up the stairs. *He must be drunk,*

I thought. My heart pounded with apprehension. It was always worse when he'd had too much to drink. The toilet flushed, then I heard his bedroom door close. I had held my breath. Letting it out, I prayed to all the saints that he'd pass out and leave me alone.

The house fell silent, and the air grew heavy in my bedroom. I was a swimmer in a vast ocean, and sleep, the distant shore, couldn't be reached. Twisting and turning in the sticky sheets, I kept hearing Patrick's words over and over like a phonograph record deep inside my head: *Goddamn lesbian bitch!* Over and over it played like the needle was stuck. All night the words screamed in my mind.

A wan light faintly etched the outline of my window as night gave in to a gray, muggy morning. It got hotter as the sun came up, but sleep refused to rescue me. Like a parched plain with no horizon, an endless Sunday lay before me. My head throbbed painfully. I lacked the energy to move, so I just lay there watching the daylight devour the darkness.

I must have dozed for a while because the next thing I knew Gus's angry voice was rising from the kitchen below.

"Mina, it's time for mass. Are you coming with me or are you going to sleep the whole goddamn day?" I didn't move or answer. "If you're not down here right off, I'm leaving. Do you hear me, girl?"

I kept my eyes shut, waiting for more ranting, but there was a long silence. Then the front door slammed, jarring the whole house, and I was alone with pain. Turning toward the wall, I buried my head deep in the pillow and let the tears that had been aching to come take me at last.

11

MINA ARENHOLT—A REAL WOMAN NOW

Graduation was a complete disaster, followed by a dismal dinner at Chuck's Steak House on Roosevelt Avenue. The dinner was Aunt Willie's treat that went along with the check she had given me earlier.

All through the meal her steady stream of cheery conversation masked her dislike about including Gus in the invitation—and she was pulling it off rather well. Her German accent deepened, and I could tell she was pleased at Gus's discomfort. She enjoyed every grimace and grunt he made as he noisily consumed his steak. Tiring of the game, she suggested a trip to the little girls' room. I knew she wanted to ask the questions I was dreading.

"Mina, you've pulled a long face all evening. This is the day you have looked forward to with so much anticipation. What's wrong?" She stood behind me as I washed my hands. The mirror reflected a small, fragile woman with short henna hair.

Age had traced a pattern of worry across her broad features. Her eyes held mine, and I knew to be careful with my answers. Bracing myself, I thought how tired and old she looked and how she resembled Mama. Suddenly I missed Mama terribly, and I realized I hadn't thought about her in a long time.

Frown lines furrowed the space between Aunt Willie's eyes. "How is it you look so sad, *Liebchen?* You've hardly spoken a word all evening. You didn't seem to enjoy the congratulations of your friends after the ceremony. When Sister Mary Frances embraced you and wished you well, you turned away with hardly a word. That was rude. After all, Sister was your favorite teacher." She shook her head. "I just don't understand you tonight. Tell me now, what has come over you?"

I swallowed hard and reached for a paper towel. I knew I would have to say something. "Aunt Willie, graduation isn't all that important, really. I can't generate much enthusiasm for all the fuss. Please don't worry. I'm OK. Really I am." My words sounded lame as I took my time wiping my hands.

"Is it because Katy couldn't be here?" Her eyes were full of concern as she struggled to understand.

"Yes, I suppose that's it." I tried to sound casual. I had said earlier that Katy was sick. Embroidering the story, I said the doctor had insisted Katy stay in bed because she had a temperature of 102°. It was a pretty elaborate lie, but it was all I could think of on the spur of the moment. It must have been convincing because now Aunt Willie clucked her tongue and made small sounds of sympathy that made me feel awful for deceiving her. Still, what could I do? I couldn't tell her the truth because, after all, I didn't know the truth myself. But I was pretty sure what happened the other night was the real reason Katy hadn't shown up. Like something undigested, the thought lay in the pit of my stomach. I'd felt this queasiness start in the auditorium while I was watching for Katy. All during the ceremony I kept staring at her empty chair in front of mine, knowing something dreadful must have happened and that I was to blame.

As we left the ladies' room I prayed I'd get through dinner

without having to answer more questions or manufacture more lies.

I forced down the gravy-drenched roast beef as best I could and somehow got through the ice cream and cake that followed. As usual, Aunt Willie did all the talking. Gus sulked in silence, stuffing his mouth noisily like always. Watching him, I felt an almost uncontrollable urge to scream. Instead, I wiped my mouth daintily and clutched the napkin in my lap to keep my hands from shaking.

At last it was over. Aunt Willie rummaged through her enormous black handbag and paid the bill. "That was good, ya?" You enjoyed, Mina?" She beamed, not bothering to include Gus with her smile.

On the way home in the taxi no one spoke. When we got to the house she hugged me close, saying how proud she was of me and that I looked really beautiful in my home-made dress.

"Good night, Gus." Her voice was abrupt. "I hope you enjoyed dinner." Her words clearly implied she didn't give a damn whether he had or not.

He mumbled a perfunctory, "Yeah, thanks," and lurched out of the backseat. Without another word he climbed the front steps and let himself in the front door.

I fought the tears that wanted to come and kissed Aunt Willie's cheek. "Thank you so much," I choked, then dashed up the steps, stumbling over the hem of my long skirt. I caught myself from falling just as the sobs rose in my throat. At the door, I stood for a moment, trying to catch my breath. As I fumbled with my key, I heard the cab pull away from the curb. "Mother of God, pray for me," I gasped as the door closed behind me.

The house was dark and smelled stale from being shut

up all evening. Going straight to my room, I heard Gus rummaging in the kitchen below. The fridge door banged. He was looking for a beer as usual. I prayed he wouldn't bother me. I pulled my dress over my head and flung it on the floor in the back of my closet. I didn't want to see that damn dress again. Just looking at it brought back the pain of the night in Katy's room. I decided to throw it out with the trash in the morning.

It was weird. There had been no call from Katy all week. And even more ominous, she hadn't shown up for class the previous week or made it to graduation rehearsal. I hadn't called for fear Mary or Patrick would answer the phone. Of course, I'd been imagining the worst, and the worst was that I might never hear from Katy again. I even tried to convince myself Katy really was sick.

I decided my best move was to get in touch with Mary Alice. Maybe she'd call Katy for me. Mary Alice would think it strange I didn't know what was up with Katy, but I'd think of a cover story. I had to know what was going on.

The roast beef sat like a hunk of lead in my stomach so I went to the bathroom and took an Alka-Seltzer. Not even bothering to put on my nightie, I crawled under the sheets, praying with all my strength that Gus would leave me alone. My supplication apparently didn't have time to get through to the Almighty because I heard his footsteps down the hall. The turn of the door knob tightened my abdominal muscles. Sitting upright in the darkness, I waited for the door to open, my heart rapping like a jackhammer against my ribs.

The dim outline of his body slipped into the room and his low chuckle broke the silence. His laugh had a disturbing, almost intimate quality that raised the hair on the back of my neck.

It was way out of character, a laugh like that, and I was at a loss as to its meaning. His bare feet made no sound coming toward me. His long johns made him ghostlike in the darkness.

"Well, our little Mina's all grown up now, graduated proper-like and ready to take her place in the big wide world," he said sarcastically as he sat heavily on the edge of my bed. I shuddered as he groped for me. His fingers tightened over my hand, pressing it hard against the mattress, and his face came close. I smelled the beer on his breath. "It's about time I started treating you like the woman you are. No more kid stuff, eh? Time we got down to the real thing. This will be the night you'll remember. I promise you, Mina, darlin'." He laughed again. His stale breath scorched my face. I started to shake and drew my knees to my chest.

"Tonight you'll know what it's like to be a real woman," he said. His slobbering mouth covered mine, and his tongue pushed past my teeth and filled my mouth. I was panicked and choked with terror. I wretched and gagged.

"What are you doing?" I pushed him away, and with the back of my hand I tried to wipe away the foul taste of his mouth. I thought by talking I could stop what I feared was coming, but before I could think of what to say, he stood up and fumbled with the buttons on his underwear. Hopping from one foot to the other, he struggled out of his long johns, stamped them under his feet, and stood naked in the half light. He was breathing hard. The bedsprings protested angrily as he sank back on the mattress and grabbed for me again. I couldn't move.

"Please, Gus, for God's sake, don't!" Sobs ate my words and weakness drained me into complete helplessness.

"Goddamn it! Mina, use your head. Don't make me

spell it out for you. Just move over and give me room." He threw his leg over my waist, falling heavily on all fours on top of me. In that moment I knew I was lost.

He grabbed the sheet I was clutching. He flung it away, and I felt his hairy legs tighten around me. His laugh was shrill like a woman's.

"You're pretty foxy, aren't you, Mina? Damn! I like a broad who sleeps bare. You knew it would turn me on, didn't you? Well, you won't be disappointed."

His hands were squeezing my breasts. "Gorgeous!" he gasped as his fingers dug into my flesh. I winced and pleaded for him to stop. His breath rattled deep in his throat as his wet mouth found my breasts. His teeth bit into my soft skin.

"Stop! You're hurting me!" I cried. "For God's sake, stop, Gus!"

"Jesus, I could eat you alive," he moaned as he sucked at one breast then the other.

A strange sensation came over me. He was hurting me terribly, but at the same time I was excited. What he was doing was disgusting, and yet part of me felt an unbelievable urgency. Just as that urgency became almost more than I could bear, he took his mouth away, and his hand moved downward. Groping roughly, his fingers opened me and then with a ripping pain he was inside me. Screams burst from my lungs; louder and louder they echoed in the darkness.

"Damn it! You're as dry as a bone. Relax, and for chrissake shut up!" He spit noisily into his cupped palm and rubbed himself to go deeper. Pushing my legs apart, he pinned me hard to the squeaking mattress. His body was wet with sweat, and guttural moans accompanied each wrenching thrust. The pounding became more violent and my screams grew weaker.

I'm giving up, I thought, and began to cry. But the crying seemed to come from someone else, like the screams had before. It was an odd sensation. I was there, but I couldn't determine who was crying or who was hearing the crying.

All of a sudden his body convulsed. He arched above me.

"Oh, shit! Oh, shit!" he gasped. A horrible animal sound burst from him. His hands clutched my breasts, and the full weight of his body collapsed on mine. For an awful moment I couldn't breathe. He didn't move. He was suffocating me. *This is how it feels to die.* Suddenly a rush of air filled my lungs, and with it came the strength to push him off me.

Like a dead man he rolled to the far side of the bed and immediately began to snore. But he wasn't dead. And lying in the twisted sheets I knew that I was alive too...because the pain told me so.

12

THE *SHIDDACH*

"Bubbe, are you awake? May I come in to talk?" Chana's voice was unsteady as she knocked tentatively at her grandmother's door. It was after 11. Perhaps Bubbe was already asleep, she thought. But no, a thin sliver of light crept from under the door.

In her nightie and a thin cotton robe, Chana stood barefoot in the hall, trembling and listening, her ear close to the door. "Please don't let them hear me," she prayed silently to a God she wasn't sure existed. Her mother and Mendel had retired earlier. Only a dim night-light glowed faintly in the nursery where little Moishe slept. The house was quiet, and the beating of her heart sounded loud in her ears. She knocked again.

"Chanala, darling, come in, come in." Her grandmother's voice was cheerful as always. Chana turned the knob soundlessly and stepped into the warmly lit room.

Sarah Blumenthal sat propped among her pillows. The lamp at the bedside bathed her tiny figure in a soft radiance. A book lay open on her lap. Pinching her spectacles from her thin nose, she peered expectantly at Chana. Her faded blue eyes filled with questioning concern. "My goodness child, what is it? At this hour you should be asleep already. Are you ill, Chanala? You look so pale. What's the matter, darling?"

"No, I'm fine, Bubbe. I just want to talk." The braided

rug felt warm and reassuring under her bare feet.

Sarah clucked her tongue against her teeth. "Look at you padding about with no slippers. Come quick, get under the covers before you catch your death. I don't know why your mother keeps the furnace so low all the time." She shook her head. "Just to save a few pennies. What's the point if we all come down with chills and fever?"

Chana climbed into the high bed and cuddled close to her grandmother. Pulling the covers to her chin, she was relaxed by the warmth of the bed. She didn't know how to begin. Lying quiet for a moment, Chana tried to pull her thoughts together as she stared at the oversize dark roses of the wallpaper. She'd heard Sarah complain on more than one occasion, *I wish your mother could do something about that atrocious paper,* and she remembered the resignation in Bubbe's voice, *but this is Mendel's house, and he doesn't see fit to change anything, so what's to do? I live with it.* Chana knew it was one more thing that made Bubbe a stranger like herself in this somber household.

Sarah pulled her close. "Well, child, what is it? Has the cat run off with your tongue? A problem with school? *Nu?* So tell me." Her wrinkled hand reached for Chana's. "Lord, your hands are chunks of ice yet. Tell me, Chanala, what's going on? Why are you creeping about the house in the middle of the night when you should be fast sleeping in your bed?"

"Bubbe, I..." A huge lump hurt deep in her throat. She held tightly to the old woman's hand and hoped she could put her fears into words before the tears came.

"They can't do this to me," she began in a trembling voice. "Please, Bubbe, you have to help me. You're the only one who will listen. Tell me, please, what should I do?" She rested her head on the old woman's shoulder and let the tears come.

Sarah's thin arms cradled Chana, rocking her tenderly. "*Oy vay iz mir, mine crynehel. Nein, nein*, Chanala, don't cry, my *anekel*. Shush now," she crooned softly, stroking the tousled hair as Chana's tears dampened the ruffled bosom of her flannel nightgown.

"Have you talked with Mama? What does she say?" Sarah knew what was disturbing her granddaughter so she steadied her voice, hoping to calm the girl.

Chana sat up. Her eyes searched the woman's face. This was the familiar Bubbe, the one she could rely on to make everything OK. Even when Chana was small, when she had the sniffles or a tummy ache, Bubbe's magical power could make things better. She was sure the soft words and gentle touch would work their spell again. They had to.

Chana's voice was steadier now, "Yes, I've talked to Mama. She called me to her room after supper. She said the Rebbe's assistant, Gabai Zevi, had a meeting with her and Mendel yesterday afternoon. Avrum Rosten's parents were there too. They've set the betrothal ceremony for 7 o'clock Thursday evening at the synagogue. The *Ketuba* will be signed by everyone, and my life will be ruined." Chana began to sob. "I might as well be dead."

Bubbe patted her shoulder, "*Nein, nein,* my Chanala."

"Bubbe, you knew they were going to do this all along, didn't you?" Chana's flooded eyes were pleading. "Why didn't you tell me? Now there's so little time. Please help me. You're the only one I can turn to. No one else will listen. It's all been decided, but maybe Mama will listen to you. Tell her I can't get married. I'll die first. You can make them listen. I know you can." The words tumbled over her sobs. "Oh, Bubbe, Avrum Rosten is so ugly with that gap between his front teeth. His *payess* are greasy and he smells bad. I don't think he ever takes a bath! Oh, Lord, Bubbe, what am I going to do? Mama won't listen to me. She just runs on about what a good match it is because he's first in his class at Yeshiva University and everyone knows he'll be a great Talmud scholar one day. She said Mendel informed the Rebbe, and the Rebbe's already given his blessing."

Chana's eyes blazed as her words came faster. "Bubbe, tell Mama I can't stand him. Please tell them to stop this awful *Shiddach*. Avrum's so horrid. He never talks to me; he just looks past me like I don't exist. Please talk to Mendel and Mama and make them understand how I feel. Mama says it's final; it's all been decided and the Rebbe gave his blessing. She says it's a match the whole community approves. She's so pleased with herself, and I can't change her mind no matter what I say. They're swallowing me up, Bubbe. Can't you do something?"

Never in all her 70 years had Sarah felt as helpless as she did now looking into the eyes of her beloved granddaughter. What could she say to this child, the light of her life? She shook her head. "Chanala, the words are not mine to say that will change what is happening. I wish with all my heart I had the ear of your mother and Mendel, but I know they will refuse to hear me. I don't have the power. I'm just an old woman in the house of my daughter's husband. You must understand, Chanala, Miriam listens only to Mendel, not to me."

The Hasidic world had long ago devoured her Miriam. Now it was about to consume her Chana too, and she was powerless to stop it.

The day before, she'd had heated words with her

daughter about the decisions made at the Gabai's office. Miriam's face had shone with delight at her accomplishment, and she'd brushed Sarah's protests aside with a rush of excited words.

"No more will they say my daughter isn't from the nicest people, Bubbe. When she is married to Avrum Rosten she will no longer be considered 'half Jew' and be looked down on by the community. It's been agreed they will be supported by both families. They will live in Nathan and Leah Rosten's home until Avrum finishes his studies at Yeshiva University. Mendel has worked hard to bring this about. He's a good father to my Chana and overjoyed at the Rebbe's blessing. He's told me the *Riboyne Shel O'lem* wants it. So it will be."

Sarah had persisted in trying to convince her daughter that the child was much too young. She pointed out that Chana should finish school before any wedding was considered. "I can't imagine what you and Mendel are thinking of to do such a thing," she said sharply.

"Mama, it's not for you to question me or Mendel in this matter," Miriam shot back. "You don't understand about these things, so don't meddle. This marriage is best for Chana and the family. She will be considered a *Kalleh Moid*, a true Hasidic bride. The members of the *Tzaddikim* sit for the betrothal ceremony in synagogue next Thursday evening." Her last words had been full of anger. "I'll say no more, except to remind you again not to interfere. It is not your place to do so."

Sarah knew any further pleading would be useless.

In the big bed she held her granddaughter close and shook her head sadly. "What is done, is done, Chanala, my darling. I know it's like a bad dream you're having, but I can't make it go away. I wish I could. It's out of my hands already." She retrieved a handkerchief from the bosom of her nightdress and pressed it gently in Chana's hands. "Dry your eyes, my Bubeleh. Tears won't help a bit. Let me tell you a story." Sarah plumped the pillows at their backs and put her arm around Chana's shoulder.

"It happened a long time ago, even before your Mama was born. There were two young boys who lived in a small town in upstate New York. They were very close friends, almost like brothers. When they were in high school one of the boys had to move with his parents to Chicago, but before he left, the two friends made a promise that their children would be joined in marriage one day. Over the years they kept in touch. The boy who moved to Chicago married a girl from Decatur and eventually grew wealthy in the ladies' ready-to-wear business. In a year's time their first son was born. The boy who stayed in the small town also married, and two years after, a daughter was born to them."

Chana turned to her grandmother. "Bubbe, you were the girl born in the small town, weren't you? Of course, now I remember. The town was Plattsburg, right? You used to tell me stories of your growing up there."

"Yes, Bubeleh, you're right and much too smart already. Well, not to worry. Let me get on with the rest of my story. The baby born in Chicago grew into a brilliant young man. He studied at Northwestern University. His father was proud of him and hoped he might study for the Rabbinate. One day Saul Blumenthal remembered the promise given to his boyhood friend, and a marriage was arranged between their two children.

"So, since you know who I'm talking about, I'll use names for the rest of the story. I was appalled and crushed by what had been planned for me, but Papa explained it was expected of a dutiful daughter in a respected Jewish family. Papa was the law in our household, so no amount of crying on my part swayed him. Mama said it was tradition and I should try to make the best of it. So my fate was sealed and they took me to Chicago on the train. To this day I remember how I felt when I met your grandfather for the first time. Such a whirlwind of emotions. I'll never forget. I was facing a tall stranger who I would spend the rest of my life with. There were tears in my eyes, and it was hard for me to look at him, but his dark eyes met mine and he smiled as he took my hand. Through my tears I saw he was the most handsome man I had ever met. Looking in my eyes he said, 'No need to cry, Sarah Miller, but if you must, remember, it is written in the *Kabbalah*: 'God counts the tears of women.' " In that moment I knew I had met my soul mate, my destined one, my *Bechertah*."

Tears of remembrance glistened in the old woman's eyes. She turned to Chana, "Who knows, Bubeleh, perhaps you should also be so lucky. You might find Avrum is your *Bechertah* after all. His looks can't compare with those of your grandfather, but who's to know how you will feel when you get to know each other?

"Perhaps it won't be as bad as you think. It could turn out to be a good match. Who's to know what the future holds, darling?" She was trying her best to make her voice reassuring, but in her heart she was afraid the match would be nothing but a disaster. How was it possible, she thought, that such a thing as this was still forced on children by their parents? How could people still live with the customs of the old country?

Her fingers caressed Chana's rumpled hair. She sighed

to herself. Yes, she was a stranger among them and just an old woman. She couldn't stand up against the whole *Lubavitcher* community. All she could do was hold this child she loved dearly, kiss her good night, and pray it would all work out.

"Go now. Get back to your room. It's getting late already and you need your sleep, darling."

Chana clung to Sarah for a moment before climbing out of the warm bed. "All right, Bubbe. Maybe we can talk later. I loved your story." Her voice was almost inaudible. "You and Grandpa were lucky."

"Yes, we'll talk more later, Chanala. Try to sleep well. Things will look brighter in the morning."

At the door, Chana turned to the tiny woman sitting in her big bed. *Bubbe looks so frail and old*, she thought as she closed the door softly behind her. Numbed by the realization that her last hope had been crushed, Chana made her way down the dark hall to her room.

She was just a girl and a half Jew in their eyes. They would do as they pleased with her. "Oh, Papa," she wailed, "I wish you were here to take me away from all this." But only the pillow heard her cry as it gathered her tears.

13

THE *TZADDIKIM*

The old men silently took their seats at a long oak table in the middle of the great hall of the synagogue. All wore black caftans and skullcaps. Rebbe Schneerson lowered himself into an ornately carved chair at the far end of the table. His broad fur hat made a dark halo above his white hair and flowing beard. A richly embroidered white caftan draped his frail body. The congregation often compared him with pictures of the old prophets, and some said he resembled the *Baal Shem Tov*. High above, an immense chandelier bathed the assembled figures in an almost mystical light. Paneled walls faintly captured the glow, filling the cavernous hall with shadows. As in a Rembrandt painting, the pale faces at the table struck bright accents in the darkness. The Ark, built into the front wall, was barely visible, as was the Rebbe's red-cushioned chair on its right. A sheaf of papers lay on the polished table in front of the Gabai, who sat stiffly at the Rebbe's left. He shuffled them nervously while the *Tzaddikim* sat motionless, waiting for the ceremony to proceed.

In an upper room of the synagogue, the women friends of the two families hovered about Chana. The room was hot and filled with nervous excitement. Everyone seemed to be talking at once. Flushed matrons buzzed around Chana, showering her with good wishes laced now and again with liberal servings of advice. She felt smothered and slightly faint, but sitting pale and quiet in the seat of honor she managed a slight smile and nod for each well-wisher.

Miriam stood at Chana's side, one hand resting lightly on her daughter's shoulder, eyes bright with pride at the attention given to her oldest child. This was a dream come true. The influential women of the community were accepting Chana as one of their own. She silently thanked the Master of the Universe. The women ate sponge cake and drank sweet wine as they wished the bride a prosperous and fruitful life.

Pessie bent close to Chana, speaking softly as she pressed a small wineglass into her friend's hand. "Please don't look so sad, little sister. This should be a happy night for you. Everything will be all right. You'll see. We'll talk later. I'll come to your room like always." She straightened up with difficulty, her small body grotesque with the approach of her second child, due within a few weeks.

Chana held out her hand to steady Pessie and smiled. "That will be good. I have so much to tell you. I'll wait up for you."

Rivke, Yakov's wife, pushed her way through the press of chattering women, a tray of macaroons in her hand. As she held it before Chana's face, her voice was shrill: "A grateful bride brings a healthy appetite to her own betrothal ceremony."

Chana shook her head and turned away. But Rivke, taking delight in her future sister-in-law's refusal, persisted. "Come, you should eat. What's not to like? Be grateful to your parents for arranging such a fine *Shiddach*." Her words were intended for all to hear.

Miriam frowned, but Chana hardly noticed Rivke's sarcasm. She searched the room for her grandmother. *Where has Bubbe gone?* she wondered as she swallowed the sweet wine, trying to wash down the lump of despair lodged in her throat. She was suffocating with the heat of so many bodies pressing about her chair. She felt faint, but most of all she felt terribly alone. Only the event held interest for the women in the room; they had little concern for her. In fact, they ignored her entirely as they gossiped among themselves. She knew all they expected from her was a proper amount of gratitude, expressed with just the right tone of humility. When they did pay her attention, their eyes were sharp and critical, anticipating she would stumble in her new role as *Kalleh Moid.*

It would be good to be alone with Pessie when the terrible evening was over, Chana reflected sadly. Her friend was quite occupied with her year-old son and impending delivery. They hadn't seen much of each other, nor shared the closeness enjoyed in the early days when Pessie first joined the family.

As Sarah Blumenthal threw open the door, all eyes turned expectantly toward her. She had been stationed in the hall outside to listen and report the progress of the *Tzaddikim* in the temple auditorium below.

"Shush!" She raised her hand. "Shush, now, everyone listen!" The room fell silent. Chana caught her breath, holding it tight in her chest as she strained with the others to hear. Faintly from far below came the unmistakable sound of breaking china.

"The plate has been broken," whispered Miriam.

Another woman exclaimed in a hushed whisper, "The destruction of Jerusalem."

The men below shouted exuberantly, "*Mazel Tov! Mazel Tov!*"

In the quiet that followed, the voice of the Rebbe rose, intoning passages from the Talmud. All in the upper room were transfixed as they strained to hear his words. Then, after the Rebbe, in a thin voice Avrum Rosten began his discourse. The women above listened with misty eyes, remembering their own bridegroom speaking the same words at their *Shiddach* ceremonies.

After Avrum's speech there were sounds of chairs being moved across the floor. The table was being made ready for food to be brought in. The washing of hands would come next, and after the blessing of the bread, the feasting and drinking would begin. Singing swelled from below, and suddenly the women in the upper room came alive with shrieks of laughter and shouts of "*Mazel Tov!*"

Everyone embraced each other laughing and crying, and the room was filled with joyous excitement. Miriam's voice was ecstatic. "They have done it! The handkerchief has been held by both families. Now all is legal. All is binding!" Miriam embraced her new *Kalleh Moid*, overlooking the despair on her daughter's face. Chana turned her head away, and Miriam never noticed the tears streaking her daughter's cheeks.

Pessie clapped her hands and sang with the others, but her eyes were full of concern as she watched her friend sitting forlornly in the seat of honor.

Bubbe went quietly to her granddaughter. Taking her hands she spoke softly, "Chanala, it is done already." She bent close, "Chana, I'm so sorry. Oy! What else can I say, darling? Maybe it will turn out well in the end. I pray time will bring you happiness, Bubeleh." She tried to make her words sound cheerful, but she knew her gesture was hollow, and not for a minute did she believe her own words.

From below the singing grew louder as the groom was raised in his chair above the heads of the celebrants. High on the shoulders of the shuffling men, he was passed from one to the other as they circled the room. The old songs rang loud, accompanied by the stomping of feet. Finally, as exhaustion overcame them, they returned to their seats at the long table to groggily intone the grace at the close of the *Tzaddikim*. On unsteady feet they walked into the starry night and back to their homes.

Long before that, however, the women started saying their good-byes. As they left the upper room they formed small groups to walk up President Street. Strolling under the linden trees along the parkway, Miriam put her arm around Chana's waist and gave her a hug. "I'm so proud of my *Kalleh Moid*, my little girl bride. Everyone agrees a fine match was made here tonight. You will be the most beautiful *Kalleh* of the year, my Chanala."

Bubbe walked in silence beside them as Miriam chattered on. "Next week, Thursday evening, the families will meet at our house for the signing of the conditions. The Gabai told me he will pen the Aramaic form himself. It will be signed by both families. Mendel says the Rebbe recommends Tuesday the 18th of next month as an auspicious day. If the Rostens approve, it will be the wedding night."

Chana bit her lip to keep from protesting and shaming her mother in front of the women who walked with them. She wanted to cry out, "No, Mama, no!" But she held the words inside.

Bubbe noticed how cold Chana's trembling hand was in hers. Saying nothing, she held tightly to her icy fingers, and her heart wept for the child she loved.

14

CHANA STERN—THE LETTER

Dearest Papa,

You've been dead almost four years. I miss you so much. No one here can help me, not even Bubbe. I know there's no address I can put on this letter, but wherever you are, I hope my thoughts reach you.

Since the betrothal ceremony and the signing of the marriage contract, the days have piled up with a terrible heaviness, each one a vice that presses the very life from me.

Tonight what happened shouldn't happen to anyone. They took away my countenance. When I look in the mirror I see a complete stranger. They destroyed the person I've known and made me into one of their own. I am powerless and alone. Even Bubbe turned her head when she saw what their shears had done.

They took great delight in their task and sang as my curls fell. I was glad tears blinded me so I couldn't see the strands lying limply on the floor.

Mama was radiant all the while. Afterward she took my hand and whispered, "It's tradition that the bride should weep when her hair is shorn. So, Chanala, cry as others have done through the centuries. My little Kalleh, it will purify your heart for the ceremony Thursday evening."

Papa, you wouldn't know Mama. She's not the same as when the four of us lived in the city. Since she married Mendel and became a convert, she's so different. She belongs to the Hasidic world, heart and soul. Bubbe and I hardly matter to her anymore, especially since the baby came. Little Moishe is her pride and joy. He's going on four now, and Mama and Mendel call him "boychick." Bubbe can't talk with Mama like in the old days, and it's been ages since Mama really saw me. She only sees a Hasidic daughter making a fine marriage. She doesn't remember the growing-up years when we were all together and happy on Riverside Drive.

Bubbe isn't the same either. I've tried to talk to her, but it's no use. She's given up where Mama's concerned, so in a way she's given up on me too. When Bubbe tries to tell her how unhappy I am, Mama says it's not her place to interfere in Dubovitch family matters. My heart is full of despair, and I see the same despair reflected in Bubbe's face.

But to get back to what happened last night: The women surrounded me, each holding a lighted candle. Pessie held the mirror for me to see. In the flickering light, I saw their handiwork and wept. They left ragged strands of my hair sticking out above my ears. My head looks too small for my body and I don't recognize myself at all. Now there is an ugly, shorn stranger looking back at me in the mirror. But they weren't finished with me.

Next they bound my head with a rough kerchief, and all of them escorted me to the mikva. *Do you know what a* mikva *is? Perhaps you do, but I never heard you use the word. It's a place for ritual bathing. The one they took me to is just for* Lubavitchers. *The other Hasidic courts, the* Satmorers *and the* Bobavers, *have their own. The Lubavitchers'* mikva *is within walking distance of our house on President Street and not far from the synagogue. The place looks like the swimming pool at the Shelton*

Hotel where you used to take me swimming. Remember? Only this one isn't for swimming. It's shallow all over and lined with colored tile. In this pool, swimming is definitely forbidden.

Mama, Bubbe, Pessie, and the others walked me there. When we reached the vestibule, everyone hugged me and wished me well. Mama took me inside and turned me over to an attendant, a heavy woman in a long-sleeve smock. She took hold of my arm. Her pale eyes measured me without expression. Her rough, red hands were dry against my flesh. I immediately hated her and looked for Mama, but she had disappeared.

I started to shake as the fat one led me down a dim hall to a small cubicle. Inside, she motioned for me to sit on a tiny wooden stool. Without a word she produced a pair of gleaming steel clippers from the pocket of her smock. "Hold out your hands" were the first words she spoke to me. Her voice was as flat as the look she gave me. Grasping my hand she started to cut my fingernails. She took precise care to clip them as short as possible and never once did she heed my protests when her clippers jabbed into my flesh. With great difficulty she got to her knees on the tile floor and removed my shoes and stockings. The same procedure reduced my toenails to mere stubs.

All the while this was happening, she was muttering in Yiddish under her breath. Next she did a strange thing: Carefully gathering the nail clippings in a fine handkerchief, she deposited them into a bronze bowl, then put a lighted match to the small bundle. She sang under her breath in Hebrew as the flames consumed the contents of the bowl. The flames died into smoke, and the room reeked with the sickly smell of burning flesh.

Without asking, she started to undress me. As I stood naked before her, she pulled a thin cotton shift over my head. My feet were cramped and stiff from the cold floor. I was miserable. I kept looking at Mama, but she didn't seem to notice me. Her eyes were closed. She was rocking to and fro, her head bent in prayer.

The old woman took me by the arm and walked me to the edge of the pool. She descended the steps into the tepid water, pulling me after her. Mama stood by silently, her eyes still closed in prayer. The woman's singing grew louder. All at once she grabbed me. Putting one hand over my nose and mouth, she forced me backward. The water rushed over my head as my feet left the bottom. She held me down. Water filled my nostrils and roared in my ears. I was sure I was drowning and panic took possession of me. I fought to find the bottom with my feet as my arms flew in all directions, grabbing helplessly at the water. Just as I was about to give up the fight, her big arms pulled me to the surface. I gulped air, but before I could get another breath she pushed me back under. This she did two more times, and each time she brought me up for air, I heard her shout, "This is a kosher daughter of Israel." The words ricocheted off the walls.

Papa, I was sure I was going to pass out. My ears were ringing and everything was spinning. As I closed my eyes to steady the world, she pushed me toward the steps at the side of the pool, and I was free of the water.

The next thing I remember, I was in the dressing room drying myself off with a coarse towel I found on the bench. My tormentor had disappeared. Shaking, I rubbed my hair dry and got into my clothes. When I left the dressing room, Mama pressed a $5 bill into the big one's hand. They *exchanged a few quiet words, and then Mama came toward me and took me in her arms.*

"Chanala, Chanala," she murmured as she held me tight.

The dam broke. I buried my face in the warm curve of her neck. For a moment the Mama I knew was back, holding me close like in the old days when I was little.

"I'm so proud," she whispered.

We held each other like that for a long time.

Now I must bring this letter to a close because I am exhausted. I miss you so much, Papa. I know you've heard me. I love you.

Your daughter,
Chana

P.S. I'll keep this letter always.

15

MAZEL TOV

Up in Chana's room the women laughed and chattered like a flock of magpies as they finished dressing the bride. Then, still flushed with merriment, they all left the house for the synagogue. The *Lubavitcher* compound at 770 Eastern Parkway was a short walk from the house on President Street. There they gathered in an upper room overlooking the synagogue's courtyard. The women fussed over Chana, preparing her for the ceremony that would take place later under the stars.

Rays from the setting sun filtered through the shuttered windows, making thin bars of gold across the floor. Chana's voluminous gown of white voile billowed about her feet. In the fading light its folds turned a tawny cream. The boned bodice allowed her only quick, short breaths. Sitting uncomfortably in the cushioned bridal chair, she felt light-headed as the elderly matrons and young women crowded around her. Talking to one another, they raised such a babble that Chana's ears ached.

At the far end of the room, Bubbe helped Miriam unpack the heavy lace veil that had been handed down from one generation to the other. They draped the heirloom over a long table and reverently smoothed the richly patterned lace.

Perspiration trickled from under Chana's wig, soaking the reddish-brown strands at the nape of her neck. The *shaytl* fit poorly and was uncomfortably tight. She wondered why Mrs. Levi hadn't done a better job after all the tedious visits she and Mama had made to the old woman's wig shop. As she dabbed the back of her neck with her handkerchief, a sharp rap sounded at the door. A breathless silence replaced the noise and confusion and all eyes focused on the double doors at the far end of the room. Miriam brushed a curl from her cheek, nervously straightened the sash of her lavender gown, and moved quickly to open the door.

Accompanied by Yakov and David, Avrum Rosten stepped timidly over the threshold. They were followed by six students from Avrum's class at the university wearing black fedoras straight and low over their curled *payess*. Yakov and David wore the customary fur hat, as did the groom, who was resplendent in a white silk caftan. Avrum's hat rested uneasily above his pale countenance, and his neatly groomed sidelocks curled stiffly in front of his protruding ears. Visibly uneasy, he perspired profusely as he made his way to Chana.

Chana shuddered. Why hadn't the good Lord seen fit to provide Avrum with at least a ghost of a chin? Lowering her head, she fixed her eyes on her hands. Tears threatened to come. All morning they'd been waiting just behind her eyelids. She fought valiantly one more time to hold them back. She would never let these people see how she felt.

Avrum approached her chair, eyes cast down in compliance with tradition. The *mitzvahs* commanded he shouldn't look on his bride until they met under the *chuppa*.

Shifting his feet, he cleared his throat. Glancing at Yakov for support, he launched into a discourse on the obligations of a Hasidic bride and dutiful wife. His eyes were focused on the floor near Chana's feet. When he came to the end of his dissertation, the women who stood behind Chana came forward and tossed handfuls of grain over the startled couple to ensure a union blessed by many children.

Miriam and Bubbe, the veil supported between them, approached the bride and groom. Giving one end to Avrum, they lifted the gossamer fabric over Chana's head with a ballet-like gesture. It descended over her, falling to the floor about her chair. A strong sensation of suffocation choked her. She gasped for air as the weight of the veil threatened to dislodge her wig. "Now, they have me for sure," she thought. "I'm trapped, just as Jonah was when the whale swallowed him." It was such a bizarre idea she suddenly felt like laughing or maybe crying—she didn't know which.

       🙚   🙚   🙚

By 8 o'clock guests began to fill the courtyard where folding chairs were arranged in rows. A red-carpeted aisle led to a magnificent white silk *chuppa*. The bridal canopy was supported by four ribboned poles festooned with bunches of fragrant stephanotis.

The guests held small white candles in special cardboard holders and the night came alive with hundreds of flickering lights.

Families greeted each other in hushed voices, then quietly took their seats—the women and small children on one side of the red carpet, the men and young boys on the other. The women dressed in their *shabbas* finery were a colorful contrast to the bearded men clad in black opposite them. Whispering softly in Yiddish, they waited for the groom to appear.

Suddenly a hoarse whisper rose above their murmuring, "The *Rhosen* is coming!" Heads turned, and someone else exclaimed, "See, he comes with his men." All eyes were fixed on the procession moving slowly down the red carpet.

Avrum Rosten walked languidly between his brothers-in-law-to-be, Yakov and David. Paler than ever, he leaned heavily on them as if he were unable to stand by himself. Again, tradition was being served; the deliberate show of frailty demonstrated to the guests that he had fasted properly as required by the *mitzvahs*. All nodded with approval at the groom's elegant display of weakness.

Nathan and Lea Rosten walked behind Avrum, doing little to conceal their satisfaction. They beamed openly and nodded to friends. This day would mark their lives forever. They would be allied with the prestigious Dubovitch family, and everyone knew Rov Dubovitch had the ear of the Rebbe himself. They couldn't have made a better match for their son, and the dowry had been more than they had hoped for.

Behind them came the Yeshiva students. Young faces gravely solemn, they marched in a tight group, ritual fringe hanging beneath their black coats. With stiff-brimmed black hats fixed at the same angle, they were six carbon copies of sober adolescence, all sporting the delicate beginnings of beard and mustache.

Next came the bridegroom in a white linen *kittel* tied at the waist with a black silk cord. An enormous fur hat dwarfed his sallow features. Hesitantly he took his place beside the Rebbe who stood waiting under the *chuppa*. The Rebbe's fringed *tallis* and gold-banded shawl made him a biblical figure straight out of the old testament.

The crowd stirred as all heads turned to the tiny figure of the bride, led by her sister-in-law, Pessie. The two made their way majestically down the aisle. Chana seemed to float toward the group waiting under the canopy. Rivke followed, watching that the bride's train flowed properly behind her. Chana's face was completely hidden by the folds of her veil.

The Rebbe stepped forward and, with a slightly palsied hand, lifted the veil from Chana's face, then slowly let it fall again. The gesture was met by a loud wailing from the women's section. The sound of their lament rose and swelled in the starry night, a magnificent tribute to the plight of women through the ages. Before the ceremony, Miriam carefully coached her daughter to weep so all could hear. Chana didn't have to pretend, but, setting her jaw, she refused to cry out. She wouldn't give them that. She let the tears course down her cheeks behind the privacy of her veil.

The Rebbe held a goblet of red wine in his trembling hand. His voice wavered slightly as he intoned the ancient betrothal benediction. First he gave the cup to Avrum to drink, then turned and offered it to Chana. Pessie lifted the veil, and Chana brought the cup to her lips. Her hand shook, and some drops fell, staining the pristine folds of her skirt. Like blood on new snow, they spread darkly on the pale fabric. The wine was sweet and thick on the back of her tongue. She tried not to gag and swallowed hard.

Rivke and Pessie came forward to stand beside the bride. Taking her by the hand, the three slowly circled the groom. Chana felt dizzy as they repeated their circle seven times. The audience sang as the group made slow turns around Avrum. Chana spoke the Hebrew words she had studied. Rivke and Pessie joined in the chant, but their voices were barely audible above the loud audience.

The Rebbe took the marriage contract from the Gabai

and read from the scroll. The Aramaic words filled the thin air with a strange cadence. All held their breath to listen. Next, the Rebbe offered a quill pen to Chana and, trembling, she put her name on the parchment. Avrum fumbled, searching for his gold-rimmed spectacles, his hands also unsteady as he took the pen to write his name beside hers.

Pessie lifted the veil from Chana's tear-soaked face. Avrum took her right hand in his left, and with his right hand he slipped a plain gold ring on her index finger, speaking loudly in English for all to hear, "Behold thou art consecrated unto me according to the laws of Moses and Israel."

The Rebbe raised a glass wrapped in a fine cloth and laid it at their feet. With a shrill crack it broke into shards as Avrum, still holding Chana's hand, ground it under his heel. This brought the congregation to their feet. "*Mazel Tov, Mazel Tov!*" they roared, and the courtyard erupted with loud stomping and clapping. "*Mazel Tov, Mazel Tov!*" echoed in the night.

As the tumult rose about them, Avrum grasped Chana's arm and turned her toward the aisle. "Come quickly, follow me." With long strides he pulled her down the red carpet toward the synagogue door. "Try to look happy," he hissed. "Everyone is looking." Avrum stumbled over her long gown. She tried to smile and did her best to keep up with him.

꙳ ꙳ ꙳

In a room prepared for the bride and groom on the second floor of the synagogue, a small table for two awaited them. Here the newlyweds would share their first meal together. Everything had been kept hot under silver salvers. A bucket with champagne stood next to the groom's chair. Macaroons and *kugel* were arranged artfully on a cut-glass plate. Here they would break their fast, and the marriage would be considered consummated.

After Avrum seated Chana, he poured a glass of wine. "Here, maybe this will put some color in your cheeks and a smile on your lips. You really look sick. Are you sure you're all right? Maybe I should call one of your women."

"No need, Avrum, I'm all right," Chana answered, keeping her gaze fixed on the glass in her hand. Sipping slowly, she hoped the wine would soothe the ache behind her eyes.

Avrum sat stiffly opposite her and poured a glass for himself. As the wine found her stomach, Chana realized she was ravenously hungry. Cupping the glass with both hands, she drank deeply and began to relax. She felt a bit light-headed but definitely better.

Settling into her chair, she began to study the man who was now her husband. Watching him sip his wine, she noticed he kept his eyes cast down as he spoke. Immediately the thought came: *I will be sitting across from this man every meal, year in and year out, for the rest of my life. Oh, God! How am I going to cope with that?*

Soon the wine began to ease the pain in her head, making a drowsy warm place there. The present is painful enough, she decided. Why should I add to the burden by fretting about a future I have no control over?

At that moment the roast chicken smelled irresistible. The aroma of the borscht, steaming in the tureen in front of her, was all she wanted to concern herself with.

Avrum ladled some of the dark broth into a bowl and set it before her. His pale eyes met hers for a moment. An embarrassed half smile parted his thin lips. Realizing she didn't know what to say, she bent over the soup bowl and gratefully broke her fast.

They ate in silence. With each glass of wine, Avrum's cheeks grew flushed. Tiny beads of perspiration edged his upper lip. Wiping his mouth delicately with his napkin, he leaned forward and raised his fourth glass of champagne. In a voice suddenly bold from the wine he exclaimed, "Chana, my *Kalleh*, you are truly radiant!" Eyes raised to the ceiling, he exclaimed, "*Riboyne Shel O'lem*! What more should a man ask for?" Putting his glass down, he continued. "My heart is full. By the Torah, I will be a good husband to you, Chana, I promise." His eyes were moist as he finished this out-of-character declaration.

At that moment Chana was not sure what she was feeling. The wine was making everything a little out of focus. There had been a moment when she almost laughed at his exaggerated gestures. Instead she took one more swallow from her glass and reached for a macaroon.

While the bride and groom dined privately, the men in the hall below were singing and dancing wildly. The music furnished by the *Klezmorim*, a group of *Ashkenazi* musicians known for lively Russian folk tunes, rang through the lower hall. With wine and song, the men waited for the groom to join them. Then they would raise him high on their shoulders and dance in circles about the room, passing him from one to the other until all were exhausted and the wine was gone.

In a separate room the women celebrated more quietly. With wine and sweet cakes, there was much merriment and excited chatter. Soft singing and slow dancing filled their time until Chana's return from the nuptial feast.

At the end of the evening, the two parties came together to conclude the festivities by dancing the traditional *Mitsveh Tintzl*. Male relatives danced with the bride while holding opposite ends of a white silk handkerchief to make sure contact was not made between them.

The *Mitsveh Tintzl* marked the close of the first day of the wedding celebration. During the next seven days there would be quiet evening gatherings for the families and friends of the bride and groom. After the seventh day the community would return to its usual sober existence.

16

LEAVING THE OLD LIFE

It had been a week since Mina's graduation and the night Gus forced her to go all the way. She'd made a phone call to the city yesterday. There were openings for waitresses at Schrafft's on 57th Street. It wasn't her idea of a great summer, but Aunt Willie had cut the ad out of the paper. Handing it to her niece, she suggested it would be a good way to supplement the graduation check.

"After all," she said, "you have to come up with $200 more to meet your tuition for secretarial school in the fall."

Mina never fancied herself a waitress, but it wasn't easy arguing with Aunt Willie. Some weeks ago her aunt decided secretarial school was the sensible thing to do. Not having any other ideas for the future, Mina agreed.

Here it was the morning of her interview and she was sitting at her dressing table wondering if she should wear her hair up. Switching on the dresser light, she anxiously studied her face in the mirror. Did no longer being a virgin show? Would people see it, like on a printed page? Strange thought, but there it was. Looking closer, she decided it was lack of sleep that made her uneasy this morning. Sleep hadn't been her friend since that night in Katy's room. She leaned closer to the mirror. Her mouth did look different, sort of hard. *Oh, damn!* Mina thought. *There I go again. I guess that's the way guilt works on a person.* Her eyes did look strange. Would Katy see it? Like a tiger, the question leapt at her out of nowhere. Katy—the pain and the joy—was always waiting there. She would never let Katy know what Gus had done. She'd never see Katy again, so enough. No more thinking. It hurt too much.

She pulled a brush through her hair. Twisting it in a French roll, she fastened it high on the back of her head. Fluffing out a pompadour over her forehead, Mina smiled for the mirror. She began to feel better as she applied rouge to her cheeks. The effect wasn't bad after all. She composed her mouth and carefully outlined her lips with color.

Her mind returned to the interview, and she began composing what she would say when she got to town. Recapping her lipstick, she dropped it into her purse and gave one more look in the mirror. Picking up her hat and gloves, she rushed downstairs.

Gus had already left for the bakery. The dirty dishes lay piled in the sink, a humiliating reminder of the night before. After drinking more beer than usual, he'd come up behind her as she stood at the sink. Grabbing her breasts, he pushed his body against her. She felt his hardness between her buttocks.

"Forget the damn dishes. I can't wait," he rasped, his breath hot on her neck. He reeked of beer as his wet mouth covered hers. Pushing her to the floor, he pinned her with his weight and took her right there on the kitchen floor in front of the sink.

Mina stared at the food-encrusted dishes, and a wave of nausea removed any desire for breakfast. Staring at the spot on the linoleum, she was sure the scuffed pattern would be forever etched in her memory. She was shaking now, remembering the pain and humiliation. She had to get out. Slamming the back door behind her, she ran for the bus stop.

Her stomach settled after she boarded the bus. Getting off at Roosevelt Avenue, she joined the crowd of early commuters climbing the stairs to the elevated platform, making it just in time to slip through the closing doors of the D train.

All the way to Queen's Plaza her thoughts kept pace with the thumping of the car's wheels against the rails. *Who am I, anyway? Who is this person I've become? Katy's father called me a lesbian. Certainly I'm not the Mina Arenholt of two weeks ago.*

Arenholt. God, she hated that name! It represented Gus and all she despised. The sound was guttural and unpleasant. Why had Mama done that to her? How could she have made that man her father?

The old hurt and loss were laid bare again with all their familiar pain. What would her real father have been like? Surely things would have been different if he had lived. She swayed with the motion of the train, and the clack of the wheels seemed to repeat: *Different, different, different.* In a flash of anger she thought, *Why did my father desert me like that?* Then, almost immediately, familiar guilt replaced the anger. How could she think such things about that face-less man who had loved her mother so long ago? Oh, she was very familiar with the queasiness in the pit of her stomach. It was almost always with her. Guilt was her uncomfortable and constant companion these days; it followed her relentlessly, closer than her own shadow. It permeated every cell of her body like a raging virus.

She remembered the night years ago when Gus had first come to her room. It was then guilt had first anchored itself in her head. More than once she experienced a shiver of delight when he fondled her breasts, but when he demanded she touch him with her hands and mouth in that disgusting way she couldn't help but gag in revulsion.

What did it all mean? When Katy caressed her nipples she'd been consumed by exquisite waves of pleasure. Was it the same? To think that was impossible, but here she was comparing the two. Katy. Gus. Certainly they had no connection. It all seemed beyond reason to think they were the same.

Her head ached. She could hear Gus's voice rasping in her ear: *I know you like it, Mina. You can't fool me. I know you mean yes when you say no.* His coarse laugh flooded her thoughts, and again she heard him: *You really make me hot. You know how to turn me on, and I know you do it on purpose, you little bitch.*

Things were getting out of hand. Not only was intercourse painful and revolting, but with all the other emotions she had to deal with, fear of getting pregnant was foremost. Gus had refused to use any protection. She had begged him to use a condom, but he'd growled, "Hell, no. There ain't no feeling when you wear one of them rubbers."

Words rang in her head along with the rattling of the cars: *Not anymore, never again, never again.* Like a flame spreading from below her stomach to her head her cheeks burned, and in that moment she grew aware of another sensation. It filled her up and joined the anger to become something entirely new. As the train slowed for Queen's Plaza a calm came over her, and she knew what she had to do.

When the train stopped and the doors opened, she merged with the crowd on the platform. Suddenly she was filled with exhilaration. Her body was light. She felt really powerful for the first time in her life.

Descending to the lower level, her feet hardly touched

the stairs. As she stood waiting for the Express, a rush of hot air swirled about her. When the train screamed to a stop, a surge of bodies swept her into the waiting car.

She squeezed herself next to a large black woman whose spread legs guarded an immense paper shopping bag. The heavy woman shifted her weight until Mina was pushed hard against an old man with a thin gray beard. He wore a black hat and held *The Daily Forward*, a Jewish newspaper, close to his face. It brushed his nose with each jolt of the train.

As the train roared under the river, she gathered the comfort of her anger. Tonight she would have it out with Gus and that was all there was to it. She would never let him do it to her again. All of a sudden she was soaring. It was a glorious feeling, and she rode it all the way to the 57th Street station.

The interview went well, perhaps due to her newfound resolve and confidence. The manager, a Mr. Blumfield, seemed pleased with her and what she wrote on the application. As he smiled impersonally at her, his questions were clipped and brief. Finally, he extended a pudgy hand.

"Very good, Miss Arenholt. I hope you'll be happy here with us." A stiff smile smoothed his sallow features. "We're just one big happy family at Schrafft's. Please report for training on Monday morning. Be here promptly at 7. That will give you time to pick up your uniform before indoctrination begins at 8."

She decided to take the bus back to Jackson Heights. It took longer than the train, but the day was clear and warm. She loved the view from the upper deck, and there was really no reason for her to rush back to the house. Why not enjoy the afternoon?

Beneath the Triborough Bridge the river shone with startling brilliance under the early afternoon sun. Her plan to confront Gus took shape in her mind as she transferred to the number 7 bus at Roosevelt Avenue, and by the time she got off, she had things well settled as to what she would say to him after supper.

It was stuffy and hot when she let herself into the house. She went straight to the kitchen and threw open the back door. There was the mess in the sink waiting for her. A fly probed jerkily across the crusted bottom of the frying pan, then proceeded in quick dashes to explore the rest of the dishes. Staring at the remnants of last night's meal, she thought, *how symbolic*. How like the stuff in front of her, her life had become—unpleasant, sticky, and just plain dirty. It was going to change.

Tossing her hat and purse on the kitchen table, she grabbed her apron and faced the challenge before her. The hot water felt good and clean while she scrubbed away at pots and pans. She hummed as clean dishes piled in the drainer. She laughed and sang, *"Life is just a bowl of cherries. Don't take it serious, it's too mysterious...."* Then the phone rang.

Grabbing a dish towel to dry her hands, she hurried to the living room and picked up the receiver. She was still laughing when Mary Alice's shrill voice came through.

"Is that you, Mina? What's so funny? How about letting me in on the joke?"

Mina swallowed the remains of her mirth. "Oh, nothing really. I'm just happy about landing a job in the city, that's all."

"What do you mean *a job*? I thought you were all set for secretarial school. Gee, I was hoping we could bum around together and maybe go to the beach once in a while this summer. What kind of a job is it anyway?"

Mina didn't feel much like talking. Her mind was full of how she was going to handle Gus, and now mouthy Mary Alice was trying to extract the particulars about her new job so she could phone the news all over Jackson Heights.

"It's just a temporary thing. A fill-in until school starts. I answered an ad for waitresses at Schrafft's on 57th Street. It's no big deal. You don't have to spread it all over town, you know."

Mary Alice sounded miffed. "Well, I guess you're not interested in what I heard about Katy Conklin."

Mina's heart jumped into her throat. "What did you hear? Tell me." She almost choked on the words.

There was a long pause at the other end of the wire and a stickiness oozed from Mary Alice's voice as if she were lapping chocolate syrup from a spoon. "Well..." she drew out the word for dramatic effect. "My mother saw Mrs. Conklin at Altar Guild yesterday afternoon. Mother asked how Katy was doing because she heard Katy missed graduation on account of being sick. Mrs. Conklin said Katy was fine. But you'll never believe what she said next." Another pregnant pause.

Mina's heart skipped a beat. She pressed the receiver hard against her ear so she wouldn't miss any of what Mary Alice was saying.

"Katy has entered the Convent of the Sacred Heart in Albany. Can you believe it?"

The words struck Mina like a sharp blow to the solar plexus, and she was sure she would never draw another breath. It was finished. She would die standing right there with the phone in her hand. She couldn't have heard correctly. Mary Alice must be putting her on.

Mary Alice continued. "Her folks took her on the train two days after graduation."

Oh, Mother of God! It's no joke. It's for real. Her legs went limp. She grabbed the phone stand for support.

"Mina? Did you hear what I said? Say something, for heaven's sake. Did you know she was going to do that?" Now Mary Alice's words were ripping her life apart. "You're Katy's best friend. She must have told you something. Imagine Katy being a nun! It's too unbelievable. Come on, Mina, don't tell me you didn't know. Why didn't you tell us she was going to do a thing like that? Well, honestly. It's completely unreal. Well, say something, damn it!" Mary Alice was breathing hard as she waited for an explanation.

Mina's hand shook so violently the receiver slipped from her fingers. It swung loose on its cord, just missing the floor. Slowly she picked it up and replaced it on the hook.

They had sent her love away and she would never see Katy again as long as she lived. Dear Jesus, was this some kind of terrible nightmare? Was God punishing them for what they had done in Katy's room? How could the Conklins have done this to Katy? *It hurts so much it must be real,* she thought. Only something real could bring so much pain.

She stood staring at the black instrument that had shattered her life. The phone suddenly sprang to life again, ringing loudly. Mary Alice hadn't had enough. She wanted more. Ignoring the phone, Mina slowly climbed the stairs as the shrill ringing reverberated through the empty house. It gave up only after Mina had closed the door of her room and fallen on the bed.

It was hot, and the air was dead in her room, but she

was too drained to get up and raise the window so she just lay still, staring at the ceiling. After a while she heard the clock downstairs strike four. That brought her to her senses. Gus would be getting home by 5.

Suddenly she knew she couldn't face another night under the same roof with him. She had to get out of the house before he got home. All her plans for facing up to him had melted under the weight of losing Katy. She needed to be with someone. A terrible loneliness suffocated her.

Leaping up, she dove into the closet, found her mother's old suitcase on the top shelf, and threw it on the bed. Pulling clothes off hangers, she emptied her closet and her dresser drawers. Stuffing everything into the cracked leather bag, she sat on the lid to lock the latches. Struggling downstairs with it, she felt light-headed and slightly giddy.

Her aunt would be home from work by the time she got to Astoria. She'd be safe there. Many times Aunt Willie had said, "Come stay with me. I have room, *Liebchen*." Now she was on her way to do just that.

For the last time, Mina closed and locked the front door. Dropping the key in the mail slot she heard it fall with a hollow sound on the bare floor inside. She didn't need it anymore. She was never coming back.

17

THE ESCAPE

Lea Rosten's parlor smelled musty. The lace curtains were drawn against the late afternoon sun, shrouding the room in half-light. Miriam sat stiffly on the horsehair sofa under the faded litho of Rebbe Schneerson in an ornate gold frame. Her face was pale. She clenched a balled-up handkerchief with white-knuckled fingers.

Lea had called her early that morning to come and talk. Miriam hadn't liked the sound of her voice. It boded no good, she was sure. When Lea had opened the door a few minutes ago, Miriam knew from her dark countenance that things had come to a critical juncture in the Rosten household. For some time now she'd been painfully aware that her daughter's marriage was not going well. Rumors had reached her that Chana was behaving strangely for a new bride. There were hushed whispers in Shul and darting glances in her direction as the cantor's voice rose to the latticed gallery where she sat with the other women of the congregation.

When they'd met at the door, Lea's words were clipped, her voice tight. Her whole demeanor filled Miriam with dread.

"We are concerned about our daughter-in-law. Perhaps you can talk some sense into Chana before we have to take the matter to the *Gabai* for the Rebbe's consideration. She's upstairs in her room. I'll tell her you're here. I hope you can make her understand her obligations in this house as a wife and daughter-in-law are not being met."

Without waiting for Miriam's reply, Lea spun on her heel and made for the door. There she turned to face Miriam once more. "I hope you understand the gravity of the situation, Mrs. Dubovitch." With that she disappeared into the hall, leaving her sharp words suspended in the quiet of the room.

Miriam listened to Lea's impatient footsteps on the stairs. The whole house fell silent, and she heard the beating of her own heart as she sat waiting for the confrontation that was soon to come. Chana appeared at the doorway almost immediately. With a hesitant smile, she approached her mother.

"Hello, Mama." Her voice was low but steady. "How are you, Mama? It's been a long time. I'm glad you've come." She stretched out her arms, and they held each other close for a brief moment. Then they settled uncomfortably on the lumpy couch, and an awkward silence fell between them. Miriam spoke first.

"What's this I'm hearing from your mother-in-law, Chana?"

There was a painful pause during which Chana kept her eyes fixed on her hands clasped in her lap. Finally, she spoke softly, "It's no good, Mama. It's no good at all."

Miriam's chin rose defensively, and her eyes grew hard. "What do you mean? What's no good, Chana?" she asked, her voice full of impatience. Silence sat between them like a stranger.

Chana's words grew stronger. "Mama, I can't live here any longer. I've discussed my situation with Bubbe, and she agrees with me that I can no longer stay in this marriage. I must leave as soon as possible."

Fighting a wave of panic, Miriam caught her breath. Why was the All-Forgiving One, the All-Compassionate Lord of the Universe letting this happen? With great difficulty she recaptured her breath, and hot anger came with it, burning her cheeks and leaving her mouth dry of words. How could Chana do this to her? What would Mendel say? What would the community think? How could her daughter bring such shame to the family? There must be some way to keep this terrible thing from ruining all their lives. One after another, frightening thoughts seared through her mind, but she could find no words to answer her daughter.

"Bubbe has spoken to Dr. Solomon," Chana said, lowering her voice. "He and Rose have offered me their hospitality. I plan to stay with them until I can make other arrangements. The Rostens mustn't know I'm leaving. Oh, Mama, there isn't any other way. Please don't look at me like that." Chana reached for her mother's hand, but Miriam drew it away quickly.

"Don't touch me." She glared at Chana as she rose to her feet. "I won't let you bring this shameful thing into our lives. You are an ungrateful girl. How can you possibly think to get away with this? You are a married woman now. You can't just leave a marriage." She was breathing hard as she confronted her daughter.

"Mama, keep your voice down," Chana pleaded. "I'm afraid if they know what I'm planning, they'll try to stop me. Mama, if you love me, please don't give me away." There were tears in Chana's eyes now. "I can't stay in this marriage. I can't bear another night in this house, so I'm leaving after supper. I'll tell them I'm going to visit Pessie to bring her the booties I finished for the baby. I won't take anything with me when I leave, so they won't guess I'm not coming back. I'll leave notes for them, and one for Avrum, of course, but I had to tell you before I left. That's why I asked Lea to phone you to come this afternoon."

Gasping, and with her eyes flashing anger, Miriam said, "Have you lost your mind, Chana? Marriages are made before God and the whole community." Her voice rose stridently. "You put yourself above the Lord of the Universe Himself? The Creator of the World? He, Himself, created marriage for His people. This is blasphemy. A daughter of mine cannot do such a thing. It's unthinkable!"

"Mama, please, they'll hear you. Please don't let me down. I couldn't bear it. You're my mother, and I love you. Bubbe said I must tell you. She said you would be angry, but because of your love for me, you would keep my secret safe. Mama, please go quietly now before Lea comes down. I'll write and explain everything, so you'll know why I have to do this, and remember, I love you, Mama."

Chana took her mother's arm and steered her into the hall where she tried to embrace her, but Miriam wrenched away, yanked open the door, and fled down the front steps.

Chana watched until her mother disappeared around the corner, then carefully closing the heavy door, she turned and slowly climbed the stairs to her room.

18

CHANA STERN—HOME AT LAST

I've lived at the Solomons' apartment on Riverside Drive for a week now, and for the first time since Papa died I feel really alive.

The first night Rose came to my room. I was in bed trying to quiet my mind before turning out the light. I knew my troubled thoughts would follow me through a long and sleepless night. She rapped softly on my door and came in. I was glad to have someone to talk to because I wasn't enjoying my own company very much.

"So you're still awake, Chana?" Her voice at my bedroom door was almost a whisper.

"Yes, Rose, come in."

She was wearing a light blue dressing gown that complimented her pale blond hair, which fell loosely about her shoulders. "I brought you a nightcap. Thought it might help you sleep." Her smile was warm as she put a cup of hot chocolate on the night table and sat at the edge of my bed. "You know, Chana, for David and me you have been the daughter we never had. These years since your mother's marriage we have heard nothing from her. She seems to have forgotten how close we once were. Fortunately, Sarah kept us informed of your growing up year after year, but her letters never prepared me for the lovely young woman you've become." She took my hand in hers.

"This is your home for as long as you like. Please know

that David and I will be here for you always. We will talk later, so rest well, my grown-up, beautiful Chanala." She bent close, and her lips touched my forehead lightly. After she closed the door I finished the chocolate quickly, switched off the light, and let the darkness fall around me.

≥a ≥a ≥a

A lot happened the following week. Bubbe came into town with disturbing news that Mama had told the Rostens where I was. She pressed a cashier's check into my hand.

"Here, this will be helpful, Bubeleh. Not to worry. We can decide what to do about that later. A big spender I'm not, so a considerable nest egg has accumulated over the years, begging to be spent. So enjoy."

"But you shouldn't," I protested. "I'm going to get a job. I can take care of myself, really I can, Bubbe."

"Yes. Yes." She shook her head. "But in the meantime, you take this. If you need more, there is plenty where that came from."

I hugged her, my tears wet against her wrinkled cheek. "I love you so much, Bubbe." I sniffed, and she put her familiar lacy handkerchief in my hand.

"Now, now, this opportunity makes an old woman happy, so take the check in good health. It brings me joy already. So no more tears. Spend wisely, my darling, and make the right choices for your new life."

"Bubbe, now that they know where I am, what do you think will happen next?" I wiped my eyes and returned her handkerchief. "Do you think they'll try to force me to come back? How could Mama do such a thing? She was terribly angry when I told her. But you said I should tell her, remember? You said, 'She's your mother and won't give your secret away.' But she did, Bubbe." I searched my grandmother's face. "What do you think they'll do now?"

"I know your mother and Mendel are going to see the Rostens tonight. They'll be planning to make some kind of move, but what I don't know. Your mother is very upset and isn't talking to me. She doesn't confide at all. Things are bad between us because she knows I'm on your side. All I can do is watch and keep my distance. I'll let you know more when I can. In the meantime, don't panic. Go about building a life for yourself, Chanala. I'll keep in touch."

After Bubbe left I told Rose what she'd said about Mama and about the meeting between the two families. Rose put her arms around me.

"Don't fret. We'll have a talk with David this evening. He might have some ideas that will help us through this."

Late in the afternoon I took a walk along the river. Throwing my head back, I filled my lungs with the salty air. The sinking sun was trapped in a smoky haze on the Jersey side. A tug towed a barge low in the water as it labored downriver against a fresh wind.

I took a deep breath. I was home at last, and oh, how I loved the smell of the river. Picking up my pace, I walked faster, feeling weightless with the sweetness of it all. When the lights came on along the parkway, I turned my steps back toward the apartment.

The doorman greeted me with a broad smile. "Evenin', Miss Stern."

I looked at him in surprise when he called me by name. Apparently the Solomons had identified me as their house-guest. *Chana Stern is really back!* I thought.

As the elevator rose, he flashed a grin. "I hope you had a fine walk, miss. My name's Tom. If you need anything, just press the buzzer. Good night, miss." His fingers brushed the visor of his cap as he swung back the gate.

I unlocked the door with the key Rose had given me. The hall light was on, but the apartment was quiet. As I hung up my jacket, I caught my reflection in the umbrella-stand mirror. My cheeks were flushed from the cold. I whipped off my scarf, ran my fingers through my short hair, and vowed never again to keep it covered with a scarf in the Hasidic manner. Feeling my old self once more, I tossed my head and shook my cropped curls as I passed the mirror and stepped into the lamp-lit living room.

"Rose, I'm back," I called out.

There was no answer. Then I saw him.

He sat stiffly on the chintz sofa. In the dim light, I recognized the black coat and straight-brimmed hat. "Avrum, what are you doing here?" I gasped.

He struggled to his feet, his voice barely audible. "Chana, Chana," he said. Shifting his weight, he seemed uncertain of what to say. A drop of perspiration coursed down his cheek. "I'm here because..." There was an uncomfortable pause as his eyes searched the floor for words.

"Sit down, Avrum, please." My voice was calmer than I felt. Grateful for that small mercy, I hoped my control would sustain me through this confrontation.

I needed as much distance as possible between us, so I took a straight chair opposite him, thankful for the wide coffee table separating us.

"Mrs. Solomon said you would be back soon. I saw her waiting for the lift when I got off and..." His voice faltered. "She said to wait for you, so here I am." He cleared his throat. "We have to talk."

"My note explained everything, Avrum," I said, keeping my voice low. "I can't be married to you anymore. Please try to understand how I feel. It was never a real marriage. You know that as well as I do. It was all the families' doing. The whole thing was a disaster from the start."

He looked so miserable that I almost lost my resolve to stay distant and calm, but I managed to resist reaching to him across the table. Realizing I'd ventured into a sensitive area, however, I didn't wish to humiliate him about his failure as a husband; for in truth, all along I'd been grateful for his impotence, but I had to press my case, and this was one tool I could use to show him the impossible nature of our situation.

After a miserable silence, he lifted his head, and his eyes were cold. "My father and your stepfather have spoken to the Rebbe," he said, and his voice was firm with a tone I'd never heard before. "Mendel's closeness to the High One allows the matter to be brought to him directly. The Rebbe has advised a meeting of the rabbis to determine what action should be taken."

His head came up, and his eyes burned with determination. "Your actions have confirmed what the Talmud says of women: They lack virtue by their very nature." He paused, and his voice softened slightly. "But if you come back with me now, I will forgive you. After all, you are really only a half Jew, and your behavior can be attributed to that. If you repent and repair your ways, the matter can be dropped."

"No, Avrum," I said. "I can't come back to you. Do what has to be done. I won't continue in this farce of a marriage."

Surprisingly, his face began to crumble, and I thought he might cry. Following him into the hall, I put my hand on his arm. "Don't think badly of me, Avrum." I felt his arm shaking under his rough serge coat.

Squaring his shoulders, he pulled away and walked stiffly toward the elevator. Hearing the hum of the lift, I closed the apartment door. Returning to the living room, I felt drained and stood for a long time watching the lights along the river.

By the time Rose returned from the basement with the laundry, my emotions were pretty much under control. I'd made my choice. It was up to me to get on with my life like Bubbe said.

All the next week I thought about my course of action. When I was growing up I wanted to become a painter, like Papa. Before he died he used to take me with him on sketching trips. The most memorable of those outings was one we took to the Catskills when I was ten.

It was the last weekend of the summer vacation. Trees were ablaze in shades of bronze and scarlet. We walked along the edge of Cater's Pond looking for the right spot to set up our easels. That warm afternoon I worked alongside him, trying to catch the scene the way he saw it—the stillness of the lake with its purple reflections of distant mountains. The sun dipped low and shadows stretched long under trees. He stood behind me, watching in silence as I put a blue wash across my sketch pad.

"That's right, Chana. Be sure your pad is still wet when you lay in your dark strokes along the shoreline. That will bring more realism to the reflections of the hills in the water."

He spoke to me like one artist to another. He treated me as a contemporary, and he made me feel proud and smart. I dipped my brush to hold more pigment and drew it across the damp paper. Suddenly the lake became real water, mirroring the distant mountains.

He nodded and smiled. "That's right," he said. "Now you've pulled the whole composition together, and you have water that really *looks* like water. I know you'll make a fine artist." I believed it was possible, and promised myself to follow in his footsteps one day.

In the apartment that night I shared my memories of Papa and the lake with Rose and David while we were eating supper.

Rose grabbed my hand. "I have an idea, Chana. Why don't you take some classes at the Art Students' League? I know Roger Brachman. He teaches life classes there. David and I met him last summer when we were in Vermont. He has a summer place in Bennington and teaches there each August. You couldn't pick a better place to study than the League, and I can arrange an introduction for you. Roger is a pompous little fellow with a fascinating Russian accent. He's the toast of the art world right now and one of the best teachers at the school. I'm sure you've seen reproductions of his nudes. He's been reviewed lately in the *Times* and *The New Yorker*. He's doing a one-man show at the Harris Gallery on 57th Street." She was almost out of breath with excitement.

"But Rose," I stammered in disbelief. "I'm just a beginner. How could I expect to be accepted for his classes?"

"Don't worry, darling. When he hears you're Harry Stern's daughter, there'll be nothing to it. By the way, he's also a bit of a snob. Nothing would stroke his ego more than having you in his class. Remember, your father's name still carries a lot of weight in artistic circles. Roger will be flattered to death having Harry Stern's daughter for a student."

Later, as I lay in bed waiting for sleep, I fantasized about being a great painter, and staring into the darkness I made a decision to go downtown and visit the Harris Gallery. The prospect of seeing Brachman's nudes excited me.

When sleep came it brought a disturbing dream of Mama and Mendel standing over me, shaking their fingers, their voices chilling and hollow, saying: *The dybbuk has you, Chana Dubovitch. The devil has you for sure. You've left us, so we declare you cherem...cherem...cherem.* Their chant followed me as I kept running down an endless corridor.

19

MINA ARENHOLT—AT THE FAIR

There was a long pause. Mary Alice was impatient on the other end of the line. "Come on, Mina, how about it? It'll be fun. Tony has a convertible. We'll go in style."

I had to think fast. I didn't really know Mary Alice's brother Tony. He was five years older than her, and I'd only seen him that one time when he came to graduation. I remembered a stocky blond with a butch haircut and that's all.

"OK, I guess I can make it," I replied with little enthusiasm. "I get off work at 3, so there won't be any problem. You know the address here at Aunt Willie's. You're sure they won't mind coming all the way to Astoria to pick me up?"

Mary Alice ignored my perfunctory acceptance. "Great!" she bubbled. "What's all this about staying at your aunt's? Doesn't your stepfather mind? Well, you can tell me about it on Saturday. We'll pick you up about 6. Oh, by the way, don't worry about Katy. I hear she's taking her new life in stride. Mom saw Mrs. Conklin at Altar Guild, and she raved about how beautiful the convent was. It's really weird Katy hasn't written to you, but maybe they don't let them write. It could be a rule or something. Anyway, we'll see you Saturday night. Bye."

After Mary Alice hung up, I told myself I was stark raving mad. I had never been on a real date before. Boys always made me nervous. Boys? Ye gods, Tony wasn't a boy; he was six years older than I was. What had I gotten myself into?

I'd phoned Mary Alice to find out if there was any news from Katy—Katy was always on my mind. I promised myself to firm up a plausible story if she asked about Katy on Saturday night.

Hanging up the phone, I went to the kitchen to start dinner. Aunt Willie would be home from the studio in an hour. She'd been a brick about my coming to stay with her and hadn't asked a lot of questions. She'd accepted my story that the commute to the city would be easier from Astoria, and that it would only be until school in the fall.

Gus called a couple of times. Aunt Willie looked at me funny when I was talking to him, but I kept my voice casual so I don't think she suspected anything. After a while, he stopped calling.

The job at Schrafft's was easier than I'd expected. Getting up at 5 A.M. was a drag, but getting off at 3 was great because I missed the rush hour.

As I scraped carrots into the sink, my mind returned to my looming date. Maybe it would be fun after all, I thought. I hadn't been to the World's Fair yet. Mary Alice was working part time in the Westinghouse Pavilion. She'd wangled a deal for four free passes to Billy Rose's Aquacade. Mary Alice had always wanted to date her brother's shipmate, Tom Flarity, so when I'd called for news of Katy, she nailed me on the spot and worked it into a double-date affair. Now I was committed to something I wasn't sure I wanted.

"Tony and Tom are stationed at the Brooklyn Navy Yard," she'd said. "They'll be shipping out in a couple of weeks, so this will be their final fling before they leave for Pearl Harbor." She'd been practically out of breath with excitement.

Well, I was committed for better or for worse, so there wasn't much I could do about it, but I hoped I wasn't an idiot for going along with her plans.

I was going on my first date, my first date with a sailor, my first trip to the World's Fair, and, oh yes, my first ride in a convertible. Suddenly it all sounded impossible, but at the same time I felt a twinge of excitement.

Sleep didn't come easy that night. When it did come it was crowded with sailors—hundreds of them in impudent white caps and tight bell-bottoms. They were all chasing me in shiny new convertibles. I woke up in a cold sweat just as they were closing in. "Oh, God," I moaned, "why didn't I say no to Mary Alice?"

ză ză ză

"I declare, I don't know what's gotten into young people," Aunt Willie frowned. "In my day, when a gentleman called he paid his respects by coming to the front door. He didn't just ring the bell and expect his date to come running." She was still complaining as she followed me into the hall.

"Don't wait up for me." I gave her a quick hug and escaped into the elevator. Privately I agreed with her. I hadn't been that impressed with Tony's cavalier attitude myself.

I was in a tizzy all day worrying about the date. When I got home from work, I had to decide what to wear and how to fix my hair. I tried on almost everything in my closet, finally settling on my green linen. It was the most sophisticated thing I had. I struggled for an hour creating a pompadour. Viewing the finished product in the bathroom mirror, I was rather pleased with myself. Maybe I could pull it off after all, I thought, but as I got off the elevator doubts took hold of me again. Shoving them aside firmly, I told myself if I had a good time tonight—and if Tony liked me—then it would prove I was OK, and that would settle my fears and my questions about being "different."

Still, butterflies did a jig in my belly as I stood on the stoop.

The car wasn't at the curb. For a terrible moment I thought they'd taken off without me. Then I saw the Ford sports coupe parked at the bus stop at the corner. Mary Alice waved from the rumble seat. My first impulse was to run.

"Come on, Mina, hurry up," she called out.

Gathering my newly created sophistication, I forced myself to walk casually.

Tony yelled, "Get the lead out, Mina, we're running late."

Holding on to my nonchalance for dear life, I climbed into the seat beside him.

He didn't pay me any attention, just ground the gears and screeched away from the curb. "OK, let's put this show on the road. Next stop, the fair!" He laughed and spun into traffic on Northern Boulevard.

Our ride to Flushing Meadows was a wild one. Tony drove like Barney Oldfield. I had no experience with a convertible, so I wasn't prepared for the blast of air that almost tore me apart. Needless to say, my hard-won pompadour was the first casualty. *Why hadn't Mary Alice warned me?* I wondered, as my hair began to unfurl.

Noticing my dilemma, Tony yelled over the roar of traffic, "You should've worn a scarf. Didn't my sister tell you we'd have the top down?"

"No," I shouted against the wind as I struggled to control the whipping strands that were all but blinding me.

Mary Alice tapped me on the head. "Never mind, we can fix it later," she yelled.

She and Tom were hitting it off. She was laughing, and her voice was shrill. Tony leaned forward to turn on the radio. His thigh pressed against mine. I tried not to notice. After spinning the dial past a number of stations, he finally brought in Artie Shaw's band playing "Traffic Jam," which seemed appropriate, since at that moment we were trapped in traffic as we got closer to Flushing Meadows.

I made a mental note that I was OK with the thigh business since it only lasted for a few seconds. Maybe he hadn't meant anything by it, or it could have been just my imagination. Relieved, I began to feel confident I might get through the evening without too much trouble. Leaning back, I started to relax. There wasn't any point in competing with the music and the traffic noise, so I kept my mouth shut and prayed I could do something decent with my hair when we got to the fair.

After leaving our car in the parking lot we joined one of the long lines to the entrance gate. Mary Alice hung on Tom's arm and tossed sappy grins up at him. Her attempt at playing coquette seemed ridiculous, but as I watched her act I wondered if I should take Tony's arm. Maybe coolness in the name of sophistication wasn't the way to play the game after all. Instead of following Mary Alice's lead, I dug my comb out of my purse and tugged at the tangles in my hair.

"Come on, doll, leave it down," Tony said. "I like my women in long hair, redheads especially. Never can tell what a redhead will do, right?" He grinned and jabbed me in the ribs with his elbow. I let my hair go and linked my arm to his. Hoping desperately I was on the right track, I donned a smile and flashed it brazenly at him.

When we got through the gate, we had our first glimpse of the huge Perisphere. It shimmered pearly white against a deepening blue sky. The last rays of the sun flashed bright on the soaring Trylon beside it. We moved slowly with the crowd down the Avenue of Nations. On each side colorful flags from every country flapped in the warm air. The dancing water of many fountains seemed to lift the gigantic globe into the evening sky. For a moment I could hardly breathe; the beauty was almost too much. Suddenly, it felt good to be alive in this place with all these people, and I was glad I'd said yes to Mary Alice. I was feeling so good I even gave Tony's arm a squeeze.

"Let's eat first," Mary Alice suggested. "The best food is at the Hofbrau House."

At the German Pavilion, tables were arranged on ascending outdoor terraces. From those vantage points people could watch the crowds pass as they enjoyed their meal. A portly waiter in tight lederhosen and woolly kneesocks showed us to our table. He tipped his Tyrolean hat as his bloodshot eyes measured us. We were on the upper terrace with a great view of the fairground. A brassy oompah band puffed its way through a lively polka. German ambiance was so thick and loud it made conversation next to impossible. Ample-breasted barmaids with three or four foaming steins in each fist spun their way between tables, joking and flirting with the customers.

"I could eat a horse, shoes and all," Tom growled as he slumped into his chair, completely forgetting to seat Mary Alice.

"You'd better settle for knockwurst," Tony yelled over the din. "Hey, *Fraulein*." He grabbed at one of the passing barmaids. "Lager for the four of us, *raus mitten!*"

"*Jawohl, mein Herr.*" She never paused, just flashed him a toothy smile and disappeared to another table.

The band fell silent for a moment, then struck the first bars of "Deutschland Über Alles." People rose from their seats and, with stiff, outstretched arms, raised their voices in the German national anthem. I suddenly remembered hearing that song on the radio as a news commentator described the march of the German army into Poland a few months before. A shiver ran through me.

The boys sat motionless. They looked angry, as if someone had flung them an insult. Mary Alice forgot to smile and sat silent. The anthem ended in a roar of *sieg heil*s, then everyone sat down and the babble of conversation resumed as the band struck up another polka.

Venting his anger on Mary Alice, Tony lashed out. "What the hell are we doing here with all these Krauts? Couldn't you have picked a better place to eat, for chrissake?"

She looked miffed. "I thought you'd like this place because they serve beer."

Just then the girl arrived with our steins. "You ready to order?" She fished a pencil from her ample cleavage.

Mary Alice retrieved her smile, and I fastened my eyes on the menu.

"I'll have wieners and sauerkraut," she chirped, ignoring her brother's dark look. "What are you having, honey?" she cooed at Tom. Everyone decided on wieners and sauerkraut, and the waitress headed toward the kitchen.

I stared at the huge mug in front of me, beginning to have some real misgivings. I'd never tasted beer before and wasn't sure I could handle it. My first impulse was to push it away, but everyone was watching. The smell reminded me of Gus, and the thought of drinking it made my stomach churn. I couldn't chicken out, though, so I grasped the heavy stein with both hands and figured if I held my breath I could down one swallow without upchucking.

I put on my face of experience and took a mouthful. It went down easier than I'd expected, and didn't taste all that bad. After the second gulp, I decided I was OK and began to relax.

Then, out of nowhere, Katy jumped into my head. What would she think if she saw me drinking beer? There it was once more. When Katy leapt into my mind it was always the same...the sweet, unbearable pain was a companion to the sound of her name. *Katy...Katy...* Only after closing my eyes and forcing down more of the foamy liquid did she begin to fade. The sound of her name blurred into the music and the racket of voices.

I kept swallowing the bitter brew to ensure she wouldn't return, and the next thing I knew I was staring at Tony through the glass bottom of my stein. He grinned at me. My face felt stiff and slightly numb as I put the empty mug down on its wet ring on the table. The band struck up "The Beer Barrel Polka." *"Roll out the barrel,"* everyone sang. *"We'll have a barrel of fun."*

The food wasn't half bad. I was really hungry, and in spite of everything, I was beginning to have a good time. Conversation came more easily. I leaned toward Tony. "Tell me, why aren't you and Tom in uniform?" I asked, hearing my voice turn husky. It sounded unfamiliar, not at all like mine. "I didn't expect to see you fellas in sport jackets and slacks," I continued. "How come you're not wearing your navy blues?"

"That's easy, doll. When off-duty we're allowed to wear 'civies.' In wartime it's a different story." Tony's arm slid over the back of my chair. His eyes grabbed mine and wouldn't let them go. I felt funny, a little dizzy, but I was also feeling pretty good.

He leaned closer, his breath loaded with beer—like Gus. I pushed the thought away and focused hard on what I hoped was a provocative smile.

"Come on, let's get out of here and see some of the sights before show time." His hand cupped my shoulder lightly and I decided I was doing just fine.

Mary Alice wanted to show us where she worked. "The Westinghouse exhibit is just at the end of this street," she said. "They have a new thing called television. It's pretty amazing. It's like a motion picture in a small box." She tried to get the boys' attention, but they weren't interested.

"Come on, nix on the scientific crap," Tom cut in. "No offense, Mary Alice, but let's find some real action. I hear they have a honky-tonk area somewhere. Maybe it's over by the Aquacade. Let's take a look...we have time."

Mary Alice looked disappointed. At the same time she wanted to please Tom, so she took his arm as we headed toward the far end of the park.

Tony's arm crept around my waist. He pulled me close. "You've got beautiful hair, Mina. Always wear it down. Makes you look sexy as hell." Lifting it from the back of my neck, he nuzzled my ear. "You're a regular redheaded Veronica Lake, you know that?"

I ducked my head and pulled away. At the same time I felt angry and ashamed of the way I was handling the moment. I was sliding into deep water and wasn't sure I could stay afloat. The best I could come up with was "Come on, Tony, I bet you use that line with all the girls." My laugh sounded shrill.

He shrugged and backed off.

We made a quick stop at a bar called Frankie's Place. The boys downed a couple of brews in nothing flat. I shook my head and said I was too full, but Mary Alice had one to keep Tom company.

When we got to the box office to pick up our tickets, it turned out two seats were in the center section and two on the side. Mary Alice was livid when she realized we weren't sitting together. But her protest didn't cut it with the ticket lady, who just shrugged.

"That's it ma'am. You want them or not? Make up your mind. You're holding up the line."

"Sorry about that," Mary Alice whined, handing Tony our tickets. "I guess we don't have much choice since they're freebies. We'll meet you two back here after the show. OK?"

It turned out we got the seats on the side of the open-air amphitheater and had to climb halfway to the stars. As soon as we got settled, Tony took off for the john. I was really angry with him for leaving me like that. I felt conspicuous sitting by myself. Slouching in my seat, I hoped people wouldn't notice I was alone.

The stars began to pierce the evening sky. A large swimming pool glowed aqua-blue far below. The orchestra began tuning up. Floodlights played slowly across an arrangement of platforms and stairs in back of the pool. Tony was gone an awful long time. *He must have had to go all the way to the entrance to find the men's room,* I thought, making a stab at being understanding. When he finally showed, he was carrying an enormous paper cup of

Schlitz. The orchestra came to life with a blast from the brass section and a roll on the kettledrums as he stumbled his way over the feet of the people in our row. Finally, he managed to slump into the seat without spilling any of his precious brew. I was still mad at him for leaving me alone so long, so I made a point of ignoring him and gave my full attention to the opening of the show.

Girls in glistening silver swimsuits appeared on the steps high above the pool. One by one they posed, then dove. *"A pretty girl is like a melody...."* They cut into the water gracefully until the pool was filled with silver streaks turning this way and that under the lights. Like dancers their arms arched and dipped to the rhythm of the song.

Putting my annoyance aside, I leaned forward to capture the spectacle. Two spotlights picked up a shining female figure on the highest platform. With outstretched arms, she held high a sequined cape. Like glittering wings it framed her gold lamé figure. Topping all her splendor was a magnificent headdress of soaring peacock feathers.

"Billy Rose presents the incomparable Esther Williams," the announcer's voice boomed after a loud fanfare from the orchestra. She stood motionless, acknowledging the roar of applause. Dropping her cape, she lifted the headdress and let it fall to her feet. Posing for a moment, she leapt into space. Then arching downward, she knifed the water in the exact center of a circle of swimmers below.

Through the applause I heard Tony's cup hit the floor and roll under the seat. The hollow sound was followed by a loud belch. I was sure that everyone was looking at us; my cheeks burned. His arm fell over my shoulder. The smell of beer on his breath pushed the image of Gus into my mind once more. I fought a wave of nausea as his face came close.

"Tony, don't," I said, squirming away, hoping to discourage him. But he got even closer. He fingered the neck of my dress. I knew right then I was in for it. "Please, Tony, don't." I reached up and brushed his hand away.

"Come on, doll, be a sport. You're a redhead, remember? For chrissake, loosen up and act like one."

I glared at him, praying he'd read the meaning of my look. Grunting in disgust, he moved away.

In the next number Esther Williams was an Indian maiden resplendent in a tall, feathered headdress. To the accompaniment of drums she dove over a torrent of water cascading into the pool. Torches, held by the swimmers below, made it appear she was plunging into a lake of fire. The strains of Jerome Kern's "Indian Love Call" swelled to blend the spectacle of fire on water.

The awesome scene in the pool eased the discomfort I'd felt a few moments ago. Relaxing a bit, I began to enjoy the show. Once more Tony reached for my hand. Strangely enough, I was relieved he wasn't mad at me and let him hold it since he'd made no other move. I figured if that was all he expected, I could handle it. Maybe I'd been wrong getting so upset.

After a few moments, the hand that held mine dropped from the arm of our seat to his thigh and slid between his legs. His grip was so strong I couldn't pull my hand away. He pressed my fingers against his hardness. I felt his breath, hot and full of beer, in my face. Panic, then rage, took over.

Making a fist with my other hand, I hauled off and hit

him as hard as I could. His head snapped back against the seat. Eyes wide with surprise, his features froze in an incredulous stare. His hand dropped mine and flew to his face. At that moment he looked so comical that I swallowed a hysterical impulse to laugh. My cheeks burned, and for a glorious moment I tasted the sweetness of power.

"Shit!" he spat. "What the hell do you think you're doing?" He wiped his mouth, checking for blood.

My knuckles smarted; I'd landed a pretty solid punch. Laughter erupted around us. Someone yelled, "Attagirl, babe."

He dabbed his lip with a handkerchief, hunkered down in his seat, and made a more detailed check of the damage.

For the rest of the performance he kept as much distance between us as our seats would allow. He didn't utter a word, and I didn't feel like talking.

After the show, as we descended the stairs to the street, he walked ahead, ignoring me completely. I had a hard time keeping up with him. It was obvious he didn't want anyone to think he was with me. His pace increased until we reached the ticket office. As we waited for Mary Alice and Tom, I noticed his lip was swelling and had turned an ugly shade of purple.

When they showed up, Mary Alice was leaning all over Tom. They were holding hands and acting like a couple of ninnies. Without tearing his eyes from Mary Alice, Tom suggested we hit one of the bars for a nightcap before heading home.

"Yeah, let's. How about it, you two?" Mary Alice gave me a hard look that plainly said I'd better say yes.

Then Tony's fat lip registered with her. Puzzled, she

nudged Tom, directing her gaze toward Tony. An awkward silence followed. "What the hell?" Tom dropped Mary Alice's hand and turned Tony toward the light for a better look. "What happened? Who decked you?" He looked at me for an explanation.

Tony glared and didn't answer.

"So you don't want to tell all?" Tom chided. "Well, that's OK, you can 'fess up later. In the meantime, how about a beer before we head out? Whaddaya say?"

"Nothin' doing," Tony said with a nasty edge to his voice. "I've had enough for one night." Grabbing my arm, he pushed me ahead of him. "Get going. I want to beat the mob out of the parking lot."

All the way across the fair grounds, Tom and Mary Alice kept trying to find out what was up, but Tony held onto his stony silence and walked faster and faster. When we got to the car, Mary Alice glared at me. "I'll talk to you later," she said under her breath as she climbed into the rumble seat. I could tell she was bent out of shape about having her date with Tom cut short.

Tony got in and slammed the door, leaving me to fend for myself. I didn't say a word, just got in and slammed my door too. Tony made it clear to everyone that I was the big offender in the caper.

I didn't give a damn. I just wanted the evening to end.

He drove in sanctimonious silence all the way to Astoria. When we pulled in front of the apartment, he leaned across me and unlocked the door. "Good night, Mina." His voice was almost inaudible. Motionless, he waited for me to get out.

I set my jaw and lurched out of the car. Slamming the door as hard as I could, I stumbled up the front steps, shaking with rage and humiliation. On the way up in the elevator, I prayed to all the saints in heaven that Aunt Willie wasn't waiting up for me. All I wanted to do was fall in bed and put the whole damn dating business behind me forever. I knew I never wanted to deal with a situation like that again.

20

CHEREM

With a sigh, Rose replaced the receiver and leaned back in her chair. She could almost hear her mother's voice: *This I need, yes? All right, already, this shouldn't happen to a dog. It's enough to make you hit your head against a stone wall.* Why the Yiddish words of her dead mother should be so loud in her head, she didn't know. Perhaps the echo from the past formed a perfect frame for her own frustration.

How could her oldest and dearest friend do such a thing to her own daughter? Miriam had surely gone over the edge this time. In the last few years Rose had tried her best to understand Miriam's journey into Hasidism, but she could no longer give her friend the support she gave in the past. This turn of events went beyond religiousness and piety and straight into madness itself.

She rubbed the back of her neck to relieve a throbbing ache. The desk clock said 4:30. She'd been on the phone for over an hour. Sarah Blumenthal's news had shattered her day. Bearing such ill tidings disturbed her greatly.

How was she going to tell Chana? Sarah had been so distraught that Rose had promised to talk to Chana for her. The turmoil over Chana's leaving her marriage was taking its toll on her grandmother, and she was deeply concerned about her old friend. Sarah had sounded so tired and ill on the phone. Rose decided to wait until after dinner to deliver her news. Rubbing her neck again, she returned to the kitchen.

The grandfather clock in the hall struck 6 when Chana let herself in. Breathlessly she called out, "Are you home, Rosala?" and rushed to the kitchen. "You'll never guess what I did. Never in a million years. Lord, that smells good. What's cooking?" Chana gave Rose a quick kiss. "Is David home yet? I'll wait till we're at the table to tell you what I've been up to."

"We're just having leftovers. I made a stew of sorts. David's in the den correcting papers." Rose spoke softly, her mind on the matter ahead of her. "We sit in half an hour."

"OK, that'll give me time for a quick shower."

Chana disappeared through the swinging door. Rose sighed and went to the dining room to set the table.

David had shaken his head when Rose spoke to him earlier. "It was to be expected," he said. "Too bad you have to be the one to tell her, but you did the right thing by offering to help Sarah out. I'm sorry to hear she's taking this so hard. Don't worry, old girl, I'll be in your corner all the way."

Later at the table, Chana couldn't wait to tell her news. "Well, I did it," she began eagerly. "I went downtown and signed up for classes at the Art Students' League." Pausing dramatically, she beamed at Rose and David.

Sobered for a moment by their apparent lack of enthusiasm, she plunged on. "I start Monday morning. I'm taking life drawing with McNulty, then I have an evening and a Saturday morning class with Robert Brachman himself. I bragged to him shamefully about being Harry Stern's daughter." Chana laughed. "You were right, Rose. He seemed flattered I chose to study with him. He said it pleased him to have the daughter of such a distinguished artist in his class. It was so easy; he accepted me just like that. Now I'm really scared. I've never worked in oils. I hope I don't make a fool of myself. Oh, and while I was there," she added, "I bought paints, brushes, and a sketch pad at the League store—I left them in the hall—so I'm ready to go, for better or worse. Wish me luck."

"That's wonderful, dear. I know you'll do just fine." Rose ladled a healthy portion of stew and passed it to Chana.

David's voice was warm. "That's great news, Chana." He smiled. "I know a bit about painting. If you'd like, after supper I'll check what you've bought to see if you have everything you need."

For the rest of the meal the conversation centered around Chana's prospects at the League. When they were finished, David suggested they have coffee in the living room.

After pouring, Rose set the pot down carefully on the table in front of her. Her mind searched frantically for the right beginning. Chana curled at the other end of the sofa and nestled against the cushions. The sober ticking of the grandfather clock punctuated the silence. As he waited for his wife to speak, David busied himself by filling and lighting his pipe.

Finally, Rose put her coffee cup down and cleared her throat. "I have something to tell you, Bubeleh." She turned to face Chana. "Your grandmother called while you were out. We had a long talk." Rose paused. "She told me the *Tzaddikim* handed down the decision last night." Rose paused again. "They have declared you *cherem*, Chana. You are excommunicated, and your marriage is no longer valid in the eyes of the *Lubavitcher* Court." There, she'd said it straight out. She hoped she hadn't been too abrupt.

Chana took a deep breath and put her cup down. She was surprised how steady her hand was. There was no feeling except surprise and great relief. Letting her breath out slowly, she leaned back against the cushions. "Well, that's some news, isn't it? It sure tops off my day in fine style. Does it really mean I'm free?" She looked at David for confirmation.

"Not exactly," he answered. "There's the matter of a legal divorce to satisfy the state of New York, but I think you might be able to ask for an annulment. It shouldn't be too hard to prove to the court that the marriage was never consummated. I'll talk to my lawyer and see what he says. It might be a fairly simple matter." Drawing on his pipe, he smiled reassuringly.

Rose looked distressed as she picked her next words. "That's not all Bubbe had to say."

"What more, Rose?" Chana felt a chill as she asked the question.

Taking hold of her courage, Rose looked directly at Chana, her voice wavering slightly. "Your mother and Mendel have also declared you *cherem*. They are sitting *shivah* for you this coming week." Her voice broke as she pulled a handkerchief from her sleeve.

The word *shivah* struck Chana like a physical blow, and she crumpled forward.

"Sitting *shivah*! Oh, Mama, how could you!" she wailed. Clutching herself, she rocked back and forth in her anguish. "How could you do this to me?"

David and Rose sat in silence, knowing it best she find her own way through the pain. In Rose's mind, Miriam had done the unforgivable, declaring her daughter dead. To actually sit *shivah*, have a funeral and mourn for seven days for a child who's very much alive—it was an abomination.

Rose shook with anger. David had called it nothing less than murder when they'd talked earlier. Rose couldn't go along with his harsh assessment, but she knew her friendship with Miriam was finished.

Chana's sobs began to lessen as Rose reached out and took her hand. Straightening up, Chana faced Rose. "Why didn't Bubbe tell me what was happening? Why didn't she tell me this herself?"

Rose spoke softly. "Bubbe wanted to, but she was afraid she'd break down over the phone, Chana. She's taking this very hard. I think it is making her ill. I'm sure she'll talk to you when she's feeling better. After all, you mean the world to her." She held Chana's trembling hand as she spoke.

"Didn't Mama get the letter I wrote?" Chana asked, her eyes revealing intense shock. "It explained how I felt about the marriage and why it didn't work out. I was sure once she read it she'd understand and forgive me."

"Sarah said your letter came the day before the *Tzaddikim* met. She said your mother destroyed it unopened." Rose took Chana in her arms and whispered, "I'm so sorry, Bubeleh."

The hall clock began striking 9. Chana pulled from Rose's embrace, and without a word she left the room. David knocked the ash from his pipe. Neither of them spoke as the chimes of the old clock finished marking the hour.

21

MACDOUGAL ALLEY

Mina pulled the scrap of paper from her purse and looked at it again to check the directions she'd written down earlier. The IND subway car picked up speed. Swaying jerkily, it passed 23rd Street without stopping. She felt uncomfortable. Only a few nondescript passengers were left in the littered car, and she'd never been this far downtown. By 14th Street, the car was almost empty. The people appeared to be students, bound for classes at CCNY. Mina got up, leaned on a strap by the door, and waited for the train to stop at 4th Street. On the platform she read CeeCee's instructions once more:

Take the Eighth Street exit. That puts you just a block from Macdougal Street. The alley is off Macdougal, half a block between Eighth and Washington Square.

CeeCee had assured her she couldn't possibly miss it. "But," she said, "if you do, just ask anyone. Everyone knows where Macdougal Alley is."

Once on the street, Mina headed east. Sure enough, Macdougal Street ran right into Eighth as her instructions said. Thanking the saints she wasn't lost, she walked on. Everything about this part of town was unfamiliar. The unmistakable aroma of Italian cooking, mixed with the smell of the sea, filled the warm afternoon air. There was a strange, old-world ambiance about the narrow streets. Even the sounds were different, somehow muted. It was not at all like the noisy city uptown.

Macdougal Street was paved with blocks of stone instead of asphalt. Sad, run-down walk-ups fronted abruptly on the narrow sidewalk. At the corner of one of these ancient gray buildings, she found a small sign. In faded letters it spelled MACDOUGAL ALLEY. Two-story dwellings came all the way out to meet the cobblestones. The tiny street with no sidewalk was only a short block in length. Searching, she found the door to No. 12 at the far end of the alley.

She pressed the button next to the mailbox. Looking up at the thin patch of blue sky between the buildings, she wondered if the sun ever penetrated the dark place. The cobblestones were still wet from the morning rain.

"Is that you, Mina?" CeeCee's head appeared almost immediately out the second-story window. "Come on up, the door's open."

The stairwell was musty. The narrow wooden stairs led to a small landing lit by a single dim lightbulb. CeeCee stood waiting in the open door.

"Well, you didn't get lost after all. Come on in." Her rounded, coffee-colored figure was clad loosely in a thin cotton shift. She was barefoot, her legs slightly apart, and the backlight made it clear she wore nothing underneath. "I'm so glad you came. I wasn't sure you would. You seemed hesitant yesterday when I suggested you come look at the place. *Mon dieu*, isn't it hot?"

Mina noticed again CeeCee's deliberate awareness of how her body moved. It was one of the first things she'd observed about CeeCee the first day they'd met at Schrafft's over a month ago. They'd been assigned the same shift that morning, and Mina had been immediately taken by CeeCee's graceful body as well as her dusky good looks and her exotic French accent.

CeeCee motioned her toward a worn sofa that faced a small fireplace with a cracked marble front. "Rest yourself, *ma chérie*. I'll get us some iced tea." She padded to the kitchen, her feet making just a whisper on the bare floor. Heavily lashed brown eyes flashed across the room at Mina. Startled by the flirtatious quality of her glance, Mina felt excited but also uneasy.

The tea, laced with cinnamon and spice, tasted good. CeeCee settled herself on the sofa and took a cigarette from a small wooden box on the coffee table. With swift, tapered hands she struck a match. CeeCee seemed to have an open knowledge about every gesture she made, each one precise and infinitely delicate. Inhaling deeply, she let the smoke drift from her full lips and slightly flared nostrils.

"How come you don't smoke, Mina? Did you ever try?" Her dark eyes were wide with amusement.

Mina felt awkward. She shrugged. "I don't know. I just never thought of trying it." She marveled once more at CeeCee's creamy, smooth skin, the color of light butter caramel.

A toss of her head made her dark curls dance as her frank, mischievous eyes met Mina's. "I really hope you'll consider moving in with me." Then she jumped to her feet with a fresh thought. "Would you like to look around?" Taking Mina's hand, she pulled her up. "Come, I'll show you the bedroom." Her words bubbled with laughter.

A big iron bed completely overwhelmed the tiny bedroom, leaving just enough space for one to walk around it.

A large skylight filled the high ceiling. Rays from the afternoon sun struggled through its grimy panes, filling the room with a diffused warm glow. A flowered chintz curtain enclosed a space for hanging clothes.

The kitchen was merely an extension of the living room. There was a gray slate sink under a high window that faced the blank brick wall of the building next door. With an exaggerated flourish, CeeCee opened a door next to the icebox. "Voilà! The john." There it was, an ancient water closet, circa 1910, complete with tank high on the wall over an old-fashioned wooden toilet seat. "Now you have to guess where the bathtub is." CeeCee's eyes sparkled with mirth.

"I haven't the foggiest. Don't tell me it's in another part of the building." Mina envisioned trudging outside somewhere to get washed.

"Heavens no, *ma chérie*, we're not that provincial! It's right here under your nose." She lifted the counter-top next to the sink, revealing a white porcelain tub just big enough to sit in if you brought your knees up to your chin. "We fill it from the sink. There's a drain in the bottom, so that's no problem. But you have to use the footstool under the sink to get in." Mina chuckled, picturing herself climbing over the counter buck-naked on cold winter nights.

"Of course, the apartment's best feature is the fireplace." CeeCee's graceful hand caressed the marble mantle. "You can find these only in a few of the old buildings. It comes in handy when the steam doesn't get up to the radiator, which happens a lot of the time, I'm sorry to say."

CeeCee's pitch made moving in sound fascinating. For a long time Mina had been denying how lonely she was. This offer could be the answer. CeeCee was fun to be with, so living together was beginning to make a lot of sense. Her mind raced as she accepted a refill of tea and settled back on the sofa. It was all very tempting, Mina thought. Maybe it would work out.

CeeCee lit another cigarette and blew smoke toward the ceiling. "My ex-roommate, Babe, took off for Cuernavaca, Mexico. There's a whole community of Americans down there. Mostly New York artists and writers. All pretty radical for my taste, but Babe was determined to try it." Lines deepened about her mouth, indicating things had soured between her and Babe. CeeCee took another deep drag. "I hear it's cheap living down there. Babe'll like it. She thinks she's going to write the great American novel. We didn't get along all that well toward the end, so it's probably best she's gone." She leaned back and looked straight at Mina, her eyes going soft once more.

"Hope you'll say yes to moving in. If you do, your half of the rent each month will only be 20 bucks. That shouldn't be too hard to swing. What do you say?"

Her dark eyes held Mina speechless for the moment. The fresh soap smell from CeeCee's hair, mixed with the provocative tobacco smoke hanging between them, stirred feelings Mina wasn't quite ready to deal with. Gathering her wits, Mina heard herself say in a matter-of-fact voice, "I'll have to talk to my Aunt Willie. She thinks I'm going to secretarial school in the fall. She'll probably throw a fit. Convincing her about moving into town is going to take some fancy talking." The blood rushed to her cheeks as CeeCee took her hand.

"I know you'll say yes, *chérie*. We'll get along just fine. You'll see."

"I'll let you know Monday morning," Mina said, managing to sound casual.

CeeCee fished her shoes from under the sofa. "Come on, I'll walk with you to the subway and show you Washington Square. You can pick up your train at the South entrance on 4th Street."

The park at Washington Square was crowded. Everyone seemed to enjoy the afternoon coolness after the heat of the day. Oldsters commanded the few benches in the shade of the linden trees; mothers pushed baby carriages slowly along the walks as children on roller skates skimmed by. Old men absorbed in chess games ignored the boisterous children around them. Pigeons were underfoot everywhere, busily searching the cracked sidewalk for scraps to eat.

Mina was fascinated by the massive Romanesque arch, and marveled at the centuries-old buildings that gracefully faced the slow-moving traffic. Washington Square, with its almost European charm, delighted her. Here people seemed to move to a different tempo than their fellow New Yorkers uptown.

For the next three blocks CeeCee kept up a running chatter on the benefits of Village living. "You must say yes. Please don't disappoint me. I'll be devastated if you do." CeeCee's half smile was just a hand's span away from Mina's face as they walked. The smell of her face powder and the sweet pungency that was CeeCee's alone stirred Mina once more, and her hand found CeeCee's.

Standing at the subway entrance, they were enveloped by a rush of cool air. The roar of the trains below drowned their good-bye. Pulling herself away from this new feeling, Mina turned and rushed down the stairs.

"See you tomorrow, *chérie*," CeeCee's voice echoed after her.

22

THE MEETING

The fresh June morning was giving up under the heavy onslaught of heat, so familiar to New Yorkers in early summer. Chana stood on the sidewalk for a moment studying the two nude figures on the canvas. Robert Brachman's painting was so large it completely filled the display window of the Harris Gallery. *I'll paint like that one day. I know I will*, she told herself, entranced by the two half-draped figures in the painting: A dusky girl stood next to a woman, who sat combing the child's long blond hair. The dark girl's bronze hand rested lightly on the pale shoulder of the seated woman. Her black curls were caught gracefully in a white kerchief. The two figures made a stunning contrast in light and dark, and as she studied the painting her thoughts drifted back to the events of the past few weeks.

Although she had been in Brachman's class only a short time, she was amazed at the progress she'd made, especially since handling oils and working from live models was an altogether new experience. Her swift progress now promised a talent only half dreamed a short time ago, but her joy in finding this new dimension of herself was diminished by the news that her family was sitting *shivah* for her and entering the 30 days of *shelashim*. The reality that *Kaddish* prayers for the dead were being recited twice daily for her was a sword in her heart.

Also, Bubbe's visible aging was of deep concern. Her grandmother had changed so much lately. There were drawn lines in her dear, pale face, and Chana noticed her hands shook slightly now. Bubbe had said, "Never mind what goes on with the family. Take care of Chana Stern and make her life count. After all, you know Stern means *star*. So follow your star, Bubeleh, and don't worry about me. I'll be happy already knowing you're on your way. So don't look so sad, my darling. You have a new life to find." Her eyes had glistened with tears as they hugged good-bye that day at the subway entrance, and Chana watched sadly as her grandmother haltingly made her way down the stairs to the platform below.

Now, with difficulty, Chana brought her thoughts back to the present and entered the Harris gallery. With a soft click the heavy glass door banished the heat and noise of 57th Street. A cool silence rose from the thick, gray carpet of the reception room. An oriental teak desk and carved chair were the only furnishings. A neat brass plaque rested on the polished top of the desk with the name ELI HARRIS engraved in modest letters. A gold box holding business cards lay next to the plaque. As she reached for one of the cards a man's voice startled her.

"Good morning, young lady. May I be of help to you?" Turning, she saw a slight, elderly man who appeared out of nowhere. "Eli Harris, at your service." He spoke softly.

She smiled to herself. His gray suit precisely matched the carpet, as did his thinning hair. Behind steel-rimmed glasses, his dark eyes were polite and questioning as he came forward, extending his hand. Taking hers in a warm clasp, he waited for her to speak.

"I'm studying with Brachman at the Art Students' League," Chana began. "I was told you were having a showing of his work, so I made the trip downtown this morning. I hope I'm not too early, Mr. Harris. The door was open, so I came in."

"No, no my dear, you're not too early at all. I was just opening up. You're welcome. To whom do I have the honor?" he asked, his smile deepening.

"My name is Chana Stern. I've just started studying, but I hope to be a fine painter one day. I'm particularly interested in painting the nude figure. That's why I chose Brachman as my teacher."

Eli nodded. "Stern...I seem to remember a painter by that name." He pressed his forefinger against his upper lip. "Yes, yes, now I remember. His name was Harold Stern. I knew him well. A landscape artist of some renown. Could he be a relative?"

"Harry Stern was my father. Unfortunately, he was killed in an automobile accident six years ago. He was best known for his dioramas at the Museum of Natural History." Chana caught her breath. "How wonderful you remember him, Mr. Harris."

"Well, it's a small world indeed. I'm pleased to meet the daughter of such a fine painter." He shook his head. "I didn't know of his passing. My sincere condolences, my dear. The art world is made poorer by such a loss." Then his face brightened. "Come. Follow me," he said. "I'm just opening for the day." His tongue made a soft, clucking sound. "A lucky day for me I meet my old friend's daughter who is now also becoming a painter." He pressed a button by the door. Indirect light flooded the gallery, bringing to life the paintings that lined the walls.

Caught by the splendor of the works before her, Chana gasped.

"Oh, Mr. Harris, they're wonderful. And so alive. It's as if the figures could speak at any moment."

"Well, Chana Stern, I'll leave you now. Stay and enjoy as long as you wish. I have work to do." He nodded toward a door at the end of the room. "Please come back to my office before you leave. Now enjoy. We will talk later."

Finding a low bench, Chana sat to study the paintings more carefully. She had the whole gallery to herself. She hoped it would stay that way for a while. After a few minutes she got up and examined each canvas, noting carefully how she might incorporate what she saw in her own work. She was so absorbed in the paintings she lost track of time. When she finally looked around, the gallery was full of people. She checked her watch. It was after 11. Deciding it was time to say good-bye, Chana knocked at Eli's office door.

"Is that you, Chana?" He smiled when he opened the door. "Come in, come in." He led her to a chair by his desk. "Did you enjoy Brachman's feast for the eyes and nourishment for the spirit? I hope your morning here has been a help to you. You must come as often as you like. The paintings will be here through the month of August."

Just then, there was a soft knock at the door. "Uncle Eli? It's Ben." A deep, masculine voice brought Eli to his feet. His face shone with delight as he opened the door and embraced a tall, tanned man in his early 20s.

"Ben! I can't believe you're here already. I didn't expect you until later this afternoon. Your wire said your train would get in at 5."

"How are you, Uncle?" He encircled the older man with a warm bear hug. "I made an earlier connection in

Chicago, and I came here directly from Grand Central instead of checking into my hotel. Thought we might catch lunch." Seeing Chana, his eyes brightened with interest. "I'm sorry. I didn't mean to intrude."

"No, no, come in, son, come in."

Ben picked up the large suitcase at his feet. He seemed to fill the small office, and Chana guessed he was all of six-four or six-five. "Well, I should be on my way," she said, standing up and extending her hand. "Thank you, Mr. Harris. You've been so kind. I'll drop in again before the paintings are gone."

"Not to run away so soon, my dear. I want you should meet my sister's son all the way from San Francisco. Ben Frank, this is my new friend, Chana Stern." Eli paused, noting the look that passed between them. He cleared his throat. "Ben," he said, "I'm sorry, but I have work to catch up on. A dealer I'm expecting to see will be here at 1, so lunch is out of the question. Dinner is better." Lowering his voice, he looked up at his nephew. "Perhaps Miss Stern would be so kind as to take my place and accompany you to lunch." He gave a quick glance in Chana's direction.

"That would be great. Please say you will." A beguiling expression softened the young man's strong features. "Please take pity on a poor stranger from out of town who hasn't the foggiest idea where to find a decent meal in this city."

Feeling all resistance slip away, Chana swallowed her first impulse to say she had other plans. "I know a place just a block from here," she smiled, amazed at her boldness.

When they left the gallery they started down 57th Street. The afternoon sun was growing hot. Ben shed his jacket and slung it over his shoulder. In typical male fashion he held it in the crook of one finger as he strode beside Chana. His long strides made it difficult for her to keep up. He leaned close to take her arm as they crossed Fifth Avenue, and she caught the clean, fresh smell of cologne. *Hasidic men never smell this good*, she thought. They always had the musty odor of old books about them.

At Schrafft's they took a table by the window. An attractive redhead with thick braids piled high on her head came to take their order. Chana recognized the girl as the one who had waited on her a week ago, the day the League cafeteria had been closed. Chana had crossed the street and splurged with a Schrafft's lunch. She remembered the girl's warm smile, and she wore that same friendly smile now as she wrote down their order.

Over bubbling chicken pot pies, Ben turned talkative. He explained that his family back in California owned a chain of men's stores and that he'd grown up in San Mateo just south of San Francisco. "I graduated from Berkeley," he said between large mouthfuls, "and then went on to law school at Stanford." He paused, giving her a charmingly crooked grin, and admitted, "Actually, this is my first trip to New York."

Chana returned his infectious smile.

"So, after passing the bar exam, I joined the Marines," he went on. "Applied for Officer's Candidate School. I decided to take a day to visit my Uncle Eli before reporting for duty at Quantico."

Ben toyed thoughtfully with his fork for a moment and then dropped his boyish enthusiasm as concern drew a pattern of lines about his deep set eyes. "The world is headed straight into war," he said seriously. "It's inevitable. Hitler is running roughshod over Europe and won't stop until he's finished off the Jews." Ben's eyes grew dark with anger. "He and his 'master race' are out to conquer the world, Chana. As a nation we won't let that happen, and as a Jew I can't let it happen either."

Chana nodded, her eyes as serious as his.

"I believe we'll be drawn into it within a year." He finished the last bite of his chicken pie and pushed away his plate. His voice lifted with resolve. "I wanted to serve my country the best I could, so I opted for Officer's Candidate School." His eyes glowed with a fond memory. "My dad was a marine sergeant in the last war, so it seemed like the right thing for me to do."

He stopped talking long enough to light a cigarette, and for a few moments he smoked in silence. Chana sensed he was mentally somewhere else. Then suddenly his mood brightened and an embarrassed grin erased the frown lines above his dark eyes. "Gee, that's enough about me and the seriousness of the world. I tend to get carried away." He laughed. "Now, tell me about Chana Stern. Who is she, and what is her life like in the big city of New York?"

The way he looked at her made her breath quicken, but she steadied her voice and told him a little about her family in Brooklyn and about her plans to attend Brachman's summer classes in Bennington, Vermont, in July, but that was all she could bring herself to say about her life.

When she finished he looked at her with that same beguiling smile and said, "Hey, I've got a great idea. If I shape up in boot camp and keep my nose clean, I'll be eligible for a weekend pass the second week of August. I could come up and stay with Uncle Eli and..." he paused, like a small boy asking for a goody, "would you spend some of that time with me, Chana? We could have dinner and maybe take in a show. Please say you will. It'll sure cheer me on through the hell of basic training. I hear the first six weeks is the pits."

After his eloquent plea, what could she do but say yes and write her address and phone number on a paper napkin for him? Folding it carefully, he tucked it into his wallet.

They took their time walking to Columbus Circle. There, looking at her with the same puckish grin she'd already begun to grow fond of, he took her hand. He held it for a long time. Neither of them spoke. Finally, in a voice just above a whisper, he said, "See you in August, Chana Stern."

Her heart thumped wildly as she raced down the stairs to catch her train.

That night, lying in the dark, she heard a voice out of nowhere: *No longer a Dubovitch. No longer a runaway bride, and certainly not a daughter given up for dead. Then who are you, Chana Stern? Who are you? Who are you?* The question drummed in her head until sleep swallowed her up.

23

MINA ARENHOLT—AT MACDOUGAL ALLEY

I had been putting off telling Aunt Willie I was moving into the city. In just a week I'd be living with CeeCee in No. 12 Macdougal Alley. We decided on the Fourth of July weekend for my move since we both would have those two days off.

It was Saturday morning. Aunt Willie had just washed her hair. She was sitting at her dresser, and I was rolling her hair in curlers. Mr. Potter, who worked with her in editing at the studio, had finally mustered the courage to ask her to dinner and a movie. She was as nervous as a teenager going on her first date and kept fidgeting as I wound the curls.

Seizing the moment, I fastened the last curler and met her eyes in the mirror. I let my hands drop to her shoulders. "That's it, Auntie. You should be dry in time to dress."

She smiled her thanks and started to rise, but I kept my hands on her shoulders. "Just a minute, there's something I want to speak to you about," I said, gathering my courage.

She looked impatient. "'What is it, dear?"

I almost lost my resolve, but plunged on. "Next weekend..." I began.

"You have a date with that sailor again? Is that what you're trying to tell me, Mina?" Her voice had the edge she reserved for discussing matters that displeased her.

"No, Aunt Willie, you don't have to worry on that score."

"Well, I should hope not. I didn't approve of him one bit. His manners certainly left something to be desired."

Changing my approach I started again. "I've been thinking..." I took a deep breath.

"Yes, yes, get on with it, child."

"Well, no, not just thinking." I was stammering now. "As a matter of fact, I've decided to move into the city, Aunt Willie."

Her head shot up. She whirled around and faced me. "You what?"

"I'm moving in with a girl I know at work. She has an apartment in the Village. That's in lower Manhattan, you know, down near the Battery."

"You don't have to tell me where the Village is. I wasn't born in a cabbage patch, young lady."

For a moment I thought I'd gotten away with my news, but I was wrong.

Aunt Willie's eyes got hard and her face turned scarlet. "You mean to tell me you're going off to live with a total stranger? What about your plans for secretarial school? Are you going to give that up and be a waitress all your life?" She spat out the word *waitress* like it was a bad taste in her mouth. She was breathing hard. "What happened to the money I gave you for graduation? I hope to God you haven't spent it already. That was for school, remember?" Saliva sat in the corners of her mouth. "*Gott im Himmel!* This is the thanks I get? Have you lost your mind, Mina Arenholt? Your mother must be turning in her grave." She stood up, her face inches from mine.

For an awful moment I thought she might have a stroke and I'd be to blame, but she took hold of herself, and her voice turned icy.

"What about all our plans for your future?" She pinned me with cold eyes.

I tried to explain how I felt and that I wanted a place of my own. "And besides, I like working at Schrafft's," I finished with some spunk. She was still shaking, but I could see she was running out of steam.

"After all I've done for you. How can you be such an ungrateful child?" She started to feel sorry for herself, and tears of self-pity welled in her eyes. A terrible wave of guilt seized me. I tried putting my arms around her, but she turned away from me.

"Don't be mad at me, Aunt Willie. I love you. I really do," I blubbered, running to my room. Through the closed door I could still hear her ranting. She wasn't finished with me.

"You're going to live with *commies* and *queers*—that's what you're going to do. Flesh of my flesh, living in such a place. I can't believe it. Sodom and Gomorrah, that's what it is." She was screaming. "Do you hear me, Mina? No one but Marxists and faggots live in that place."

The words *faggot* and *queer* ripped through me and reminded me of tales I'd heard about the Village but dismissed as idle gossip. For a moment I wondered if she was right. I covered my ears. Macdougal Alley was where I wanted to be, and CeeCee was whom I wanted to be with. Yes, I wanted to be with CeeCee most of all. I threw myself on the bed, buried my head in the pillow, and gave myself over to the luxury of tears.

ک‍ ک‍ ک‍

Later, after Aunt Willie left, I got my suitcase from the closet. I realized I had more things than it could hold, so I'd have to make two trips next weekend. Then I discovered my little diary was missing. Oh, God! It was still in its hiding place under my mattress back at the old house! I'd been in such a rush to get out that day four months ago that I forgot to pack it. Leaving it there with all my poems and the outpourings of my heart for Katy was unthinkable. I had to get it back. The question was how and when.

Avoiding Gus was paramount. My best bet was to get in the house while he was at early mass tomorrow. I'd have to make the trip to Jackson Heights first thing in the morning. In a panic, I realized I no longer had my house key. How to get in?

Then I recalled Gus used to keep a key to the kitchen door under an empty flowerpot on the back steps. It had been his insurance against Mama's anger when he came home drunk from the Lodge Hall. He thought he could fool her, but I knew different. Mama always heard him; she just never let on.

That night I said five Hail Marys and petitioned all the saints that my diary would still be there. Then I set my alarm for 6 and went to bed.

In the morning, I got out of the apartment before Aunt Willie was up and took the elevated to Jackson Heights. A warm rain had started by the time I caught the Roosevelt Avenue bus, and in a matter of 15 minutes I was walking up the block to the old house. I approached from the alley to make sure no one saw me. Sure enough, the flowerpot was still there. Holding my breath, I lifted it. Mother of God, I was saved. After all these years, there it was. If my luck held, Gus would still be at mass, and I'd have a chance to get in and out before he returned.

The rain was falling harder now; it trickled down the back of my neck. Everything was quiet till I saw old Mrs.

Cleary come out on her back stoop with a bag of garbage. She dumped it in the can in the alley and rushed back into the house. Thank God she didn't see me.

I turned the key in the lock as silently as I could. The house was still. The air in the kitchen was stale. The only sounds were the drone of a housefly—searching escape at a window pane—and the leaky faucet drumming a steady tat-too on the bottom of a dirty skillet.

Taking two steps at a time, I rushed up the stairs. I had to hurry in case mass let out early. I looked at my watch; I had only a few minutes to find the diary and get out. The shades were drawn against the sun and it was close and hot in my room. Kneeling by my bed, I ran my hand under the mattress. There it was! Sweet Jesus! I checked; it was still locked.

I smoothed the faded bedspread and looked around. Everything was just as I had left it and somehow appalling-ly sad. No time to get sentimental, I told myself as I closed the door softly behind me.

Deciding I'd better leave the same way I came in, I went back through the living room. Newspapers and magazines were scattered everywhere. Gus obviously had made no attempt at housekeeping for a long time. The place reeked of stale tobacco and the ashtrays were filled with butts. An empty Schlitz bottle lay on the floor by his morris chair and a half-empty one sat on top of the Philco. I could almost see him slouched there listening to the news with a bottle in his hand. Shaking the scene from my mind, I sped through the dining room. The last thing that caught my eye before I locked the kitchen door was that awful spot on the floor in front of the sink.

❧ ❧ ❧

"Cat got your tongue, girl? You've hardly said a word all evening." CeeCee shot me an amused glance. She leaned over the coffee table, pursed her full lips, and blew out the candles. It was my first night in the apartment, so she splurged by picking up goulash from Romany Marie's. She'd also brought home a straw-covered bottle of red wine to make it a real occasion. After eating, we sat close on the sagging old sofa and sipped our wine. CeeCee's arm crept around my waist, and I let my head fall on her shoulder. I was exhausted from my two trips to Astoria, and the Chianti was making me sleepy. My eyelids felt like lead as I watched the smoke from her cigarette climb to the ceiling.

After a few minutes she stubbed out the butt on one of the paper plates and said, "Your aunt wasn't too happy about you moving in here, right?" Stretching her long legs from under her, she picked up the dirty plates. "Well, no matter, *chérie*, old people get funny ideas. My mother's the same way. She hates me living in the Village, says I'll come to no good in a place like this." Laughing, she went to the kitchen.

I picked up the empty cartons and followed her to the sink.

"We can clean up in the morning," CeeCee said. "There's some wine left. Let's finish it before we turn in. You've had a full day, and you look like you could use a nightcap." She smiled, and in the dim light her white teeth shone like pearls. Her thigh pressed close as we sank back on the sofa. Her head bent to mine. I could smell the sweetness of her, and it sent my senses reeling.

"I'm so glad you're here, Mina." She spoke softly, and I fell into those dark eyes of hers. There was no escape. I was lost, and I knew it. She wanted me to make love to her, but I didn't have the slightest idea what she expected of me. Being tossed out of the ordinary and into foreign territory was throwing me for a loop. Staring at her beautiful face, I couldn't speak, and I felt like an idiot.

For weeks I'd refused to believe I wanted CeeCee the way I'd wanted Katy. Now I knew it was true, but this wanting was much stronger. I was terrified. I felt as if my body was not my own, but controlled by some terrible force.

Her breath was warm on my cheek and her eyes expectant. Throwing caution away, I bent forward, trembling, and closed my eyes. CeeCee's lips tasted of cigarettes and wine. They parted mine, holding my hunger in their softness, and I feasted again and again, my appetite insatiable. The heavy stone of doubt rolled away from the mouth of my need, and I gave myself to her delicious lips.

Breaking from me, her laughter filled the darkness. "Come on, Mina, it's time." She took my hand and we raced for the big iron bed. She pulled me to her on the yielding mattress. In a flurry of arms and legs, we shed our clothes. She guided my body to fit hers. In that moment I knew she would teach me all I had to know. Her flesh was cool, smooth like satin, fragrant and moist in all the secret places. I moved with her rhythm. The unfolding depths of her pleasure came in tender moans and quickening breath, which brought me to her again and again.

Exploring the mysterious nook between her thighs, I buried my fingers in her crisp, damp hair. My needs were met by her smooth, slow movements. We rode our passion with utter abandon; like racehorses we strained for the finish. She arched, I dove, and in a heated rush we claimed the prize together.

Lulled by the wordless sound of her satisfaction, I fell to rest on her soft belly, dizzy and intoxicated by her flavors lingering in my mouth. As sweet exhaustion possessed me, my body melded to hers, and we slept.

       ᨁ   ᨁ   ᨁ

As I opened my eyes, I remembered it was Sunday. The dingy skylight overhead was ghostlike in the light of morning.

CeeCee turned over and murmured, "Are you awake?" She cradled my head between her breasts and whispered, "I knew we were meant for this."

Her words brought the hunger back. Taking her in my arms again, I claimed what I was born to do. My eager fingers found now-familiar places. The unbelievable sweetness of her flesh meeting mine was overwhelming. I was made love to by a woman. Every fiber of my body attested to that, and there was no need to deny it any longer.

24

CHANA STERN—THE LEGACY

The early evening sun was still high over the river when my taxi pulled in front of the apartment. All smiles, Tom, the doorman, rushed to the curb, grabbed my bag, and tucked the rolled canvases under his arm. "Ev'nin, Miss Stern. Nice to see you back home safe."

I paid the cabbie and followed Tom into the lobby. He pressed the button and got a buzz right back. "The Solomons are home. I'll take you right up."

Rose stood in the doorway, waiting as I got off the elevator. "Welcome home, dear." She gave me a hug. "We missed you. You must be tired."

"I am. All I can think of is a cold shower." I kissed her cheek. Tom put my things inside the door and disappeared into the hall. Just then David came out of his study.

"Chanala! Good to have you back. This place has been much too quiet with you gone." He noticed the rolls of canvas by my suitcase. "Looks like you got a lot of work done." He picked up everything, followed me down the hall to my room, and put my things by the bed. "Join us for sherry before dinner. We're anxious to hear all about Vermont." He smiled and closed the door.

I pulled off my sticky clothes and climbed into the shower. I was toweling my hair when I noticed a large manila envelope on my desk. On top of it lay a letter with a Virginia postmark. My heart went snap, grab. All during the tedious train ride back from Vermont to the city, I'd hoped to find a letter waiting for me, and now there it was. Trembling with anticipation, I opened it. I could almost hear Ben's voice as I read:

I got the long weekend pass. Arrive Grand Central Station at noon on Friday the 16th and don't have to be back at barracks until 2100 hours Sunday. That gives us almost three whole days. I've booked a room at the St. Moritz. Can you meet me there at the sidewalk café for lunch at 1:30?

He wrote with great enthusiasm about his training, but the words *I've been thinking about you a lot and counting the days* leapt from the page. My pulse raced as I read that part again. Folding the letter carefully, I put it back in its envelope and tucked it under my pillow to enjoy later.

The manila envelope was heavy. I turned it over. BANKERS TRUST COMPANY, CHURCH ST. STATION, NEW YORK, N.Y. was printed in block letters in the upper left corner. That didn't give me a clue. I couldn't imagine why I'd be receiving anything from them. It must be some kind of advertising pitch, I thought, as I undid the metal opener. There was a thick sheaf of papers inside. On top was a letter addressed to "Miss Chana Stern":

The Private Advisory Service of Bankers Trust wishes to inform you that a trust has been set up for you by Sarah H. Blumenthal. The income from said trust is $2,000 to be distributed to you quarterly. The first payment will be sent on September 1, 1940.

There were several more pages defining the details of the trust agreement. At the bottom of the last page it said:

Please find enclosed a personal letter from Sarah Blumenthal. If you have any questions, feel free to call me at any time. C.H. Lasey, Trust Officer.

I sat there, stunned. Was this for real? What did it all mean? I was shaking with apprehension. Did Bubbe think she was going to die? I had a terrible foreboding as I opened Bubbe's letter. Why hadn't she told me about this? In her neat, old-fashioned handwriting, the letter read:

Beloved Bubeleh,

Of late, I've been thinking a lot about your future. I want you to have every opportunity for the good life. This trust I've formed for you will do just that. It will help you now. When I am no more, the remainder of a trust left to me by your grandfather will also be yours.

I haven't been too peppy lately. When I'm feeling better, I'll come to town. We'll have a nice long visit. I want to hear all about your seminar in Bennington. However, it was important for me to tend to this business right away, so I wrote Mr. Lasey. If you have any questions, he's the one to contact. Darling Chanala, not to worry. We'll see each other soon.

All my love,
Bubbe

P.S. Don't call me here at the house. It's better I should call you.

Later while we were having our sherry, I showed Rose and David the trust papers. They were as amazed as I was and said they were happy for me. They both agreed Bubbe had done the right thing.

David lit his pipe and said he had some encouraging news about my annulment. "My attorney says it's just a matter of paperwork and obtaining a court date for the hearing. I'll go with you when you have to appear in court. It shouldn't be long now." David smiled as he poured more sherry in my glass.

As I unfolded my napkin I looked at the two dear people who had done so much for me. "Everything is happening too fast, Rose," I said. "I hardly know what to think. I seem to be hurtling into a future I couldn't have dreamed of a few months ago. I want you both to know how excited I am. At the same time, I'm scared out of my wits over the outcome of all this."

Rose clucked her tongue as she passed my plate. "Don't be worried, dear. The world will still keep turning. You can sort out the details later. There's plenty of time. Now eat and enjoy."

25

CHANA STERN—A MAN IN HER LIFE

At Rose's suggestion I checked into the Henry Hudson Hotel on West 57th Street for the weekend. It's a hotel for women and within walking distance of the St. Moritz. I thought it would be more convenient for meeting Ben than expecting him to come all the way out to Riverside Drive.

I told Rose about meeting Ben, and that we planned to spend time together this weekend. She said she approved of my staying downtown, if I felt it was necessary, as long as I was in a safe environment. I assured her I'd be just fine staying at a women-only hotel.

My room was on the 18th floor, and I had a spectacular view of the river. I could see the ocean liner *Normandy* docked at her pier at the foot of 57th Street. It was odd being alone in a strange place, but I still felt exhilarated by the adventure.

I had watched the lights on the water for a long time the night before. Traffic on Eighth Avenue rumbled beneath my window. Just down the block, Roosevelt Hospital rose like an old fortress and farther down the street, like two black specters, the spires of a Catholic church reached into the night. It was muggy and hot, and the curtains at my window stirred listlessly as the sounds of the city filled my small room.

I managed only a couple of hours of restless sleep. When dawn finally consumed the lights on the river I gave up. Dressing, I took the elevator to the lobby and found the drugstore there was open. In solitary grandeur I broke my fast with black coffee and a jelly doughnut.

Getting back to my room, I took a long, cold shower. I had hours on my hands, so I lay in bed and tried to relax. I must have dozed, because the next thing I remembered someone was knocking loudly at my door. I leapt off the bed, my heart pounding out of my chest. "Who is it?" My voice was unnaturally loud in the quiet room.

"It's the maid, ma'am. I'll come back later to make up."

I looked at my watch. It was almost 11. Only two hours to dress and get over to the St. Moritz. I was assailed by a flood of doubts. Would I look OK? Had I picked the right dress at Bonwit's yesterday? I took it out of the closet and held it up to me in front of the mirror. Buying clothes was a whole new thing. Had I missed the mark this time? The floral print had appealed to me in the store, but now it didn't seem sophisticated enough. I realized I was working myself into an awful state as I hurried to dress.

Glancing at my reflection in the mirror one more time, I was sure Ben would think me a real plain Jane. *Well, I'll just have to make the best of it*, I told myself. I picked up my gloves and dashed to the elevator.

By the time I reached Columbus Circle I wished I'd taken a cab. It was getting hot, and my brown-and-white spectators were making blisters on my heels. On top of that I could feel sweat threatening to ruin my Elizabeth Arden foundation. *Damn*! I thought. *When I get to the restaurant I'll look like I've been running a marathon.*

At the café, I didn't have any trouble finding Ben's table. He jumped to his feet.

"Chana, it's so good to see you. You've made this

marine a happy man today." Holding my chair, he bent close.

I caught the familiar odor of his cologne. Every time Ben had come into my thoughts during the last month, I recalled that scent. Sitting across the table from me now, he wore the same boyish grin as the first time we met. Taking a pack of Chesterfields from his shirt pocket, he offered me one.

I shook my head and said in a small voice, "I don't smoke." Darn! Why did I always feel insecure at moments like this? In the movies it looks so smart to light up. If I took up the habit, it might do wonders for my self-esteem.

After the waiter took our order, Ben leaned across the table. With his forefinger he traced the curve of my cheek. "Do you know how pretty you are, Chana Stern?"

I stuttered, "N-no, not really. I...of course not." Immediately I realized that sounded dumb. I was blushing and floundering. All my attempts at sophistication had failed miserably.

"Who are you, Chana Stern?" Ben asked, his eyes going soft and his voice intimate.

"What do you mean, 'who am I?'" I was really taken aback.

"Come on. Tell me about yourself. All you've told me so far is that you're a painter. I'm hungry to know all about you: your likes, your dislikes. Tell me. What has your life been like? I want to find the real Chana Stern."

Right away I knew I was getting into deep water. What to say? Carefully I inched slightly farther out on the conversational tight rope. "I don't know where to begin, Ben. Really, all I can think of now is enjoying this marvelous lunch. We can talk about me later." God, how could I possibly explain my life to him? Maybe someday, but not now.

At the moment all I could do was make him a present of my most provocative smile and hope it would satisfy him for the time being. "After lunch let me show you the park," I said, changing the subject. "We can walk or take a carriage like all the other tourists. What do you say?"

"Sounds great. Now, how about dessert and coffee?" He signaled the waiter.

We finished lunch with chocolate eclairs filled with ice cream. Over coffee, Ben lit a cigarette and reached across the table for my hand. "You like poetry?"

I nodded.

"How about Edgar Allan Poe?"

"Yes, we studied him in school. I remember one poem about a raven. It was kind of scary."

"Did you ever read his poem about Annabel Lee?"

I nodded again, wondering what he was getting at.

He held my hand tighter. " 'She was a child and I was a child,' " he quoted dramatically, " 'in this kingdom by the sea. We loved with a love that was more than love, I and my Annabel Lee.' I'm glad you like poetry too. Now you see, we have something in common, you and I." His eyes held mine.

I lost myself in them for a moment.

"We could be like that in this kingdom by the sea, Chana. There's so much to look forward to, just getting to know each other's likes and dislikes. Don't you agree?"

I smiled, unable to find words to answer those eyes that wouldn't let me go.

After paying the bill he suggested we go to his room before tackling the park. "OK," I said, and then immediately wondered if I'd lost my mind, for on second thought I was sure it wasn't something a lady would do. Not knowing how to take my reply back, I said nothing and followed him to the lobby.

The elevator was crowded. What would people think? Would they assume we were married? What if they could tell we weren't? I glued my eyes to a pair of feet in front of me and felt the blood rush to my cheeks.

"This is our floor," Ben said, reaching for my hand. The word "our" nailed me like a stake in the heart, and I was grateful when the elevator gate closed behind us.

As we walked down the hall, he draped an arm over my shoulder. "I have a surprise for you this evening," he said as he unlocked the door. The shades were drawn to keep out the heat, so the room was dark. His suitcase lay open on a rack. Rummaging through it, he produced a small envelope and held it out to me.

"Surprise! Two seats in the fifth row tonight for *Panama Hattie*. How about that?" The boyish grin was back. "Hope you haven't seen it already."

"No, I haven't. How wonderful, Ben! They say Ethel Merman is a smash."

He lifted the shades and motioned to a door. "The head's in there."

I looked puzzled.

He laughed. " 'Head' is Marine talk for the little girls' room. It's right through there."

In the mirror over the basin I made a quick appraisal of myself. I didn't recognize the girl I saw there. Was I really in a man's hotel room? I began to feel a bit wicked as I redid my lips. My hair had gone flat with the heat, so I ran cold water on my fingers and fluffed it out, making the curls spring back. Viewing the restoration with approval, I returned to the bedroom, my confidence more or less intact.

Ben sat by the bed smoking, one leg thrown over the arm of his chair. He leaned back and grinned. "You look gorgeous. If I wasn't so full of lunch, I could eat you up." The corner of his eyes crinkled with amusement. "Well, let's shove off and do the park."

Out on the sidewalk he took my arm. "Shall we see if we can find a carriage? It's too hot to walk."

We found one in front of the Plaza Hotel, and the cabbie tipped his hat as we climbed aboard. As we turned into the park the noise of the city seemed to fade. The air was cool under the green arch of trees, and the ancient mare's hooves drummed a sleepy cadence on the pavement.

Ben pulled me close, and my head found a comfortable niche on his broad shoulder. Ever so lightly his thigh touched mine. For the first time I noticed his hands: fingers long and bronzed by the sun, a delicate forest of hairs just beneath the knuckles. A khaki watchband circled one tanned wrist. His jacket was rough against my cheek. There it was again...that intoxicating cologne provocatively blended, this time with tweed and tobacco smoke.

Neither of us spoke for a long time. Then he took my hand in his.

"Chana, I've made a decision about my life. I love being a Marine, and I'm thinking of putting in for flight training when I get my commission. If I'm accepted, I'll go straight to Dallas for basic training." He leaned back, and his eyes searched the patches of blue sky passing over our heads. "If we do get into war," he said seriously, "I want to meet the enemy up there. Grunts have a dirty time of it on the ground."

He looked down at me and his voice turned thoughtful. "I've heard battle tests a man like love tests a woman. I believe the saying is true. What do you think, Chanala? Do you think love tests a woman in the same way?" His eyes held mine.

I couldn't answer. I just nodded, acutely aware that our bodies were touching. His hand started speaking to my knee. Ever so slightly, his fingers caressed the skin just below the hem of my dress and came to rest there. I didn't move; I just closed my eyes and let the sensation have me.

After a few moments I realized I had to reclaim myself. Fixing my attention on the elderly driver sitting high in front of us, I took the knee-exploring hand in mine and held it firmly for the rest of the ride.

&a &a &a

The evening was a revelation! The Amsterdam Theater was a veritable wonderland. As the lights went down I whispered, "Can you believe it, Ben? This is a first for me."

"You mean this is the first Broadway musical you've been to?"

"This is the first time I've ever been in a theater."

"Then this is an occasion to be remembered. Where have you been all your life, Chanala?"

At that moment the orchestra came to life. His question made me wonder again how long it would be before he'd ask me about my past. But as the music swelled I put that troublesome thought aside.

Ethel Merman's raucous songs, delivered with startling brilliance and energy, filled me with wonder. I could hardly believe such magic and splendor was happening to me.

When the show let out we joined the crowd moving up 42nd Street in search of after-show entertainment. "How about a drink before we head back to your hotel?" Ben's arm crept around my waist. It felt good, and I leaned into his warmth.

"OK," I said, surprised by my daring. But why not? After all, my first drink in a bar would make a perfect ending to a day of many firsts.

We approached a place ablaze in green neon. Over the door, flickering letters spelled KELLEY'S STABLE. People were pushing past us to get in.

"This must be a popular place. Shall we give it a try?" Ben took my arm, and we let the crowd take us inside.

The floor was covered with sawdust, of all things. Cigarette butts and bits of trash littered the grainy stuff that clung to our shoes. The air, blue with cigarette smoke, made my eyes burn. People stood at a long bar, and at the far end of the room a group of musicians loudly celebrated the blues. Noise and laughter filled the tavern.

"I've heard about music like this," Ben shouted in my ear. "They call it 'jamming.' People gather in bars like this to hear musicians improvise—it's all spontaneous. None of them get paid. They play for the love of it. Some really famous artists show up to jam all night...or until the free drinks run out."

There wasn't a table to be had, so we stood with the others at the bar. The place was hot, and everyone seemed hypnotized by the primitive cadences rocking the room. Sipping my beer cautiously, I realized I wasn't cut out to be much of a drinker. I really didn't like the taste at all, but I kept smiling at Ben until my cheeks ached.

In the cab on the way back to my hotel I let him kiss me. He didn't stop with just one. With each kiss I found I was becoming more of a participant. A strange feeling like I was coming undone took hold of me, but somehow I didn't care. Each kiss was more intoxicating than the one preceding it. When the cab finally pulled up to the Henry Hudson and stopped, Ben held me tight as his tongue pushed past my teeth to fill my mouth. I melted under this new sensation. It thrilled my body in a way I had never known before.

The cab driver flipped the meter off and sat motionless, waiting.

Ben whispered, "I think I'm falling in love with you." Then, after playfully kissing the tip of my nose, he added, "I'll call for you in the morning. About 10. Sleep well, my Chanabel Lee."

Later, in the comfort of my bed, I refused to entertain any sense of guilt and accepted my body's newfound sensuality as part of my new life. As I fell into sleep I promised myself I'd go with my new life joyously, no matter where it led me.

26

CHANA STERN—IN THE RAIN

The next morning Ben surprised me. A pale blue convertible, top down, was parked in front of the hotel.

"Good morning, star of my heart. Your chariot awaits," he said with a Sir Walter flourish as he held the door open and bowed me into the front seat.

"How did you manage this? Are you a magician as well as a marine?" Delighted, I laughed at him as the soft leather gave deliciously around my body.

Sliding into the driver's seat, he gave me a quick hug, then started the motor. "This elegant vehicle belongs to Uncle Eli," he said. "He's making a gift of it for our day together. Would you like to drive out on the Island? You know, I've never been properly introduced to your Atlantic Ocean. How about making a day of it at the beach? I took the liberty of having my hotel put up a lunch for us. It's in the basket on the backseat. What do you say?"

"That sounds perfect. Let's go," I said.

Turning off Eighth Avenue, we headed east on 58th Street. "Here," he said, handing me a road map. "You can be my navigator and tell me how to get out of the city to Long Island."

Unfolding the map, I studied it for a few minutes. "From here the Queensborough Bridge is our best bet. This will be quite an adventure," I said, grinning at him. "I've never been farther out on the Island than Brooklyn."

Fortunately we found Flushing easily. Ben picked up some gas and more accurate information on how to get to Jones Beach. After about an hour's drive he suggested we find a stretch of beach of our own instead of fighting the crowds at the public one. For a while we had caught enticing glimpses of the ocean beyond the passing dunes.

He turned out of traffic onto a winding little road. There were scrub-covered sandy dunes on either side. The road finally petered out, and there it was before us: a vast expanse of blue with white breakers charging a long, deserted beach.

Killing the motor, he stretched his arms over his head. "Well, here we are. I guess we walk the rest of the way." He grabbed my hand. "Hungry? Come on."

"I'm starving," I replied as I took the clean salt air deep into my lungs. We found a blanket in the trunk. Ben retrieved the lunch basket from the backseat, and we started toward the beach. To walk more easily, I took my shoes off and carried them. The warm sand was gritty between my toes, but it felt good as it gave softly under my feet.

"Let's spread our blanket in the lea of this dune. We'll be sheltered from the wind, and it's not too far from here to the water." He fell to his knees and spread the blanket for us to sit on.

I flopped down beside him. "Oh, Ben, it's so beautiful. I've never seen anything like this. But you know, it's just as I imagined, only much more grand." Closing my eyes, I felt the sun on my face. I breathed in the freshness from the sea. "This is the first time I've been to a beach. I had no idea that the ocean was so big, so utterly magnificent."

"Well, then this day belongs to you. I give you the whole Atlantic Ocean for your very own." Pointing to large gray-and-white birds running stiff-legged in the wet sand, he said, "And I give you all the seagulls as well." Melded with the wind, his infectious laughter made my heart sing. I couldn't remember being so happy.

The picnic basket proved to be a gourmet experience beyond all expectations. Along with delicate turkey sandwiches there were strawberry tarts and an assortment of imported cheese wedges. In the bottom of the basket were two bottles of wine, one red and the other white. Ben poured some of the red for me. The hotel had thought of everything, even crystal goblets.

For a moment he held his glass to catch the sun, then lightly touched it to mine. "Here's to us and our 'Kingdom by the Sea.'" We drank, and his dark eyes captured mine once more.

After finishing the wine and the goodies, we lay back on the blanket and let the sun make us drowsy. Our shoulders touched; my arm lay against his. His fingers found my hand and held it gently. I liked the feel of him stretched beside me. We didn't speak—the sound of the waves was enough.

It wasn't long, however, before the sun became too much. Ben raised himself on one elbow and looked down at me. "It's getting hot. How about a walk up the beach?"

Barefoot, we ran toward the water. He grasped my hand tightly as we faced the waves. Several large breakers chased us back up the steep sand. Then a really big one caught us off-guard, and in a flash he scooped me up in his arms. The water drenched his slacks and swirled about his knees. Holding me high above the water, he kissed me hard. My mouth tasted of salt spray as he put me down beyond the reach of the next wave, then we locked hands and started up the beach.

"You were right, Ben, when you said you didn't know much about my life." I paused, wondering where to go from there.

"You mentioned living in Brooklyn, but the address you gave me was Riverside Drive, in the city."

"That's right. I'm staying temporarily with friends of my parents." All at once I felt the dam break. I wanted to share who I was with him. The words came tumbling one after the other as we walked. I told him of Mama's conversion and her marriage to Mendel after Papa's death.

We found a large piece of driftwood far up the beach and sat on it. I continued telling him the way it was, being a Dubovitch and living on President Street.

He listened quietly, his eyes on the horizon, as if he were seeing it all where the sky met the sea.

When I came to the part about my arranged marriage, he looked at me in disbelief.

"So you see, Ben, you've been dating a married woman. Are you shocked?" Up went my chin. Making light of the fact that I was still married seemed the best way to break the news, but my courage began to desert me when he didn't answer right away. He just kept his eyes on the water. Holding my breath, I hoped I hadn't been too cavalier coming out with it like that. I couldn't bring myself to look at him.

Then he took hold of my arms and turned me slowly until I faced him. I could tell his crooked smile covered a mixture of emotions, and I was afraid.

In a voice so low I could hardly hear it over the roar of the sea, he said, "Chanala, darling, it's true I've never dated a married woman. Am I shocked? Not in the least, because you are the most adorable woman in the world and the best

<![CDATA[<>]]>

thing that's ever happened to me." Framing my cheeks with his hands, he brought my face to his and covered my lips gently with his own. Time stood still. One after another I heard the breakers climb the sand then retreat to form again while the sun flooded the water with a dazzling brilliance.

Sometime later we became aware that the sun no longer warmed our backs. The sea, once sparkling blue, had turned an angry gray. Behind us black clouds devoured the sun and a cold wind flattened the sea grass on the dunes.

"We'd better make it back to the car before the storm breaks." Ben pulled me up, and we ran back the way we had come. As we struggled with the car top, splashing drops began to pelt us. The wind flung rain in our faces as we finally got the canvas top over the windshield. We were sweating, soaked, and breathing hard when the full force of the storm hit.

In the shelter of the front seat, Ben laughed. "That was a close call. We'd better stay put until this lets up. There's a bottle of wine left. Let's break it out." He reached into the basket on the backseat and came up with the bottle of white.

In the car mirror, I checked the damage to my hair and ran a comb through my wet curls.

"Here you are, my lady."

I took the glass with a smile and sipped the dry wine, letting my head rest on the back of my seat. He leaned forward and turned on the radio. There was a blast of static. After searching the dial, he finally brought in an orchestra, mellow and clear: *"When the deep purple falls over sleepy garden walls and the...."*

"Ah, that's better." He bent close and nibbled at my left earlobe. We didn't talk; there was just the old song and the sound of the rain. He hummed softly as he pleasured the hollow place at the base of my throat. The sensation was delightful beyond measure and played havoc with my senses.

As we finished our drinks, Helen O'Connell began seducing the microphone with a rendition of "Green Eyes." The wine was making me just a bit light-headed. I seemed to be someone I didn't know very well. I wondered what that meant.

As he drew me closer, I began to slip away, going soft to his touch. He raised me up and deftly slipped under me, and I found myself straddling his lap, my dress bunched above my knees. His tongue found its place as his lips devoured mine. The buttons of my blouse gave way to his fingers, and before I knew what was happening he'd released the hooks of my bra. My bare breasts tumbled into his searching hands. Cupping them eagerly, his tongue visited each nipple, and spasms of unbelievable pleasure surged through my whole body. Just as I thought I could bear it no longer, he artfully pulled my panties aside. He moved swiftly, and as our bodies joined, an unequivocal pain took me by surprise. It was exquisite pain, and I greedily pressed against his hardness as each of us pursued our pleasure. All of a sudden, he stiffened and held me hard. I tried desperately to catch up with him, but he moaned, and under me his body went limp. Giving it all up and falling weakly against him, I heard the rain and someone gasping for breath. Suddenly, I realized that someone was me...unfulfilled...empty...utterly alone. As the storm raged, I wept.

27

NO. 12 MACDOUGAL ALLEY

Mina heard CeeCee's feet on the stairs. She straightened up and quickly wrapped a towel turban-style about her head. Her back hurt from leaning over the slate sink. Once more she promised she'd get her hair cut. Since it had gotten so long, washing it in the high sink was a real back-breaker.

CeeCee burst through the door. "We go Italian all the way tonight. Look at the stuff I got. We eat big for sure. You hungry, *chérie*?" CeeCee's dark eyes danced at Mina as she dumped the heavy shopping bag on the kitchen table. "I've got a big surprise for you, love, but we eat first, so give me a hand." She pulled from the bag a carton of warm spaghetti sauce. "From Raffeto's, no less!" Next she produced a package of vermicelli and a large, raffia-wrapped bottle of Chianti. Last of all she drew forth a football-shaped loaf of bread. "Voilà! From Zito's Bakery over on Bleeker Street." Laughing, she tossed it across the table.

Mina caught it and sniffed the sesame-covered crust. It smelled deliciously of garlic. All at once Mina was filled with such happiness. Lately she had examined and savored all aspects of what it meant to be connected to another human being: to go to sleep and wake up each day beside CeeCee, to feel her warm body, to share the sunlight of each morning—a joy to be treasured. It was a new and miraculous feeling, knowing love comes to life when two women, two selves, merge. Even the smell of CeeCee on her pillow brought extravagant tears of happiness, and just thinking of how lucky they were to have found each other was an erotic pastime she enjoyed in quiet moments alone. There was no doubt in Mina's mind: Theirs was a union made in heaven, and it would surely last for all time.

After dinner they sat close on the old sofa. CeeCee lit a cigarette and put it between Mina's lips. She liked the taste of tobacco now. She found it exciting and intimate to share a cigarette with her lover.

Mina broke the silence. "OK, what's the secret I had to wait until after dinner for?"

CeeCee exhaled slowly, deliberately building the suspense. Then she began to laugh at Mina's impatience. "I got you a job," she said.

"You what?" Mina sat up. "What do you mean, you got me a job? I already have one, you know."

"This is just for Saturdays. It's this way: Fat Suzie walked out of Brachman's class this morning saying she'd never be back. Seems he got snippy with her about the way she was holding a pose. Everyone was talking about it in the cafeteria. I had a thought, so I cornered the little Russian in the hall later and told him I knew someone to take Suzie's place.

"At first he didn't listen to me, but he came around when I told him she was much slimmer and better-looking than Suzie." CeeCee took a long drag before continuing. "He said he'd give her a try, and for her to be at his class before 9." She grinned at Mina. "So the job's yours if you want it. You can come along with me, and I'll show you the ropes. It'll be fun. What do you say?"

"But CeeCee, I don't know the first thing about modeling. You know that."

"Don't worry, it's a snap. Nothing to it. I can teach you all you have to know before Saturday. Come on, Mina, just think of the dough you'll be making. You can have a field day at Klein's with the extra bucks. How about it, are you game?"

"I know you like your Saturday job at the League, CeeCee, but do you really think I could pull it off? I've never done anything like that. Oh, Lord! I'd have to take my clothes off like you do! I could never stand buck naked in front of all those people." The thought brought Mina to her feet. "I can't do it. It's all so gross. How could you think I would do such a thing, CeeCee?"

"Calm down, it's no big deal. Nobody cares about your being naked. The students only look at you as an object, like a piece of fruit or something. You'll get used to it in no time."

"But there'd be men looking at me. I'd die of embarrassment," Mina said, knowing she was weakening. She'd do anything to please CeeCee—even the unthinkable like baring herself in front of a bunch of students. Besides, the promise of extra money was tempting. After all, she rationalized, it couldn't be that hard thinking of herself as an apple or a grapefruit. "OK, I'll try it next Saturday and see how it goes. Maybe I won't die of embarrassment after all." She started giggling at the thought of how Aunt Willie might react if she found out.

"That's my *chérie*." CeeCee squeezed her hand. "Come on, let's hit the sack." She picked up the half-empty bottle. "Bring your glass. We'll finish this in bed."

≈ ≈ ≈

Often on Saturday nights, Mina and CeeCee walked over to The Lauralie near Waverly Place. There was a loose company of young lesbians who hung out together in the

Village. They had accepted Mina immediately, with easy good humor, taking CeeCee's new lover into the "sisterhood" without a second thought. With more or less understanding, they all cared for—and about—each other. No matter who was involved with whom, there was always a place to stay and an open ear for anyone who wandered into the Group.

However imperfect they might seem to the straight world, they had built a community where they could at least survive within the society they perceived so hostile.

Mina found the gay bars provocative and challenging, although at times she wasn't sure if she really liked them. The Lauralie, the most popular of all the lesbian bars, was not far from No. 12. There, with beers in their hands, they'd stand with the others, trying to decide whether to brave the tiny postage-stamp floor for a slow dance.

From the beginning the regulars had extended Mina their friendship as well as a roving eye on occasion. When it was known that she and CeeCee were steady lovers, however, they backed off and left her alone.

Sunday mornings in August, when Macdougal Alley gave no air to cool No. 12, they brown-bagged peanut butter and jelly sandwiches and took the train to Gay Point beach. Coming home later to nurse painful sunburns never lessened the adventure of a day by the ocean. Mina was happier than ever, and CeeCee was the door to that happiness. Even the pointed looks their coworkers sometimes shot their way didn't tarnish the luster of each day.

Workweeks always started with doughnuts and coffee at The Griddle on Second Avenue at the corner of St. Mark's Place. Fortified, they'd rush to the Astor Place subway for the long ride uptown.

The next Saturday came all too soon for Mina. She was terribly nervous about the modeling job and had trouble with her crumb-covered doughnut. Only by gulping down the steaming coffee did she manage to wash it past the lump of apprehension in her throat. All the way uptown she sat next to CeeCee, tensely clutching her overnight case. CeeCee had advised bringing a robe and slippers for when she wasn't posing. Friday night, on the way home from work, Mina had splurged at Klein's and spent her first modeling check before she got it, buying a green-and-blue silk kimono with red dragonflies painted on the sleeves. It lay neatly folded in the overnight case along with her scuffs and a comb. This was the day she'd have to put all privacy aside and bare her body to everyone—all for a measly buck and a half an hour.

Holy Jesus, Mary, and Joseph, I hope I survive the humiliation, she said to herself as the train hurtled toward their stop at Columbus Circle.

28

CHANA STERN—A STRANGE MEETING

I had decided to channel all my energy into my painting, even though thoughts of Ben were with me constantly. I tried to keep my perspective clear on that score.

One morning—after being complimented by Brachman—I registered for his Saturday session. Thus I had a full week of classes.

That particular morning he stood by my easel for a long time, watching me work. I waited nervously for his critique. Finally, he cleared his throat. "You paint with great passion, Chana," he said, speaking softly so only I could hear. "It's unusual for a woman painter to have such an eye for the erotic. Men will envy your renderings of the female figure."

Wrapped in the aura of his praise, I promised myself to work harder than ever.

My first quarterly check from Bankers Trust had arrived and was tucked safely in my checking account, allowing me to move downtown. I always wanted to be on my own, and Bubbe's generosity had made that come into being. The Henry Hudson Hotel was a natural choice since it was only two blocks from the League.

When I told Rose I was moving, her mouth drew into a sharp line of disapproval, but David actually looked pleased for me. "Go for it, Chana," he said. "Just don't forget us completely. We'll miss you, so be sure to keep in touch."

I had moved in only a week before, but I'd gotten quickly settled into my new quarters high up on the tenth floor. By Saturday morning I was filled with a wonderful sense of freedom as I walked down 57th Street. On my way upstairs to Brachman's class, I stopped to pick up a new canvas at the League store.

An already-hot sun flooded the studio, so all the windows were raised to catch what little air was moving. The smell of paint and turpentine greeted me as it did every morning. Most of the students had found their places. I gathered my things from my locker and set up my easel in my regular spot by the window.

Promptly at 9, Brachman made his grand entrance and took his usual stiff stance in front of the model stand. "Are we ready to work?" he asked. "We have a new model this morning. Suzie's no longer with us, so I hope you all have a fresh canvas." Hands on hips, he impatiently addressed the curtained cubicle behind the stand. "Time is not to be wasted, Miss Arenholt. Please come out and mount the stand."

The room fell silent. All eyes were on the visibly quivering curtain. It opened. A slim figure in a blue-and-green kimono stepped timidly onto the small platform. Clutching her robe about her as if she were cold, she stood motionless, eyes cast down.

"Come, come, we have work to do. Don't just stand there." Brachman was losing his patience. "Please drop your robe, Miss...? What name do you go by? Arenholt is much too clumsy."

"You can call me Mina, sir," she answered, still not raising her head. Then her hands fluttered to the folds of the kimono, and it fell from her shoulders to the floor.

I caught my breath at the beauty and slimness of her

almost boyish figure. Raising her head, she fixed her gaze at a point above Brachman's head as if trying to isolate herself from him and everyone in the studio. Her defiant gesture clearly indicated she had never worked as a model. Poor girl.

Heavy braids were pinned high on her head. They were a lustrous golden red and framed her pale face provocatively. Where had I seen hair like that? Of course! She was the girl who had waited on Ben and me at Schrafft's, and that wasn't the first time I'd seen her either. She'd waited on me once before some weeks ago. The thought of Ben drew me away from the class and the strange coincidence of seeing this girl on the model stand. For a moment I was back there in the car with Ben and feeling the conflicting emotions of that night in the rain.

"Please give me your attention, Mina." Brachman's sharp voice brought me back to the present. "We will take a standing pose." He stepped up to the stand and, as if she were a puppet, arranged her limbs until he was satisfied. "Ah, good. Now hold that pose and remember it, please. That is the look I want."

The light from the high window gave her white skin a pale translucence. One arm was raised so that her hand rested languidly on top of those coppery braids, and her head was bent as she gazed down at the kimono held loosely in her other hand. Its folds fell gracefully to the floor.

Inspired by the charm of the pose, I got to work and quickly blocked in the drawing. Slowly she came to life on my canvas. By lunch break I had already begun to lay in the dark areas. When I finally checked my watch I noticed she had left the stand, and the students were leaving the studio. Reluctantly I put my brushes down, took off my smock, and headed for the rest room.

When I got to the cafeteria it was crowded. I picked up a tray and went through the line. Looking for a place to sit, I noticed our model sitting alone at a table at the far end of the room.

"May I join you, Mina?" I set my tray down next to hers. "We've met before, you know," I said smiling. "At Schrafft's, some weeks ago. Do you remember?"

At first she looked surprised, then smiled back at me in recognition. "Of course. You were sitting at my station by the window. You were with a tall, good-looking man. How odd to meet again like this. Please, sit down. I'm just waiting for my friend."

In a gesture of modesty, she pulled the kimono close about her. I noticed red dragonflies painted on the sleeves. Her green eyes, flecked with amber, held mine for a moment, and I saw just a hint of freckles across the bridge of her nose. She seemed to glow with an inner beauty that had completely escaped me when I was rendering the contours of her body with my brush.

"I'm Chana Stern," I said, holding out my hand. "May I call you Mina? I haven't seen you here before. Am I right in assuming you're new at modeling and this is your first day at the League?"

Her grip was firm and warm. "Yes, this is my first day. My friend CeeCee, who also models here, got me the job. I know absolutely nothing about the modeling profession. Did my inexperience show all that much?"

"Not really. You did very well. You seemed just a bit nervous, but from what I saw this morning I'd say you were a born model. You don't have anything to worry about."

A dusky girl with dark cropped hair approached and set her tray next to Mina's. She wore a flowered shift and mules, and her dark eyes were questioning.

"Chana," Mina said, "this is my friend CeeCee LaClaire." Mina moved her tray to make room. "CeeCee, this is Chana Stern. She's studying with Brachman. She's just given me the greatest compliment by saying I'm born for the modeling game. Can you believe it?"

"Sure, I can," CeeCee said, smiling. "I told you there wasn't anything to it." She turned to Chana. "Hi, Chana. Have you been studying long with the mad Russian? I hear he's a real tyrant. Did he give my girl a bad time?" She draped her arm over the back of Mina's chair.

"Well, he was a bit impatient with her at first," I said, noticing the possessive way CeeCee acted with Mina.

CeeCee attacked her bowl of stew as if she were starving. "God, am I hungry," she said, laughing. "Did you have trouble holding the pose, *chérie*?" Her free hand covered Mina's.

"Yes. My arms and legs felt like they'd turned to stone. I could hardly move at the breaks, but after a while I realized it was like dancing without moving. I used to take ballet a long time ago. Did I ever tell you about my ambitions to be a ballerina, CeeCee?"

I got the feeling they had forgotten me, so I broke in. "Which instructor do you model for, CeeCee?"

"Rafael Sawyer," she replied, not taking her eyes off Mina. "He gives me plenty of slack. He's a real pussycat. That's him over there paying the cashier. You'll get to know everyone in no time."

She was directing all her attention to Mina, and I was beginning to feel like a third wheel. I'd finished, so I picked up my tray. "Nice to make your acquaintance, CeeCee. I'll see you back in class, Mina." I took off and headed for the lavatory, thinking to myself, *What a strange meeting that was...and how beautiful Mina's green eyes were as they held mine for a moment.*

29

ELEGY

As she sat on the subway train the old questions descended over Mina once more, this time with a vengeance. In truth, they had never really left her—not since that awful afternoon in Katy's room, not since they'd sent Katy away to the convent. Always there, just behind her consciousness, they lay waiting to take over. Her quiet times were their playground. Now in full command, they obliterated all other thoughts.

Swaying with the motion of the train, Mina could do nothing to stop the questions from claiming their answer. She was to blame, had always been to blame, and would always be to blame. *Blame. Blame.* The cars screeched and slammed their way under the river toward Queens Plaza. The hateful taste of black coffee lay rancid in her mouth. CeeCee had made her drink a cup before she left the apartment. Now she was on her way to see Katy for the last time. Katy was dead. The wheels kept pounding the rails. *Dead. Dead. Dead.*

She didn't seem to belong to herself. She felt disoriented. Deliberately letting the roar of the train die on her ear, she gave in to the pain of remembering:

Katy, Katy, she thought, *how could you leave like that? We never had our summers at the beach like we planned. We'll never read Walt Whitman together again. I never mailed you the poem I wrote when they sent you away to the convent. I wanted to send it to you but didn't dare. We never told each other of the passion we felt. It was so new for us, and we shared such a small trip in time.* Mina's temples throbbed, and she couldn't stop the rush of thoughts.

How could I have told CeeCee only last week that "nothing on earth could equal the happiness" she and I shared? I forgot you, Katy, in the need of my body for another woman. Forgive me.

Mina remembered how Mary Alice's voice sounded, so strange and tight, when she'd answered the phone on Tuesday night. It was after 11 o'clock. Her heart, frozen with dread, had known instantly that something awful had happened the moment she'd heard Mary Alice's flat-sounding words, unnatural and faraway. "The Conklins got a phone call from the mother superior at the convent," Mary Alice had begun without preamble. "She told them they'd found Katy's body crouched in the shower." There was a pause. "She slashed her wrists, Mina." Mary Alice paused again. "The water was still running, so there wasn't much blood. They said she'd been dead for hours." Mina made no reply, so Mary Alice continued.

"They're burying her on Sunday over in Flushing. Just the family will be at the funeral home, but we can go to the grave site together. I'll meet you at the Woodhaven gate house at 3 o'clock."

Somehow she had answered Mary Alice, but her words had rung hollow, even in her own ears. "All right," she whispered. "I'll meet you there." Then, pushing the phone away as if to rid herself of the hateful news, she let her head fall to the kitchen table and didn't move.

CeeCee had come padding into the kitchen then, wiping sleep from her eyes. "What's going on?" she asked groggily.

"Who's calling at this hour?" The offhanded manner of CeeCee's question struck Mina like a physical blow. Already raw and bruised, she felt an overwhelming need to be alone at that moment. "I'll tell you tomorrow," was all she could manage as she pulled herself up, brushed by CeeCee, and stumbled back into the bedroom.

Enormous, a pale moon looked down from the skylight. Dry-eyed, Mina watched it until the scalding tears came to dissolve its ghostly shape and drain her heart.

      🙠 🙠 🙠

Mary Alice was wearing black. Mina felt miserable and inappropriate in her leather jacket and slacks. Mary Alice hugged her warmly—an unusual gesture, Mina thought. Not at all like the old Mary Alice. Tears kept pushing behind her eyelids. Blinking them back hard, she took a deep breath and reached for Mary Alice's hand.

They walked up the hill, the way the gatekeeper had pointed. A sharp wind, preceding the forward edge of winter, blew cold in their faces. Clouds loomed gray behind the leafless trees. At the top of the hill, beneath the skeleton of an ancient elm, two burly grave attendants were pulling the lowering straps from the open grave. Picking up the still-living flowers, they tossed them in a trash bin and started shoveling dirt into the gaping hole. Holding hands, Mina and Mary Alice watched as the workmen smoothed the raw mound of earth with their shovels.

Too late. It was all over. Everyone had left. There were no sounds of weeping. No black-clad cleric reading the final words. Reluctant to leave, they stood watching the somber ritual under the old tree. The grave attendants gathered the tools of their trade. Then, rolling the trash bin before them, they disappeared over the far side of the hill.

No hallowed ground for a suicide, Mina thought, feeling the sting of tears again. Just a lonely place on the top of a hill with a careless wind to scatter dead leaves across the grass where Katy sleeps. Walking down the hill with Mary Alice's hand in hers, Mina felt the chill of that cold wind against her back.

Parting at the subway, she said, "Come visit sometime, Mary Alice. I'll show you the Village." Mary Alice nodded and said she would, but Mina knew they'd never see each other again.

On the way back to town, the first lines of a poem formed in Mina's mind—a poem she would dedicate to Katy and write beside the old ones in the little green diary:

Giving up the moment we call today
We perish each alone
No need to weep
For I've heard, in hushed tones,
Of a life beyond the stars.

30

CHANA STERN—THE SOLUTION

I was beginning to panic so I bought a bottle of castor oil and a box of bromo quinine pills at the hotel pharmacy. I missed my period last month. I didn't think much about it at the time. I'd been late before, but now several weeks had gone by, and my uneasiness had turned to terror. On top of everything, Ben hadn't called as promised. There was just a postcard two weeks ago:

I'm stretched pretty thin for time these days. Been in the field a lot. The phone in the barracks is always busy. I'll try to call this weekend. Love, Ben.

The weekend came, and he hadn't called. That was ten days ago.

The phone was ringing when I reached my room. Fumbling in my purse for my key, I almost dropped the pills and the bottle of castor oil. Throwing everything on the bed, I made a grab for the phone.

"Hello?" There was a pause before I heard his voice.

"Chana? How are you? I'm sorry it's been so long, but we're coming up on graduation so they've kept us pretty busy. Can you come down to Washington weekend after next? I can get a two-day pass. I'll book us a reservation at the Hay Adams."

My legs gave way, and I sat down hard on the bed. I

couldn't answer right away. The best I could come up with was, "I'll try to make it, Ben. I'll write and let you know." It had been so long since I'd heard his voice, all I could think of was *This is a stranger I'm talking to.* There were so many emotions crowding in on me, I didn't know which was real. My heart felt as if it were breaking. Never in my life had I felt so alone, and hearing his voice only underlined my solitary state.

"Great," he said hurriedly. "I've got to go now. Ten people are waiting to use the phone. Please say you'll meet me in D.C., Chana. We'll have a ball." Before I could reply I heard a jumble of voices in the background and a click as the phone went dead. Numb, I sat for several minutes trying to sort out my feelings. Then I picked up the bottle of castor oil and went to the bathroom. Gagging, I managed to swallow it all.

Dinner was out of the question, so I lay down on the bed, my mouth foul with the oily taste. I stared into the darkness, waiting for what would happen next.

Ben's call and the proposed trip to Washington paled as wave after wave of nausea engulfed me. For what seemed hours, I tossed and turned, fighting the gripping misery. My stomach finally gave up the fight around midnight. Making a desperate dash, I fell on my knees in the bathroom. With my arms embracing the toilet bowl, I vomited all I had swallowed. After a wrenching series of dry heaves, the diarrhea came, leaving me shaking with exhaustion. It wasn't until first light that I finally collapsed back on my bed and slept.

Bubbe came to town the next day. I skipped my class at the League and met her at the Russian Tea Room. After the castor oil my stomach was still in turmoil, but somehow I made it through lunch. I didn't feel much like talking so I suggested a movie. We decided on *Flying Down to Rio* at the Music Hall.

I hardly watched the show. My mind churned with all kinds of thoughts. First of all, I had to find out for sure whether I was pregnant. That meant seeing a doctor, but how to find one? I couldn't ask anyone I knew. Bubbe, Rose...they were out of the question. This was something I had to do on my own, but how? That was the question that ran circles in my head as flanks of pretty girls standing on the wings of airplanes sang, "Oh, Rio, Rio by the sea, oh..."

Still dwelling on the problem at hand, I remembered that most hotels had a doctor on call. I'd stop at the desk and ask when I got back to the Henry Hudson.

I took Bubbe's arm as we walked across Columbus Circle. I was happy to see her looking so well after the scare she'd given us all. As we approached the subway, I screwed up my courage and asked about Mama.

"Everyone is fine," Bubbe said. "Yudel's starting at Yeshiva University this fall, and the boychick is as precocious as ever. Mendel spoils him beyond all reason." Disapproval loaded her voice.

I could see she wasn't going to tell me anything about Mama. I tried hard not to feel the pain, knowing the pain was hers also. So I kissed her and held her for a moment. Then she was gone.

A week later, the doctor recommended by the desk clerk gave me the results of my rabbit test. I was pregnant. Trying to be kind, he said he might be able to help, but to him, help meant giving me the address of a home for unwed mothers run by a friend of his in Queens. "Anything else," he said, "would be illegal."

After I left his office, I walked back up Eighth Avenue toward the hotel. I was about to cross the street when an ambulance screamed by and careened into the emergency entrance of Roosevelt Hospital. Startled, I pulled back onto the curb and waited for my heart to settle down. *I can't have this baby*, I thought. *No one must know. No one else can take care of this. Only me. It's all up to me now.*

Back in my room, I gulped down the bromo quinine pills. I woke up the next morning with my ears ringing so hard I could hardly hear, my head aching unmercifully, and I was still pregnant. All I could think of were stories of kitchen-table butchers and women bleeding to death after going to one of those awful abortion places down some dark alley.

Saturday morning I was in an awful state. I'd thrown up my coffee and sweet roll, but I decided to try going to class anyway. Mina and CeeCee had become my only friends. We'd gotten together at No. 12 several times in the past few weeks. I found them comfortable to be with. Now I needed to talk to someone. I wasn't sure what I would say to them, but just being with them seemed important.

I continued feeling weak and shaky all morning. Mina sought me with her eyes before she took the pose. Her nod and half smile touched me. I knew she was someone who cared. The warmth of that smile carried me through the next three hours.

My canvas was almost finished, but I still had to catch what I wanted in Mina's eyes. The warm look she'd given me a few minutes ago was exactly what I was striving for, so I bent all my efforts on bringing that look to the canvas. Concentrating on the soft contours of Mina's face calmed my nerves. By 11:30, however, I was feeling light-headed again, and the nausea returned.

Putting my brushes down, I rushed for the ladies' room. I reached a stall just in time to fight the dry heaves. They left me feeling faint, so I sat on the seat and put my head over my knees. When everything stopped swimming, I went to the washbowl and splashed cold water on my face. As I wiped my cheeks I was shocked at the pale, drawn face that stared back at me from the mirror. Just at that moment, Mina burst through the door.

"I thought lunch break would never come. My legs are paralyzed. Hi, Chana. My God, what's the matter? You look awful." She came close. Turning me to the light, she gasped, "You look like hell. What's going on?" Her recognition of my state made the tears well up. I didn't care. I was beyond acting brave. My shoulders were shaking. She took me in her arms. The feel of her body was all I needed. The dam broke and I clung to her, sobbing.

Just then, other people came in. Talking loudly, they lit cigarettes and dashed for the stalls.

"Come on, we'd better get to the cafeteria before the crowd descends," Mina said gently. "We'll get a table and you can tell me what's going on. If you feel like talking about it, that is." Her arm was still around my shoulders as we took the stairs up to the cafeteria. It made me feel comforted and protected.

I shook my head when she asked if I wanted to get something to eat. I sat at the little table and watched as she went through the line.

When Mina put her full tray down on the table, my stomach took another turn. I tried not to look at the food. She put a glass of water in my hand.

"Maybe I can get you an Alka-Seltzer. I'll ask the cashier."

I shook my head, not daring to speak for fear it might make me dash for the john again.

CeeCee came over to the table, full of good cheer. "Hello, Chana. How did your class go? You're not eating? Don't tell me you're on a diet, *chérie*." Her clipped manner annoyed Mina.

"Knock it off, CeeCee. Chana's not feeling well."

"No offense, *mes amies*." She dashed off to fill her tray. When she returned her voice softened. "Sorry, Chana. What's happening here? You coming down with the flu or something?"

"Not exactly." Figuring I might as well come right out with it, I said, "No. I'm not sick." I lowered my voice but kept it steady. "I'm pregnant."

Stunned, they just stared at me without saying a word. I began to wish I hadn't come out with it like that.

"*Mon Dieu*, Chana, that's a lot more serious than the flu. You have a man who'll take responsibility for this?" CeeCee lit a cigarette and inhaled deeply. Mina took hold of my hand.

"Is this the marine's baby?" Mina said.

I nodded, not wanting to put into words what was tearing at my heart. The thought of Ben hurt too much. Even mentioning his name was painful.

"My God. Does he know?" Mina asked, her beautiful green eyes full of concern.

"No. And he never will. I have to take care of this by myself. It's my problem." My voice broke. "The only thing is, I don't know what to do." I felt the tears catching up with me again.

CeeCee leaned forward. "Who's this marine person? You never mentioned anything to me about a marine in your life, Chana."

"I met him two months ago. I told Mina about him. I didn't think you'd be interested. I certainly didn't think anything like this would happen. We had an affair one weekend, and I haven't seen him since."

"Goddamn. They storm the beach, then next thing you know they're gone. You're better off getting rid of that son of a bitch, and you sure don't want any marine's baby to take care of." CeeCee cocked her head to one side. "We have a big problem here for sure." Then her eyes brightened. "It just might be that I can help, Chana..." She paused and glanced about the crowded room. "...but this is no place to discuss such matters."

We arranged to meet Sunday at their place in the Village. I was beginning to feel a lot better knowing I wasn't alone with my problem.

☙ ☙ ☙

"The thing we're up against is time," CeeCee said as she lit a cigarette. We sat on the floor, eating off the coffee table. Mina had brought in Chinese, and there was an assortment of paper cartons in front of us. My appetite was still a little dicey so all I had was tea and a fortune cookie that promised me I'd meet a tall, dark stranger and move to a foreign country. We all laughed at that.

"I've missed only one period," I began. "The doctor said he thought I was six weeks gone."

Her face serious, CeeCee took a long drag and looked me straight in the eye. "It has to be this week, so listen up. There's this woman, Tante Marie. She's a longtime friend of Ma Mère. She lives downstairs in the same building. She's a black Island woman like Ma Mère, so they became easy friends way back when we first landed in New York.

"When Tante found out we were from Port-au-Prince

she took Ma Mère and me under her wing. Haitian women have a strong bond. She even got Ma Mère a job as a cleaning lady for the library on 135th Street. Being from a foreign country, it wasn't easy for a black woman with a small child in a new place. Especially when the child was light enough to pass as white."

CeeCee blew smoke toward the ceiling. "I remember Tante used to hand out peppermint sticks to all the kids in the building. We were so poor there was never enough money to buy luxuries like candy. She made a big thing about warning us never to set foot in candy stores. 'That's where white slavers hang out,' she said."

CeeCee stubbed out her cigarette before going on. "I guess that's why she always bought candy for us kids. We all loved Tante. She was special to us. Her flat was the nicest in the building. The overstuffed chairs in her parlor had doilies pinned to them." CeeCee smiled, remembering. "And there were real lace curtains at her windows.

"Oh, she was rich compared to the rest of the tenants. No one ever asked how she got so rich, but it was well known she could look into a person's face and tell right off what they were going to do even before they did it."

Picking up her chopsticks, she shrugged. "Some said she practiced voodoo, but Ma Mère told me Tante studied the root truths from the wise women of Port-au-Prince, and those were the skills that made her all that money."

CeeCee's black eyes stared pointedly at me from under their thick lashes. "You got $300, *chérie*? That's what Tante charges for taking care of problems like yours."

"Yes," I said, my throat dry in spite of the tea I was sipping.

"CeeCee," Mina said, "are you sure this is the right

thing to do? After all, I've heard stories about...you know...." Her voice sounded thin in the quiet room.

"Tante Marie's a powerful woman, Mina. Many times birthing babies as well as solving the problems of women in trouble. She knows what to do, so don't worry. She'll take care of Chana just fine, you'll see. We go as soon as I can arrange it."

CeeCee set the time for next Sunday. They said they'd pick me up at noon.

🙿 🙿 🙿

I was so nervous all I could manage for breakfast that morning was a cup of black coffee. At CeeCee's instructions I'd bought a box of Kotex wrapped in plain brown paper at the hotel pharmacy. Back in my room I packed my overnight case because they wanted me to go home with them to the Village afterward.

As I sat on my bed waiting for their call, my mind was overwhelmed with terrible pictures of myself bleeding and being taken to a hospital emergency room to die. What would they tell Mama and Bubbe about me? Suddenly I was furious with Ben. He was to blame. How could he have done this to me? But even as I raged at him, something deep in my conscience whispered hard questions: *Why had I let him? Wasn't it just as much my fault as his?*

Shaking my head violently, I pushed those thoughts firmly away. Besides, the anger felt better than fear, so I hung on to it. Next came disbelief. I couldn't believe this was happening to me. I wanted to pretend I had never met him and that I'd never been someone who could be treated in such a manner. Right then I swore I would never let any man have me like that again.

I was reaching for the anger once more when the phone

rang. They were waiting in the lobby.

All the way to Harlem on the subway Mina kept hold of my hand. CeeCee didn't say much. She seemed occupied with her own thoughts. When the train pulled into the 125th Street station she jumped up. "Let's go. This is our stop."

Cold gusts of wind swept up Lenox Avenue. Black families dressed in their Sunday best were emptying the churches and swarming the sidewalks. No one paid any attention to three young women walking north. At 134th Street, CeeCee slowed in front of a gray, turn-of-the-century apartment building. "Here we are. Tante's on the second floor." She punched the buzzer in the dingy hall.

Shifting the box of Kotex to her other arm, Mina grabbed my hand. I was glad she was there. I wasn't always at ease with CeeCee, but Mina was different.

CeeCee turned to me and asked in a matter-of-fact tone, "You brought the money?"

I nodded.

Upstairs the hall was dark. One naked bulb didn't give much light. My heart pounded in my throat. A little black woman opened the door a crack and peered out suspiciously. She recognized CeeCee right away and beckoned us in. A kerchief bound her nappy gray hair. A nondescript wrapper hung loosely on her thin body, and her bony black feet were thrust stockingless into ancient carpet slippers. A toothless smile crinkled the lines around her bright black eyes. "*Mon petit chou-chou*!" she croaked as she embraced CeeCee.

Launching into a torrent of French, they ignored Mina and me. Then with a dry laugh the old woman faced us. "Which one of you comes to be helped by Tante Marie?"

"This is the one, Tante." CeeCee put her hand on my shoulder. That was all the introduction I got. She didn't ask my name or anything.

"Come, come, no time to waste." She motioned us down a narrow hall to a plain but neatly furnished room with a table and small bed. The two of them spoke briefly again in patois. Then CeeCee turned to me. "I'm going upstairs to visit with Ma Mère while Tante does her work. Mina will stay here with you, Chana. Don't be scared," She patted my arm. "I'll be back in a little while."

"*Mais oui, ma petite*, go see your Ma Mère. She hasn't seen you for a long time. Everything will be fine here. Her friend can stay, no problem."

CeeCee closed the door and was gone.

"You take off your dress and panties while I make ready." She went to the table at one end of the room. Taking a kettle off the hot plate, she poured water over a narrow rubber tube lying in a shallow basin. "Take your time while I boil this. You'll be fine. Not to worry. When this is over, no more troubles. You'll see." Her dry laugh did nothing to reassure me, and I began to tremble.

Mina helped me pull my dress over my head and whispered, "I'll be right here with you all the time, Chana."

My breath was coming in short gasps. Realizing I was probably hyperventilating, I made a concerted effort to slow my breathing. I was shaking hard now and had to sit down to pull off my underpants. Embarrassed by my nakedness in front of this strange little woman, I curled my legs under me and made myself as small as possible on the hard bed.

Putting on thin rubber gloves, she looked over at me. "Lie back now. Relax. Don't you be frightened." She came close, and with a surprising amount of tenderness, her black eyes fixed on mine. I couldn't tell from her sharp features just how old she was, but I guessed by the grizzled hair escaping from her kerchief that she was a grandmother many times over.

"You scared? Don't be, *ma chère*." Picking up the basin she set it on the edge of the bed. "Now you just try to relax and bring your legs up so." She eased my feet apart. "That's right. This is nothing I wouldn't do for my own grand-daughter. It's good you only six weeks...you not far gone. No worry. Tonight you hurt some. Be like bad cramps. You have cramps before?"

I nodded, my teeth clenched against what I knew was coming.

As her hands worked between my legs, Mina sat by my head. I clutched her hand and fought the tears. Tante was peering intently as she worked. I held my breath as I felt her pass the thin tube into my cervix, then up into my uterus. The pain was excruciating but didn't last long. It lay inside me, coiled and ready to do its work. Tante explained it was to stay there overnight. "When it hardens, it does its work."

I heard her explanation through a fog of agony.

"When you get home you go right to bed. You got some aspirin?" Her voice was almost motherly. "You take two or three. The tube is in place now. When it's ready, it comes back down. The heavy bleeding will start then and voilà! no more baby. Now, see? That's all there is to it. Not so bad, eh?" She patted my trembling leg. "It's all done, *ma petite*. You can get dressed now. You brought some Kotex? You wear a couple pads on the way home." She pulled off her rubber gloves. "You start bleeding hard later on, but don't be worried. That's the way it works."

I turned my head and noticed CeeCee standing in the doorway. She and Tante embraced as they said their good-byes. Mina helped me with my coat. Tante Marie was smiling broadly at us. I noticed several teeth missing as I handed her three $100 bills. Nodding, she tucked them in the pocket of her smock.

"*Merci, ma chérie.* That's special price because you're a friend of my *chou-chou.*"

My legs were trembling. Mina put her arm around me to steady me as I walked to the door. Tante's last words were, "You call if there's any trouble, but not to worry. There'll be just a few cramps, that's all. *Au revoir, mes amies. Bonne chance!*"

      ❧   ❧   ❧

The subway ride home seemed endless. *I'm going to be all right*, I told myself over and over. *There's nothing to worry about. Just a few cramps, that's all, then it'll be done.* I kept reassuring myself as I sat between Mina and CeeCee on the train, feeling the cramps coming. *It's like having my period. All I have to do is get through tomorrow, then it'll all be over and no more baby.* The cramps got worse, and I leaned forward against the pain.

Mina put her arm around me. "Are you OK?" she asked with a worried look.

"It's just the cramps, like Tante said," I managed under my breath. After what seemed like ages of rocking back and forth with the motion of the train, the pains got worse. I was beginning to think the ride would never end. I let my head fall on Mina's shoulder and tried to steady my breathing to ease the misery in my belly. Finally, after many stops and jolting starts, I felt CeeCee's hand on my knee.

"Come on, Chana. This is our stop." She and Mina

helped me to my feet. "Not much of a walk. You'll be fine, *chérie*. Just take your time and lean on us. We'll be back at No. 12 before you know it."

I got even more shaky climbing the stairs from the subway to the street, but the cramps lessened as I walked. Stopping at the corner of Macdougal Street, CeeCee paid for a bottle of brandy at the liquor store and put it in her purse. "My treat, *chérie*. You take a couple of shots when we get home. Make you feel better, you'll see."

I sat at the kitchen table and downed two full shot glasses of the strong stuff while they made up the couch. Mina plumped the pillows and turned down the cover. "Now take off your clothes and crawl in," she said. "Here, I'll give you a hand."

I held my arms up like a small child and let her pull the dress over my head. The brandy hit my empty stomach with a jolt and began its magic. Not only did it ease the pain, but it dulled the sharp edge of fear that was tearing me apart. I pulled the blanket up to my chin and felt the warmth consume me.

Hours later, pushed into wakefulness by painful spasms in my groin, I opened my eyes. It was dark. Groping for reality, abject terror took over until I remembered where I was and what was happening to me. Muffled murmurs from the bedroom and the creaking bed springs confirmed what I'd suspected for some time. CeeCee and Mina were lovers. Even though I had noticed their closeness, the way they touched each other, the endearing looks that flashed between them, I hadn't been able to accept it, but there it was. Strange. I didn't feel any shock listening to their passion behind the closed curtain.

"*Mon Dieu! Mon Dieu!* Oh, Mina, *ma chérie*,"

CeeCee's voice came in breathless gasps. Mina murmured softly, but I couldn't make out the words. When all was quiet, sadness overwhelmed me, and I felt forgotten and terribly alone.

The reflection of the moon on the brick wall outside the kitchen window was the only light in the apartment. The gripping spasms grew stronger. Then there was a searing pain in my abdomen. I felt a surge of hot wetness and made a dash for the toilet. The rest of the night was filled with the agony of rushing back and forth from my couch to the old water closet. In the early light of morning, doubled over with pain, I passed alarmingly large clots into the bowl and came face to face with the fact that I might die.

Tante had promised I'd be all right, but what if she were wrong? I had never seen such clots before. I pictured myself dying there in the dark, sitting alone on the ancient wooden toilet seat while Mina and CeeCee made love in the other room. Self-pity overwhelmed me. I wanted to call out to them, but I didn't. Then a tremendous cramp bore down on me, and I watched a gray lump fall from my body into the bowl. I wondered if that was the embryo. I felt like I was going to faint. Finally, I staggered back to the couch. The bleeding was heavier than ever, but I was relieved to see it was dark in color. I had read somewhere that hemorrhaging was indicated only when bright scarlet appeared.

It was dawn when I finally felt the catheter work its way out of me. I staggered into the kitchen with the ugly instrument of my salvation, wrapped it in a piece of newspaper, and threw the awful thing into the garbage can under the sink. Cold light was filtering through the kitchen window as I reached for the bottle of aspirin. I took three and hoped they'd stay down. The pains were easing some, and I wondered if it was really all over. Falling back onto the couch, I let myself drown in the merciful ocean of sleep.

31

MINA ARENHOLT—Letting Go

When I opened the door to the apartment I knew something was wrong. The place was too quiet. I was sure CeeCee would be home before me. She'd gone up to Harlem to spend Thanksgiving with her mother. I'd spent my two days off in Astoria with Aunt Willie. Things hadn't been going well with CeeCee and me lately. It all started the week Chana stayed with us after her abortion. CeeCee had begun spending most of her evenings at The Lauralie in the company of Tinka and Joan from the Group. Hanging out in gay bars was CeeCee's way of handling turmoil.

During Chana's recovery I'd made a point to be with her as much as possible, to help her feel she wasn't alone. After work I'd cook supper for us, and we'd talk until it was time to turn in. Even at that time I think my heart knew what my head refused to understand about CeeCee. Part of me insisted it couldn't be happening, but a small bothersome voice kept whispering, *Life with CeeCee is coming to an end.*

I couldn't forget how CeeCee was unwilling to listen to my pain over Katy's death. I hardly knew how to address the guilt and agony hanging over me at that terrible time. I'd tried every way I could to make CeeCee understand how it had been with Katy and me, but she said she wasn't interested in tales of lost loves. "Let the dead bury the dead," she'd said.

One night during her stay with us Chana took me in her arms after I broke down. I sobbed as I told her of that gray day in the lonely cemetery, and Chana and I talked that night like CeeCee and I had never done. The possibility of life without CeeCee had troubled me for quite a long time, but in my heart I knew a breakup was going to happen sooner or later. It helped talking to Chana. There was a warmth in her I'd never found in CeeCee. Chana told me about her life in Brooklyn and about her unbelievable Hasidic marriage. Our intimacy during those evenings together dulled my heartbreak over CeeCee's obvious unconcern and cooling passion.

Now as I walked through the dark living room, the quiet hung in the air like a living presence. Trying to dissolve it, I went into the kitchen quickly and switched on the light. Oh, God. There it was on the table. A plain white envelope propped up between the sugar bowl and the salt shaker. I stared at it, not wanting to touch it. I knew if I picked it up, it would validate its reality. I was an actor in a second-rate melodrama. My knees shook. *There must have been something I could have done to prevent this,* I told myself as my trembling fingers finally broke the seal. CeeCee's precise and slanting script danced blithely across the page:

Heard from Babe last week. She's writing a column for an American newspaper in Cuernavaca. Says it's a great place to live and there's a job waiting there for me if I want it. So I'm off to Mexico.

We never spoke about it, but we both know it's over and time to move on. Better this way, ma petite. *Have a good life,* chérie.

I'll always remember,
CeeCee

Crushing the note in my fist, I threw it in the fireplace. It lay curled in the grate, a wounded white thing against the chunks of black coal. Trembling, I lit a cigarette, then touched the burning match to it and took a deep drag as I watched it flame and turn to ash.

That night I mourned for CeeCee alone in the big iron bed, lost in a wilderness of grief like I'd never mourned Katy. This was physical. CeeCee and I had lived together for six months. We had been part of each other. Now the CeeCee part of me was gone. The worst, however, was remembering we'd said it was "forever." Without CeeCee, the place called *tomorrow* was too painful to even contemplate, so all through that long night I focused only on *yesterday,* reliving all our precious moments there in the dark. The heartbreak of holding on seemed easier than that of letting go. Just the thought of connecting again with another human being was frightening. For the second time in my life, love had been snatched away—and I was helpless. I knew there was nothing I could do to change what had happened, so I wept.

32

MINA ARENHOLT—THE BAR SCENE

Four days had passed since I'd found the note that brought my world to an end. The psychic discord of the awful event still tore at my heart. I kept thinking there must be something I could do to end this agony.

At times a cold fury started behind my eyes; it froze, grabbing all reason from me.

That night, when sleep was impossible, dawn found me wandering Macdougal Street. I passed the night in Washington Square sitting on one cold bench after another, full of anger and rage. I paced the predawn smothered in the cloud of my own pain, until finally exhausted, I dragged myself up the stairs to the dark apartment and fell into bed. As I closed my eyes I knew it was only an hour or so before I'd have to dress and face the ride uptown to work.

When I reported in it was obvious the girls knew about CeeCee's departure for Mexico. She'd turned in her notice the week before and had said nothing to me about it. Pretending I knew was hard, but I kept on smiling and said I was glad she'd gotten the opportunity to go.

Their sidelong glances ravaged me, but I added bravely, "She was a great roommate. Lots of fun. I'll miss her." I was determined not to let the hurt show.

The next night, Tinka's call was a lifeline thrown to my drowning. Her voice, overdrawn with cheerfulness, assaulted my depressed state. "Hey, Mina. Joan and I thought we'd make a night of it. Want to come along?"

Grateful for the invitation and not wanting to face another endless night alone, I said OK. The two of them came by and picked me up around 7 o'clock. Tinka's frank eyes measured me. "You look like hell," she said. "It's about time you got out of the apartment." Joan gave me a hug, and we took off for The Lauralie.

As we settled at a table, Joan said, "There are plenty of women to choose from here. All you have to do is take your pick, Mina."

I looked around and shuddered. I really hated this sort of thing. I didn't know why I even came. Gay bars had always made me uneasy. Deep down they reminded me of what I was, making me feel guilty and uncomfortable in my own skin. I lit a cigarette and tried to look casual. Queers came in all sizes, shapes, and colors. Queers could be rich, poor, "butch," or "femme." Like drinkers, they were terribly insecure. Some were quiet and shy, others full of boast and rhetoric. The tough ones sported stubby, black combs in the back pockets of their tight pants, wore sturdy shoes, and slicked their hair back like men.

I took a long drag on my cigarette and let my thoughts continue. They hustled drinks, their voices reverberating in the dark recesses of the room. Some hiked up their shoulders like marines, ran hands over their crotches, and seldom made direct eye contact.

Femmes came in all categories too, from voluptuous to vulgar. Some were even demure. They wore their hair like Veronica Lake and kept their eyes cast down. Others were blatant sex machines with fake eyelashes, dark lipstick, and push-up bras. They'd lean over the table to make sure their cleavage was seen as they languidly sipped daiquiris and smoked exotic Murad cigarettes.

I surveyed the room. The Lauralie was strictly lesbian. It was favored by the Group because it was relatively quiet and less threatening than the Tender Trap or Tony's over on Bleeker Street. I remembered the hostess at the Trap. She was called Dara and prided herself on being a loose version of Jean Harlow. White-blond and blowsy, her job was to see that all glasses were full and that the women didn't paw each other too obviously or duck into the rest rooms for sex. She enforced the rules, kept order, and saw that the jukebox kept playing.

There was a gay bar over by NYU called Sappho's, which was famous for its drag queen hostess, Lollie LaToure. Dressed in sequins and ostrich feathers, Lollie called everyone *ma petite* and stared suspiciously at you through outrageously long blue eyelashes. She ruled over a world turned upside down where men dressed as women and danced with women dressed as men. Butches in various stages of machismo gyrated with their femmes on a tiny dance floor. Loud and smoky, it was a zoo of grinding pelvises and it didn't close until after 4. I'd gone there with CeeCee one night. She was intrigued by the atmosphere, but the place turned my stomach. We never went back.

In comparison, The Lauralie was almost ladylike, but I didn't feel comfortable in any of the gay bars, and once again I found myself wondering what I was doing here. Nervously I fished in my purse for another cigarette.

Joan and Tinka left the table to dance as "I'll Never Smile Again" drifted across the dance floor. Frank Sinatra caressed the words with such tenderness, I felt my heart

would break. *"Until I smile at you, I'll never love again...."*
Oh, God, he was singing directly to my own heartbreak. In
the dim light couples nestled cheek-to-cheek as they swayed
to Tommy Dorsey's music. I couldn't just sit there listening.
If I did, I knew I would cry, so gulping down the hurtful
lump in my throat, I got up and went to the bar for another beer even though I hated the stuff. Too many bad memories came with its malty taste. I'd make this one last all
evening, I told myself.

Back at the table I lit up another cigarette, trying to
look like a regular who was used to the nightly search for a
flickering eye. I was feeling more and more like a fish out of
water and had just about made up my mind to split and
walk home when the proprietor, Big Lu, dressed in a large-
flowered muumuu, came swaying over and sat down.

"You lonesome, honey?" Her bangle bracelets clinked
as her hand covered mine. "For a fiver I can bring a real
pretty filly over to keep you company."

"Well, I was just about to leave," I stammered, but Big
Lu was already on her feet.

"Don't go, honey. I'll be right back."

I couldn't breathe. Oh, God, what was I getting into?
When Big Lu came back she said, "You can pay me now."

Before I knew it, I had my wallet out of my purse. Big
Lu grabbed the bill from my hand and disappeared again in
the direction of the bar.

Holy Jesus, I've lost my mind for sure. A drop of
sweat inched its way down between my breasts, and my
mouth went cotton-dry. I took a swallow of beer and tried
desperately to appear casual. It wasn't long before Big Lu
was back with a girl in her early 20s. She was bird-thin
with dark hair teased into an immense pompadour that

accentuated her coarse features. Her eyes were expressionless and sullen.

My face felt stiff, but I managed a limp smile that she didn't seem to notice at all. She was carrying a large purse, a cigarette, and a tall drink. Big Lu looked at me and said, "This is her. Dolly, baby, this is—what's your name, honey?"

"Mina," I said, going clammy all over.

"Well," Big Lu chirped, "here's Dolly. Dolly, this is Mina. Now you kids have fun!" With a conspiratorial wink, she took off in the direction of the bar.

Dolly sat down, moving her chair close to me. I wanted to pull away; instead I froze. *I can't sit here and do nothing*, I thought. But what to say next? I didn't seem to have any words left in me. After a long, awkward pause I said, "So, you're Dolly. Dolly what?" That was all I could manage.

"Just Dolly." Her eyes narrowed.

"Oh! That's fine. You been here long?"

"Yes, out in the bar."

"I didn't see you when I came in with my friends."

"Well, I was there. I didn't see you either."

"You come here often?"

"Sometimes."

Another long pause, then, "Are you a friend of Big Lu's?" I asked.

Her face went blank. "Yeah, sort of." She stubbed out her cigarette and took a long gulp of her drink. Giving no indication she was interested in my line of conversation, she pulled a small mirror out of her purse and proceeded to fuss with her hair.

I couldn't stand the silence so I asked her if I could buy her another drink.

"Maybe when I finish this one. You in a hurry or something?"

Just then the jukebox stopped playing and the silence closed in once more. Tinka and Joan came back to the table. Joan flashed a knowing smile in my direction. I felt my cheeks burn. I introduced them, and a brief exchange of banter followed. Then, turning to Dolly, I asked her what she did. She twirled the swizzle stick in her drink as if she hadn't heard my question.

Tinka pressed on, her question more articulate. "Where do you work, Dolly?"

"In a broker's office."

"Wow! That's great," Joan chimed in. "How do you like it?"

"What's to like? It's just a job." She dug a pack of cigarettes out of her purse. "You got a light?" I fumbled for my lighter. As she leaned toward me I got a whiff of body odor and Taboo so strong it turned my stomach. She took a long drag, and her thigh went after mine. Beginning to panic, I gave Joan a pointed look. "I've got to powder my nose. Want to come along?" Reading my meaning, she got up and followed me to the ladies' room.

"I've got to get out of this," I began as we stood together at the washbowls. "I can't believe I actually let this happen."

"She's a real drag all right. I get the feeling she hasn't been dealt a full deck. What are you going to do?" Joan smoothed her lipstick with her little finger.

"If you'll cover for me, I'm going to duck out of here and go home. Don't worry about me. You and Tinka stay and have fun, but I can't take any more. You both were great about wanting to cheer me up. Thanks for trying."

I pressed a dollar bill in her hand. "Do me a favor and buy Dolly a scotch and soda. I promised her another drink. Tell her I felt sick and went home. Hope the drink will get rid of her. If that doesn't do it, I'm sure Tinka can make it clear it's time for her to move on."

"OK. And don't worry about us. I hate to see you walk home by yourself." She gave me a hug. "You sure you're all right?"

I nodded.

"We'll keep in touch, then. Sorry tonight didn't work out."

Not wanting to explain to Big Lu, I avoided her on the way out. The cold air felt good, and I made up my mind to avoid gay bars in the future. I knew I'd find the apartment dark and empty when I got back. There wouldn't be anyone to talk with or to exult with, no one to share laughter with, or a cigarette before bed, but somehow it didn't matter as much as I had thought it would. CeeCee was gone, but a lot of the pain had already miraculously vanished. I just felt terribly alone as I walked back to Macdougal Alley.

Switching the light on in the bedroom, I sat down wearily on the edge of "our" bed. CeeCee and I never had the words between us when we needed them—not even to say good-bye. That had been the most hurtful.

Deciding not to undress, I reached for the comforter and was about to turn out the light when I noticed my green diary on the bedside table. I opened it to the page where I'd penned my last poem to Katy just a few short days ago. Finding a pencil in the drawer, I propped the pillows at my back and pulled the comforter around me.

All the losses in my life began to fly about my head like

so many gray moths. One by one I captured them and quickly wrote them down. Then, at the very top of the page I wrote: *Dedicated to CeeCee...the words we never spoke.*

33

HOLIDAY IN THE VILLAGE

"Come down to the Village over Christmas, Chana. I have that weekend off. We can cook a bird with all the fixings. It'll be fun." Mina wrapped her kimono tightly about her.

Warming her hands against her mug of coffee, Chana smiled. "I'd like that very much. I wasn't looking forward to spending the holidays in my room at the hotel."

They were sitting at a table by the window in the League cafeteria at midmorning break. Chana studied the leaden sky. "Looks like it might snow," she said. "It's sure cold enough. It was freezing in the studio. I could almost see your goose bumps, Mina. I don't see how you stand it these cold mornings."

"It was pretty drafty. I don't think the heat ever gets up to the third floor. Hope you didn't paint me all shades of blue this morning." Mina laughed. "About Christmas— why don't you come down early on the 24th? We can shop over on Bleeker Street for a small bird and all the trimmings. It's been lonely since CeeCee left," she added.

The wistful note in her voice wasn't lost on Chana. "That sounds great." She reached across the table and took Mina's hand. "Roast chicken is just the thing for the holidays. The 24th's the first day of Chanukah—you know, the feast of lights. We'll have a double celebration." Looking up at the clock over the counter, she said, "Hey, we'd better get back to class."

Later that afternoon they stood on the front steps for a moment before saying good-bye. Colored lights in the shops along 57th Street heralded the holiday; traffic moved slowly on the slick street. Blurring everything, flurries of snowflakes danced in the darkening light.

"I'll call tomorrow," Mina said, giving Chana a hug. "I'm so glad you said you'd come for Christmas." Then she dashed down the steps and was lost in the crowd on the sidewalk.

Walking back to the hotel, Chana waited for the light to change at Fifth Avenue. The wind off the river drove the snow into her eyes and stung her cheeks, but she still felt the warmth of Mina's embrace.

Chana had her strength back now. It had been tough getting back to normal after the abortion. At Thanksgiving Bubbe had come to town. Rose Solomon cooked a turkey, and they'd all had a wonderful day together. David's good news from the lawyers had cheered everyone. Her divorce was in process and would become final in a year. It had been hard looking into Bubbe's eyes that day. All Chana could think of was how hurt and disappointed Bubbe would be if she knew about the abortion.

Still grappling with a great deal of guilt and shame, Chana wondered how long it would be before she could put it all behind her and get on with life. She had written to Ben Frank the night before she went up to Harlem, explaining that a visit to D.C. was out of the question because she was down with the flu. There'd been no answer for several weeks, then only a card came saying he was off to Dallas for basic training at Love Field. His father and mother came to Quantico to see him receive his commission, he said, and he was looking forward to a long leave between Dallas and reporting for advanced flight training at Pensacola.

She was hurt, but there was a part of her that was relieved by his cavalier card. This ambivalence where Ben was concerned was puzzling because at times it seemed to crush all reason. One thing she knew for sure: She hadn't fully worked through the pain where he was concerned. There were even times when anger with herself completely overshadowed the anger at him for what he'd done that night in the rain, and she wondered at times why she hadn't said no. It didn't seem to make any sense at all, but that's just the way it was.

      ❧   ❧   ❧

The pungent aroma from wood-burning fireplaces spiced the cold afternoon air, and a wan sun bathed the old storefronts along Sixth Avenue. Struggling to keep up with Mina's long strides, Chana shifted the heavy shopping bag to the other arm. Her feet hurt. Her high-heeled pumps were making blisters on both heels. Mina had pointed out her mistake when they left Macdougal Alley. "You should have worn flats," she said.

Later when they finished their marketing, Mina suggested stopping at Bigelow's Pharmacy. "Time for a lunch break. Let's have some hot chocolate and rest our feet." There were just two seats left at the busy counter. With a grateful sigh, Chana set her shopping bag down on the mosaic-tile floor and climbed on the high stool. An elderly man smiled and leaned over the brass-trimmed oak counter. Mina gave him a broad smile.

"Mr. Ginsberg, I want you to meet my friend, Chana Stern. Chana, Mr. Ginsberg's the owner of this venerable establishment."

"Good to meet you, I'm sure, Miss Stern." Behind his

steel-rimmed spectacles his eyes sparkled with good humor. "What can I do for you two young ladies on this cold day before Christmas?"

"Hot chocolate and a cinnamon bun will do just fine for me." Mina took off her gloves and loosened her scarf.

"The same for me, Mr. Ginsberg." Chana made an approving survey of the ornate wood paneling on the mezzanine balustrade above them and the huge antique apothecary jars at each end of the long counter. "What a charming place, Mina. It looks very old."

"Yes. It dates back a century—1838 to be exact. This is one of the oldest establishments in the Village."

The pharmacy was crowded with last-minute shoppers. At the counter they were busy serving up hot meals. Chana sniffed. "Lord, what is it that smells so delicious?"

"Oh, that's their famous London broil. It's the special every Thursday night. How about us taking two orders to go?"

"Sounds fine. Then we won't have to cook tonight." Chana sipped the rich chocolate. "The Village is a wondrous place, so different from uptown. I think I might like to live here, Mina. It's another world entirely."

"I guess the word that describes it best is *bohemian,*" Mina chuckled, "although that word is sadly overworked, I'm afraid. Still, the place does have an endearing power to surprise and enchant."

Colored lights twinkled in the shop windows as they walked south. Eighth Avenue was alive with the melodious sound of carols issuing from each storefront, enticing shoppers to get with the spirit and spend.

Chana stopped for a minute in front of a secondhand furniture store. "Look," she pointed to a small brass menorah in the window. "Let's go in. It'll only take a few minutes."

The shopkeeper took the candelabra out of the window and handed it to her. "It's a fine piece, very old, miss. Only $1 since the holiday is on us already."

Chana hesitated.

"I'll throw in the candles, no charge. Light the first one in good health tonight and take this with my blessing." He dropped a string bag filled with gold-foiled chocolates shaped like coins into the paper bag.

"Chanukah gelt!" Chana exclaimed with delight as she pressed a dollar bill into his hand. "Thank you, and have a happy holiday!"

At the Macdougal Street market they made their last stop and bought a tiny fir tree from the display on the sidewalk. "I think that just about does it," Mina said. "We'd better get back to No. 12. It's getting cold."

When they got upstairs, Chana kicked off her shoes. Life was made up of many small separate incidents, Chana thought, and coming back like this to Mina's place on the first night of Chanukah was one of those she knew she'd never forget. Taking the menorah from the paper bag, she placed it reverently on the mantel. Adjusting the eight candles, she savored the warmth of the moment. *How lovely*, she thought. What a truly wonderful night, and how perfect to be sharing it with her dearest friend.

Mina brought a wooden crate from the kitchen. Placing it to one side of the fireplace, she set the little tree on it and gazed woefully at the bare branches. "We forgot ornaments. Poor thing, it looks so naked."

"How about the Chanukah gelt?" Chana emptied the string bag on the coffee table. "These will do just fine. You can call your Christmas tree properly trimmed, and I'll call it a 'Chanukah bush,' like Papa used to." They both laughed. Mina went to the bedroom to get a spool of thread to hang them.

After warming up the London broil, they ate off the coffee table in front of the fire. The pressed logs burning in the grate gave the whole room a rosy glow.

When she finished eating, Chana went to the mantle and held a match to the *Shammes* taper in the center of the menorah. Lifting it from its holder, she touched the flame to the farthest candle on the right. Replacing the *Shammes* candle to its central place, she watched the two candles for a moment as their flames grew steady and tall. Memories of holidays on Riverside Drive—when she used to light the candle on the first night—brought tears to her eyes.

Mina poured the Mogen David. It sparkled ruby-red in the old jelly glasses. She raised hers. "Happy Chanukah, Chana." Their eyes met, and the words caught in Chana's throat. "And a merry Christmas to you, Mina. I'm so happy to be here with you." She wanted to say more—her heart was so full—but those were the only words she could find.

A loud knock tore at the delicate fabric of the moment. Before Mina could reach the door, Tinka and Joan burst into the room. "We're going to the Square for the singing. Thought you might like to..." Joan's voice trailed off as she noticed Chana. "Sorry, didn't know you had company."

Tinka stood in the doorway, her eyes two question marks. She was dressed as always in her scuffed leather jacket and blue jeans. In deference to the weather she wore bright red earmuffs; otherwise she was bareheaded as usual.

Joan unwound her scarf and pulled off her gloves. Her round cheeks were rosy from the cold. After introducing everyone, Mina pressed glasses of wine in their hands. Joan admired the tree and stood with her back to the fire as she repeated her invitation, her glance now including Chana. "Would you like to go with us? It's a lovely, crisp night, and the stars are so bright. There'll be caroling under the arch in Washington Square. It's a Village tradition and quite lovely. You shouldn't miss it. Or maybe you two have something else planned?"

Almost too quickly Mina answered, "No," looking directly at Joan, hoping she caught her meaning. "We don't have any other plans." Turning to Chana she said, "How about it? A walk might be just the thing after our big meal."

"I'll get my coat." Chana disappeared into the bedroom.

Sparkling with amusement, Joan's dark eyes followed Chana, then looking straight at Mina she laughed softly and whispered, "Life seems to be looking up for you. Good luck."

Macdougal Street was oddly quiet. Their footsteps rang hollow against the rough cobblestones. There were no cars on the street. Apparently people were snug in their homes, tending to private celebrations. The whole Village seemed to be waiting for Christmas to come.

As the four of them neared the Square, they heard a faint chorus of voices lifted in song. The familiar melody, astonishingly beautiful, captured memories as it swelled in the cold night air.

Oh, little town of Bethlehem
How still we see thee lie
Above the deep and dreamless sleep
The silent stars go by....

There it was, the great arch bathed in lights. Singers with candles aglow gathered in the shelter of the majestic structure. The bare branches of the trees in the square were hung with twinkling Christmas lights. Whole families sang along with the carolers or just stood silently listening as the old songs filled the cold night air.

"How wonderful," Chana exclaimed. "Oh, Mina, I wouldn't have missed this for anything. I'm so glad we came."

The singing ended with a hushed rendition of "Silent Night" as the candlelight procession wound its way silently toward Waverly Place, and the crowd began to thin.

Slapping her arms about her body to keep warm, Tinka said, "Well, that's it for another year. It's getting awfully cold. How about ducking back to the San Remo for a nightcap?"

Mina looked at Chana, "We've had a pretty busy day, Tinka. Maybe we should get back to No. 12. Thanks anyway. We'll take a rain check on the San Remo."

As they started walking, Joan pointed to an old building on the north side of the square. "That's NYU, Chana, where I'd like to go to school." Parting at the alley with hugs and promises to get together soon, Tinka and Joan walked on south toward Bleeker Street.

Mina and Chana gratefully climbed the stairs to the apartment. It had been a long day and they were both exhausted. Only embers remained in the grate. The place was frigid. "It's too late to build up the fire again. Let's crawl into bed to keep warm," Mina suggested nervously, hoping her suggestions would not be misunderstood.

Waiting for Chana to come to bed, she pulled the covers up to her chin and gave herself to the intimacy of thought, recalling all she and CeeCee had meant to each other. Remembering the assurances they'd given each other—that their love would continue forever—made her aware once more that nothing was permanent. *Forever* was a dangerous word of no substance at all—and in the final analysis, inherently bonded to pain.

Lying there waiting for Chana, she remembered the openness, the naturalness of that loving. It had been a measurement against whatever it was she had called love in the past. They had cared tenderly and well, but there had been no one to suggest that intensity was not always wisely focused. She had wanted desperately to believe that love, once found, was all-powerful and indestructible. With Chana there was no denying she was facing again the flowering of passion, and it frightened her. *I'm like a starving woman who thinks food will cure all suffering*, she thought. *Once more I feel the hunger, and I'm afraid.*

Turning out the light in the kitchen, Chana came back to the bedroom. She stood for a moment by the side of the bed. "It's OK, my sleeping here with you?" She was hesitant, unsure of herself.

Turning back the covers, Mina said, "Of course, climb in. Where else would you sleep?" She had been afraid Chana would want to spend the night on the couch. She was sure Chana held genuine affection for her—that had been made clear many times—but beyond that, she wasn't sure. The thought crossed her mind that Chana might be confused about their relationship too. If that were the case, the best thing was to go slow.

She and Chana had never discussed CeeCee's leaving, and she wasn't quite sure whether Chana thought of CeeCee as just a roommate and nothing more. If she suspected they had been lovers, she'd never given any indication of it.

Chana snuggled under the covers and yawned. Mina caught the fragrance of Evening in Paris. "This feels good,"

Chana murmured. Mina turned out the light and stared at the stars shining through the skylight. Feeling the warmth of Chana's body next to hers, her heart began to pound wildly, for she knew once more she was anticipating that torturous journey into intimacy, and that meant she could be hurt. Among all the facets of danger lying ahead, there must be a way she could try for what she wanted without risking the agony of rejection. But these were uncharted waters. As she lay motionless beside Chana, aching to touch her and yet knowing it might destroy the sweet comfort of the moment, she prayed she could navigate these rough seas without courting a broken heart again. Chana reached for her hand and pressed it gently. "Good night, Mina. This has been a lovely day." Sighing contentedly, she turned over on her side and lay quiet. Caught in the web of Chana's breathing, Mina stared wide-eyed into the darkness, wondering what the new year might hold for them.

34

CHANA STERN—NEW LOVE

I stuffed Ben's letter, unopened, into my purse and sat down on my bed. Glancing at my watch, I noticed I was running late for my art class, but I had to think.

All week Mina had been foremost on my mind. Last night she had called about the vacant apartment below hers.

"It's up for rent," she said. Her landlady would hold off putting a sign in the window if I was interested. Lately we'd been talking about my moving to the Village. This was an opportunity to do just that if I liked the place.

Since Christmas I'd been on an emotional turntable. All I could think of was Mina and the closeness and warmth of our time together over the holidays. I'd never had such a feeling about another woman before and wondered what it meant.

Now after all this time of not hearing from Ben, suddenly he'd sent a letter. I'd been doing a pretty good job of drumming him out of my life, and I wanted to keep it that way. Reading his letter would only muddy things. Best to deal with my feelings about Mina first.

I should look at the apartment, I told myself. *I can take the train back with Mina after class*. "I'll do it," I said aloud. After actually hearing my own words, I felt better.

At first break we met in the cafeteria for coffee. "I'd like to look at the place," I said. Mina took my hand in hers and nodded. I felt my heart leap, and realized I'd just taken the first step in a long journey.

When Mrs. Rossi, Mina's landlady, opened the door to the apartment, I noticed the room was bigger than the living room upstairs. A generous window faced on the alley. "North light," I said, with approval. "This will make a perfect studio."

With a flourish Mrs. Rossi pulled down the Murphy bed on the far wall. Her gold earrings danced. "See, now thissa studio issa fine bedroom too. Only a flick of the wrist, issa pretty good, eh?"

The place was all one large room with a stove, sink, and refrigerator at one end. The toilet and bathtub were exact duplicates of those upstairs. The fireplace had been filled in, so one wall was all brick, giving the place a rather rustic feeling.

"You paint, yes? The gentleman just moved out, he was an artist too. I know you'll like thissa place just fine, Miss Stern."

I nodded, but so as not to look too eager I told her I'd consider it and let her know my decision by Sunday night.

"Only $40 a month," she added. "Of course, I gotta have two months rent in advance, you understand, and there's a $50 dolla' deposit for cleanup when you move out. You a nice lady, you be happy here. Knowing Miss Arenholt upstairs make it a fine for you, yes?" A smile broadened her plump face. After locking the door she dropped the key in her apron pocket, saying, "Until tomorrow. I'll hold the place till I hear from you."

As she left, we climbed the stairs to No. 12.

Mina went to the kitchen and came back with a bottle in her hand. "What do you think about the place downstairs,

Chana?" Feeling a little giddy, I sat down on the couch. "I know you're going to take it," she continued, handing me a glass of wine. "Let's drink a toast to your new life in the Village." Her voice softened. "I'm so glad you'll be just a few steps away. How lucky can we get?"

With an intensity that brought tears to my eyes, I answered, "I know, Mina. I feel the same way. But I wonder if *lucky* is the right word; maybe it's fate."

Mina's laugh played through me like fingers on a harp. As we raised our glasses our eyes met. I felt wonder dancing at the edge of my heart as I experienced the exquisite pleasure of her nearness. Time after time the same strange understanding had passed between us. Instinctively we seemed to know the other's thoughts.

"Stay over tonight," Mina said then. "You can see Mrs. Rossi first thing in the morning to close the deal." She opened the refrigerator. "All I've got is eggs and a brick of cheddar. How does a cheese omelet sound? And there's a heel of French bread big enough for two. That with the rest of the wine should make a fine supper."

After eating, we sat together on the sofa. Mina lit a cigarette, and we talked of art, poetry, the conduct of everyday living, and love. Mina shared with me her heartbreak over Katy's suicide. I told her of Papa's death, our move to Brooklyn, even the agonizing details of my marriage to Avrum, and the family's sitting *shivah* for me as if I were dead. Mina read some of her poems, and I cried with her when she read the one dedicated to Katy.

"You should keep up your writing," I said. "You have a real talent for the written word."

She looked at me with those marvelous green eyes. "You really think I have what it takes to be a poet, Chana?

A long time ago Katy said my poems were every bit as good as Walt Whitman's." She laughed softly, shaking her head. "But of course that was because she loved me."

"Isn't love the source of everything beautiful? Music...painting...? And most of all, love sings through the words of the poet," I said. Her face flushed charmingly and her eyes shone. My heart turned to pudding. "You're very beautiful," I said, suddenly amazed at my own daring. A moment of silence stretched between us. Then with a tenderness beyond expression, she reached for my hand.

"So are you, Chana." Her breath caught for a moment. "More beautiful than you know."

I had never heard words like that before. The realization that I had missed the best in life—someone to love me—all but stopped my heart, and I wondered why men claimed the supreme right to make such declarations to women.

       ʘ ʘ ʘ

Mina returned her diary to the bedside table, smoothed the pillow at her back and held out her hand. "Come, Chana," she said.

I sat on the edge of the bed. With her thigh against mine, my heart raced, and the smell of her was like sweet herbs. With a graceful movement of her hand, her long fingers traced the hollow at the base of her throat. The beauty of that gesture, so innocent and yet so provocative, stole my breath, and for an instant I wondered how the flesh there might feel were I to touch it. Possessed by a force I only half understood, I rose and with one quick movement slid out of my nightgown. Smiling, I held my hand out to her. Mina's eyes were two green pools waiting for my drowning as her fingers wound mine, pulling me to her. She straightened, and I gently lifted her nightgown over her head. In the circle of light I saw the small, firm breasts I had painted so many times. The nipples blossomed like young rosebuds. Our eyes met, speaking a tenderness our lips could not form. She guided my hand to her left breast and I felt her heart beating strong and fast under my fingers. Falling back among the pillows, my senses spun at the wonder of that soft, white skin. Her lips opened to mine. With a terrible urgency my body responded to the touch of her warm flesh. I reached to turn out the light, but her hand stopped mine.

"No," Mina whispered in the curve of my ear. "In the light, Chana. In the light, my love."

35

MINA ARENHOLT—THE CONFRONTATION

There it was in faded gold letters on the glass door: RADCLIFF, NUSBAUM, AND DOYLE. The corridor was poorly lit. The Tanner building's dark paneling gave off a musty odor. It was obvious the attorneys on this floor were second-rate.

I opened the door and walked in. An elderly woman sat behind an old oak desk. "I'm Mina Arenholt," I said.

"Please have a seat, Miss Arenholt. Mr. Doyle will be with you shortly." She waved a thin hand toward a row of straight-backed chairs. Picking up a dog-eared copy of *Look* magazine, I sat down to wait for Aunt Willie. Our appointment was for 11 o'clock. The Regulator clock ticked noisily, its hands showed five to.

Gus was dead. He'd been found lying on his kitchen floor, apparently dead for a couple of days. When he didn't show up for work Monday morning, Leon went to the house and found him. The medical examiner's report said the cause of death was coronary thrombosis. I felt no emotion, not even relief. Gus was part of the past, and I'd put all that behind me many months ago. It was strange how I didn't even think about the bad times anymore. For me he died the day I dropped my key in the mail slot and ran off to Astoria.

The door opened and Aunt Willie blustered in, red-faced and out of breath from climbing the stairs. She gave me a quick peck on the cheek. "How have you been,

Liebchen? I haven't heard from you since Thanksgiving."
There was that familiar edge of disapproval in her voice.

"Mr. Doyle will see you now." The receptionist indicated we should go down the hall. "It's the last door on your right." She followed us with a file of papers which she laid on the cluttered desk. "Please be seated. Mr. Doyle will be with you in a moment."

We took the two chairs in front of the long desk. With disgust written all over her broad features, Aunt Willie surveyed the dingy office. Just as she was about to give her critical assessment of the place Timothy Doyle walked in, extending his hand.

"My sincere condolences, Mrs. Frome." Turning to me he said, "And this is the late Mr. Arenholt's stepdaughter?" His handshake was limp. He sat down, cleared his throat, and picked up the papers in front of him. "A sad day for you both, I'm sure," he continued sanctimoniously, peering over half-glasses. "Gustave was a fine—"

"Let's get on with it, Mr. Doyle," Aunt Willie interrupted impatiently.

"Yes, yes, of course. I was just going to say, the late Mr. Arenholt will be missed. He was a loyal member of the Knights of Columbus and a fine pinochle player, I might add." He glanced sharply at Aunt Willie. "I don't recall seeing you at the funeral mass, Mrs. Frome. Or you, Miss Arenholt. But then there were so many members of the brotherhood there I must have missed you both." Clearing his throat once more, he adjusted his glasses and began to read.

"I, Gustave Otto Arenholt, being of sound mind..." he droned on.

What it all boiled down to was that Gus had named me the sole heir to his estate, which consisted of the house on

89th Street, the bakery, and a modest bank account. The house was free and clear, the mortgage having been paid off some years back. There were a few small liens on the business, but they could be paid off when the bakery was sold.

I told Mr. Doyle I wished to sell the house and business as soon as possible. With an oily smile, he assured me he'd be glad to take care of everything and would keep me informed of progress on the sale of the property.

When we left the office Aunt Willie suggested we have lunch at the Brass Rail on Roosevelt Avenue. Over steak sandwiches and coffee she modestly confessed that she and Mr. Potter from the studio were an item now and planned to marry in late July. "We both retire then, and we're thinking of moving to Fort Lauderdale. Wish me luck, *Liebchen*." Grinning sheepishly, she added, "I guess I'll need it, getting married again at my age."

Although a bit taken aback by her news, I managed a smile as I took her hand and told her I wished her much happiness. "Florida is a wonderful place to live. I know you'll be happy there, Aunt Willie. But before you go, I hope you'll visit me. You've never seen my place in the Village, you know."

"Yes, of course. I'll try to do that," she said. "But I don't get to the city much these days. However, I'll do my best." Her good humor waned a bit. It was easy to see she still took a dim view of my living arrangement. To cheer her up I told her I was thinking of quitting my job at Schrafft's and signing up for classes at NYU in the fall.

"With the legacy coming my way from the estate I should be able to manage nicely," I assured her. "A degree in English literature sure beats secretarial school, don't you think, Aunt Willie?"

She nodded, processing that bit of information. "Yes, of course, my dear, but I didn't know you were interested in literature. Do you think you can make a living that way?"

She had mellowed considerably by the time we reached the elevated platform. Embracing me warmly, she took off at a fast trot for the D train as it came to a screeching stop. She made it just before the doors closed. I waved as her train started to move, then stood back to wait for my Express.

36

MINA ARENHOLT—IN RETROSPECT

As I settled in my train seat for the long ride to Queens Plaza, my thoughts returned to the wonders of my new-found love. Chana and I were reinventing the world together. She'd opened me to possibilities I'd never dared contemplate. I'd learned from CeeCee how to love, survive abandonment, and live to tell the story of that experience with a certain amount of flair. Now, sometimes at night, tears came as I thought how lucky Chana and I were to have found each other. It was as if we were of one heart and mind. Ours was a unique union for which both of us had already paid numerous hells.

Very much the lady, Chana's dark curls were always perfectly tamed, her makeup impeccable. She was extremely feminine in every way. Her clothes were flamboyant and colorful, leaning toward the artistic. I, on the other hand, had my "straight" clothes, sweaters, and skirts for when I went to work, but as soon as I returned to No. 12 I jumped into the comfort of men's shirts and dungarees. In winter I stayed cozy in turtlenecks and corduroy slacks. I loved the warm, secure feel of wool against my skin and the freedom of casual clothes.

Chana and I both found a virtue in being able to live well in spite of being poor. It took effort and ingenuity as well as a sharp eye for bargains from the stalls at the public market on Essex Street. Chana was always on the hunt for peasant skirts and full artist blouses in the shops on Orchard Street. Many Sundays we had passed the morning discovering goodies in that fascinating part of the Village.

To our best friends, Tinka and Joan, we were simply Chana and Mina, without any further definition. For the rest of our Group we were just another gay couple newly in love, maybe a little more peculiar than most, traipsing around the Village with notebooks and sketch pads under our arms. Often they asked us to join them at The Lauralie or the Chicken Roost, but we always managed an excuse.

Lately we had started going to the San Remo for wine and poetry readings instead of subjecting ourselves to the hassle of the gay bars. Staring at my reflection in the dark train window with the lights of the tunnel flashing by, I recalled the night at the San Remo when I'd gotten enough courage to read some of my haikus and one special poem, still unnamed, penned from the depth of my newfound love.

Woman
touching another woman
my heart calls me
to the wisdom
of that first
raw second
of arousal

I offer myself
dear one and your eyes
shine back
filled

with the sudden
rush
of passion

a magic flower
unfolding
opening out
sweet and all-consuming
it holds us tenderly as we meet
the dark currents
of the world

Everyone had clapped when I finished, so I knew they'd understood and appreciated my work. After I finished reading Chana held my hand and whispered, "You're magnificent," and my heart swelled with pride. So, encouraged by Chana's praise and the acceptance of my audience that night, I planned to write more in an effort to earn the name "poet," in my own right.

❦ ❦ ❦

One Sunday morning early in May, the warm promise of summer filled the air. As usual Chana and I were walking along Rivington and Orchard streets looking for bargains. I spotted an ancient typewriter in a secondhand store run by a little man wearing a black *yarmulke*.

Bowing solicitously, he assured me that in spite of the machine's advanced age it was in perfect working condition. At $5.50 it was too good a bargain to pass up.

We took turns lugging the bulky thing back to Macdougal Alley. When we got it home we found that it was rather noisy, so I oiled it thoroughly and replaced the worn tape. After that it worked like a charm. In the evenings after supper I sat at the kitchen table searching for the right words to catch the essence of my thoughts. As I poked at the clattering keys and watched the letters leap to the page, I was caught by the ultimate magic of the written word. I really wanted to be a good writer. Chana had said I could be, and I hoped to fulfill her prophecy.

Chana painted downstairs as long as the light lasted. She'd given up her classes with Brachman during the week, but we still went to the League together on Saturday mornings. When I got home from the restaurant in the late afternoon I usually popped into the studio to see how her work was going. I watched as she scraped her palette and cleaned her brushes, marveling all the while at the grace of her astonishingly beautiful hands. Some evenings after supper we went back to the studio, and I posed for sketches to be used for her future paintings.

The change from "staying over" to "living together" was gradual, but in early April we'd made the major decision. No longer would Chana sleep alone in the Murphy bed downstairs. Every evening after her long afternoon of painting she joined me on the old sofa in front of the fireplace for a glass of wine before dinner. I found it glorious coming home from work, knowing the night was ours to share in the big iron bed.

Late one Saturday afternoon after we got home from the League, we walked over to Young's Hardware on Eighth Avenue and ordered a shiny metal mailbox tag with our names on it. We watched, reverently, as the machine etched the two names into the bright brass, feeling proud, excited, and a little scared. Our eyes misted and met.

Chana whispered, "How beautiful." She was trembling.

"I feel as if my heart will burst with joy and fly into a million pieces," she said in a small voice just for my ears.

I took her hand in mine and held it tight. "It's a sort of dedication, isn't it?" I murmured.

She nodded, and without a word her head found its place on my shoulder.

That joining of names became a sort of symbolic marriage to us. An irrevocable commitment forged in bronze at that moment. Without conscious articulation we knew "together" meant forever, even though there'd been no plighted troth, no ceremony, no papers signed. We were united by our love and our will alone.

37

MINA ARENHOLT—LETTERS

The day I got back from seeing the attorney with Aunt Willie, Chana was still at work. The pungent odor of turpentine was heavy in the studio. I loved that smell. It was so much a part of my Chana. She put her pallet and brushes aside and came to me. In breathless anticipation I waited for the embrace that always marked the apex of my day.

"How did it go? You look beat," she said. "Come sit and tell me everything." Smiling, her dark eyes held mine and my pulse quickened as it always did when she looked at me that way. Coming home to Chana was a real heartstopper and always a truly magical experience.

I collapsed on the small couch and lit a cigarette. She nestled close as I told her what the attorney had said. "And how was your Aunt Willie?" she asked. Her curls brushed my cheek. As her head rested on my shoulder I caught the faint pine scent of her shampoo and buried my nose in the soft ringlets.

"She's fine," I said, "and ready for the altar again. Can you believe it? She's retiring and so is Mr. Potter. They're getting married and plan to move to Florida. It'll be a good match. I'm happy for her. She's worked so hard all her life. She deserves happiness and companionship in her old age. Fort Lauderdale is just the place for them."

"I'm finished for the day," Chana said, jumping to her feet. "Let's go upstairs and relax."

"Did you pick up the mail?"

"No," she said as she locked the studio door.

Reaching in the box, I pulled out an assortment of advertisements and the gas and electric bill. There was also a large envelope addressed to Chana Stern. The globe and anchor and Ben Frank's name were in the left hand corner. The postmark read EGLIN FIELD, FLORIDA.

My heart caught in my throat. The old familiar fear flashed through me as I put it in her hand. All of a sudden I felt cold. Without a word or change of expression, Chana slipped it in the pocket of her smock. Not missing a beat, she asked casually, "What's for dinner? I hope there's enough spaghetti left from last night."

Apparently she wasn't surprised to be hearing from him. How many letters had she already gotten from him? Jealousy, like a coiled snake, took hold of me. I tried desperately to push it away, but it was still writhing in the pit of my stomach as we sat on the sofa sipping our wine. Trying to put some distance between the moment and my fear, I told her of my plan to register for classes at NYU in the fall. "I'll quit work in September. I still have the money I put away for secretarial school. That should be enough to carry me until I receive my inheritance," I explained.

"I hope you'll have time to pose for me more often then, Mina," she said. "I want to do a series of nudes to go with my other work. Eli has promised me a one-man show next winter at the Harris gallery if I can get enough paintings together. Which reminds me, I think I'll do the Brachman seminar in Vermont in August. I'd like to have a few more landscapes to add to my collection. I think your going to NYU is a wonderful idea, Mina. I'm sure Joan can show you around campus and help you get registered. Have you talked to her about your plan?"

"No, I haven't, but I will when I see her for the readings at the San Remo Saturday night. Tinka's doing an article on poetry for *The Village Voice*. This will be the second time this month the *Voice* has commissioned her to do an article."

The evening unfolded, a passion flower, rich and full, from which Chana rose to me like a flame. After the loving, she lay quiet. A trace of a smile curved her lips. I rolled over toward her. Raising myself on one arm, I looked down at her love-flushed face and the dark mass of tousled hair. Bending to kiss a damp curl that lay close to her ear, I brushed my tongue slowly down the nape of her neck to where the covers met her shoulder. A sigh parted her lips. She opened her eyes at my touch, and murmuring under her breath she gave me her mouth once more. Nestling to the curve of my back, her arm circled my waist and came to rest on my thigh. I lay quietly listening as her breath slowed into sleep, not daring to move for fear of losing the magic of her nearness.

Unaccountably, then, the jealousy that had filled my heart as I placed Ben's letter in her hand earlier came over me again, and for the rest of the night I was pursued by the dark specter of abandonment.

The next day, I tried to suppress the anguish that seemed to be drowning the life out of me, but the awful reality wouldn't leave me. The "Ben thing" was an open sore, and Chana's silence only added salt to the wound. The question was, "Should I ask her straight-out or hold my peace?" Still, I had to face the truth; I was more afraid of her answer than of not knowing, so I stayed silent.

In the daytime, when I was working at the restaurant, I coped fairly well, but at night the burden of my "wondering" overwhelmed me.

38

MINA ARENHOLT—CAUGHT!

The late July sun filtered through the dusty window of Chana's studio. I slipped out of my cotton shirt, undid the buttons of my dungarees, and flung them on the sofa. Standing naked before my love, I asked, "Will you be starting a new canvas today?"

"Yes." Chana came close and took my hand. "You are so astonishingly beautiful, Mina. You take my breath away. Undo your hair and let it fall over your shoulders." She led me to the small chair. "The light stands still here. Sit relaxed and run your fingers through your hair. The sun catches you just right." She stepped back, tilting her head to one side. "That's it, my love. Now hold that pose."

Chana worked until the light was gone and the shadows grew long in the studio. After wiping her brushes, finished for the day, she came close to me. Her hand lovingly cupped my breast as she helped me on with my shirt. Her touch unleashed the familiar excitement, and I heard myself whisper, "Chanala, Chanala," as we sank onto the sofa. In a flurry she shed her blouse and skirt and our bodies met, each surface touched with each other's rapture. From our tongues to the tip of our toes, locked in a wild rhythm, we rode each other across the need of our desire together, then apart, until sweat sheened our flesh like sweet oil.

There had been many times in the summer when I'd posed for her like this, in the afternoon, till the light faded and she could paint no more. Then came the joining, the loving. My life was my Chanala, nourished by her beyond all expectation. Lying in each other's arms as we let our ardor cool, there was a loud knock on the door.

Chana looked at me in surprise.

I heard the latch give. Oh, God! We had forgotten to fasten the bolt. Cheeks flushed and eyes still bright from our passion, Chana clutched her skirt to cover her naked-ness. I wrestled with my shirt and leapt off the couch to find myself confronting Aunt Willie. Her large frame filled the doorway. A smile of greeting drained from her face as she saw me fumbling with the buttons of my shirt. *Dear Jesus, how am I going to get out of this one?* My cheeks burned. All I could do was stammer foolishly, "Aunt Willie..." as I grabbed for my dungarees.

"What's going on here?" Her words shot at me, and before I could say anything she let me have it full bore. "Mina Margaret, what are you doing? And who's this?" she spluttered, turning her wrath on Chana. "What are you two doing half-naked like this?"

Chana's eyes were pools of terror, pleading with me for some kind of answer, but I just stood there. Holy Mary and Joseph! I came up speechless, my heart going like a trip-hammer in my chest.

"Answer me!" Aunt Willie screamed, turning scarlet. A vein throbbed at her temple.

Miraculously, some of my wits returned, and in a voice I hardly recognized as my own, I said, "She's a painter. Her name is Chana Stern. I was posing—" Then my voice deserted me.

Aunt Willie's rage turned to disgust. Loathing twisted her mouth. "I knew you'd come to no good in this place.

Holy Mother of God! That I should see this shame and degradation. Perversion, that's what it is! *Gott im Himmel*! And I've seen it with my own eyes! You'll burn in hell for what you've become. You're no longer flesh of my flesh. I deny your very existence, Mina Arenholt." She spun on her heel and slammed the door behind her.

Turning, I saw Chana's ashen face. She stood dazed, arms loose at her sides, her beautiful dark eyes staring at me in disbelief. Her face was drawn in a mask of such pain that I thought my heart would break. Rushing to her, I folded her trembling body in my arms. "Oh, Chanala, my Chanala," I moaned, "I'm so sorry. Aunt Willie must have been confused when she saw both our names on the mailbox. I never explained to her that my apartment was upstairs." She leaned against me, then her legs gave way, and she sank to the sofa. As I fell on my knees at her feet, my arms circled her waist, and I buried my head in her lap. "Oh, God! Darling, it's all my fault. Please, please forgive me, my love." She was shaking. This was her first meeting with the hostility of the straight world, and I'd brought it on her.

"I'm here—nothing can hurt you." My words tumbled one over the other. "She can't hurt us. I won't let anybody hurt us." My heart turned cold as I looked up at her drawn face. I had to make her understand. "Loving each other can't be wrong." Now I was pleading to convince myself as well. "We have to believe in our love no matter what people think. Do you understand, Chanala? It's the only way we can survive."

She was crying without making a sound. I whispered through my own tears, "Please don't cry, beloved. Remember, I'm with you always. We can face them together. It's worth all the pain. You'll see." I had to give her the courage my own heart struggled for every day of my life.

Suddenly the old fear gripped me. Would I lose her? Could love be snatched away again because of the way it was—and always would be—for us? Looking deeply into her eyes, I steadied my voice. "It isn't easy, Chana. It takes great spirit and lots of heart to face what we are. You can do it, you *must* do it, just as I do. We can find happiness in spite of them."

Her breathing steadied and with a sad little voice she said, "Of course we will." Her lips met mine lightly, and I held her close until her trembling stopped.

39

QUESTIONS

Mina stood back studying the nearly finished painting on the easel. "Chanala, I love the way you see me. When I look at this painting you've done of me I see a person I'm not familiar with at all. Beneath the color and the shape there seems to be so much more. It's as if you see past my body to something intangible within me. It's almost mystical."

A secret smile curved Chana's lips as she took a half-empty pack of Chesterfields from the pocket of her smock. "Smoke?" she asked.

"Thanks." Drawing the green-and-blue kimono around her, Mina bent to the match. Inhaling deeply, she let the smoke drift lazily from her nostrils. They both dropped to the sofa, exhausted. It had been a long session. They'd started working right after lunch and now it was almost 6:30. The little studio was hot and the light was gone.

"You have an incomparable beauty, Mina. It's deeper than form and color. It shines from you with its own light. I see that and try to bring it to the canvas." Chana let her head fall back. She studied the smoke hanging in the still air above them. Both smoked in silence for a while. Every fiber of Chana's being was raw with the need to confront the insoluble questions that had been plaguing her since that terrible confrontation with Mina's aunt in the studio several weeks ago. With sudden resolve she turned to Mina. "Tell me," she began, "how do you cope?" The question hung between them for what seemed an interminable time.

Mina caught the urgency in her voice. She realized she was about to meet the demons that stood between them at last. Playing for time, she gathered her thoughts. "What do you mean, 'how do I cope?' Cope with what?" There was a pause; neither spoke.

Chana reached for Mina's hand. "With people," she said in a tight little voice. "The way they see us. The way they think of us."

Mina's eyes met the pain in her lover's face. The silence between them deepened as she waited for Chana to continue.

"I wanted to bring Bubbe up to meet you, Mina, when she was here on Sunday, but I was afraid. I kept remembering the way your Aunt Willie looked at us, the way she looked at me with all that hate." Chana's words seemed to explode of their own intensity. "I was afraid. I was afraid Bubbe would see us the way your aunt did. That's why I didn't bring her upstairs. I'm sorry if I hurt you." Tears welled in her dark eyes and her voice broke. "Can you ever forgive me for being such a ninny? It tears me up that I didn't find the courage."

Mina clenched her fists and braced herself. She had to concentrate all her effort to answer Chana's questions in just the right manner. She'd been wondering how long it would be before Chana came to grips with who she was. How she spoke now would be crucial to the survival of their relationship. She had to show her how to survive in the "straight world" without losing herself in the accomplishment of that tricky task. Lastly, she had to show her how to find happiness in spite of the odds.

Without uttering a word, Chana got up and went to the window. With her back to the room she stood motionless, staring out at the darkening alley. Finally, with a thin smile, she turned and in a small voice said, "I almost told Bubbe about us and what we meant to each other. I wanted to so much, but I didn't. She started pummeling me with questions before I could get the words out. 'Do you a beau? Have you met any nice men lately? It's time you were thinking of settling down with a good husband,' she said. And then, 'I'm not sure the Village is the proper place to find a steady young man.'"

Chana paused. "She did mention that she approved of the studio. *Quaint* was the word she used. I saw a lot of worry in her eyes, and her voice told me she didn't really approve of my living here. Then I heard myself going on about how I would meet 'Mr. Right' one of these days and for her not to be so worried. It was then I got sick of what I was saying and almost told her I had found the 'right one' for me when she nailed me by saying, 'Chana, an unmarried woman misses the best in life. The *kabbalah* says: *One who is not married is only half a person.* Your destined one is waiting for you. It is time you found your *Bechertah*.

"That's when I lost my nerve, and I knew I couldn't tell her about us. But you see, Mina, by not telling Bubbe the truth, I feel like I'm lying to her. I don't want to lie about my life, especially to Bubbe. It tears me up having to deceive her.

"With friends here in the Village, and especially the Group, there's no problem. Until now I never thought much about our lifestyle. I was happy and that was all. Then what happened with your Aunt Willie made me stop and think, and what I think worries me. Mina, I never realized I'd have to start lying. That's why I asked how you cope."

Mina went to Chana, taking both her hands. "I knew

you were in turmoil over something." And then speaking almost sternly, Mina said, "You'd better get used to lying. You can't go around telling your loved ones the truth. You've got to know that, Chanala."

Suddenly there was a tension between them they'd never felt before. Chana was trembling.

"I do know it, Mina, but I don't have to like it." Her chin came up.

"No, you don't have to like it, you just have to *do* it. You'll get used to it."

"But Bubbe loves me; she cares about my life. It's wrong to lie to her about something so important."

"No, it's not. It would be selfish of you to want to tell her. Can't you understand that, my love?"

"Why? When all she wants is for me to be happy?"

"Oh, Chanala, darling, you're so naïve. Don't you realize no one wants you to be the way you are? Most of all the people closest to you? I don't make the rules—it's just the way the world is. If you had told her, she would see you in a way that would destroy her love for you."

"I don't believe that," Chana said, lowering her eyes. "I'm the same person I've always been. Bubbe would understand."

"You wouldn't be the same person to her. Can't you see? You'd be a stranger, a queer."

Chana turned her face away at that word.

"She'd reject you, Chana, and think of you as a pervert. She'd despise us for what we are. You must face that. To tell her about us would destroy her love for you. You must have compassion for her."

Chana shook her head. "But I can't live this way. I don't understand how you can be so accepting. How can you act so unconcerned? How did you learn?" Her voice broke. "All this makes me feel so dirty."

"I'm not saying it's easy, but it's what I've found to be practical. You saw what happened with Aunt Willie."

"But maybe you underestimate your aunt."

"No, I don't. The way she reacted is the way it always is with them. In their minds there's nothing worse than what we are."

"But Mina, maybe she's only upset. Maybe she'll come around in time."

"No, she won't. Most straight people consider lesbians an abomination. They all think we're something unnatural, and that makes them afraid of us."

"Well, then, that's their problem."

"No, it's your problem, Chana, and it's my problem too. We must hide our feelings. We have to take the responsibility to protect our love. Can't you grasp what I'm saying?"

She shook her head, "It's so hard, Mina." Tears streaked her cheeks.

"Chanala, I told you a long time ago—I don't make the rules. It's just the way it is."

Chana looked away. In that moment she almost hated Mina for making her face up to the reality she had been denying for so long.

"Remember what happened to Katy?" Mina asked. "They sent her away because of what they saw between us, and she killed herself."

"Yes, I remember. I think I'm beginning to understand, but it's hard."

"Chana, you have no right to destroy the granddaughter Bubbe's always loved. So don't entertain any false ethics about telling her the truth. It would be too cruel. What she doesn't know can't hurt her. Sometimes compassion must overrule honesty."

"Doesn't being a lesbian bother you?"

"No. Being a lesbian doesn't bother me. It's hiding it that's the problem. But I've learned to live with it."

Chana shivered. "Sometimes I feel it's a virus that spreads and rots the very core of my being. It's like an air bubble. When you're drowning you stick your mouth in it for one last breath. That's how you've lived with it, isn't it? I guess I can learn to live that way too, but it makes the world seem so small, Mina."

"That's not true. I can live in two worlds easily because you're my life, and I'll protect our love at all cost. If you want our love as much as I do, you'll be able to do it too."

Their eyes locked for an instant, and Chana knew Mina was right.

40

CHANGES FOR CHANA

Irritating grains of misery continued to rasp at Chana for weeks after she and Mina had talked in the studio that late summer afternoon. A razor's edge between right and wrong cut across her conscience more and more. Also, Ben's letters had become a problem. She found herself heading for the mailbox before Mina got home so she wouldn't have to explain their correspondence. At first she hadn't answered his letters, but when they kept coming she'd finally given in. It seemed harmless enough. He said he missed her, so she rationalized by telling herself it was her patriotic duty to keep a lonely serviceman happy. She kept her letters light and impersonal, writing only of local news, purposely ignoring and not responding to the words of endearment that closed each of his letters.

Her extreme suffering over the abortion had lessened. She hadn't forgiven Ben for that awful time in her life, but by putting those thoughts behind her, it had become easier as time went by. After all, she was partly to blame for what had happened, she reasoned.

Since the talk with Mina, the foremost questions in her mind were about her own sexuality. Sometimes she thought maybe she wasn't different after all. Keeping up the correspondence with Ben might prove just that. And maybe she wasn't even a real lesbian. It was true she had felt something for Ben last year. Because she loved Mina now, did that make a difference? She shook her head. It was all so confusing. She needed to put some distance between herself and the unsettling questions. She was looking forward to the painting seminar at Bennington. There she'd have time to think. An enormous need urged Chana now to take that time to be alone, without Mina and without the disturbance of Ben's letters. Perhaps in the country the truth about herself would be revealed.

Mina kept busy with her poetry and tried to ignore that something was wrong between them. They still made love, but the fear was always there just under the surface, waiting to take over. The verses she now wrote took on a somber tone. They dealt with life and death and mentioned very little about the quality of love.

Tinka spoke to Mina about the dark background she set her poems against. "You're showing a macabre mood these days, Mina," she said. "Is something bothering you?" They were walking home from the San Remo. That night Mina had read the revised version of her "Requiem for Katy."

Brushing aside Tinka's concern, she said, "There's nothing wrong, really. It's just that the world's in such a mess, what with the war in Europe and the talk of our getting into it. Perhaps it has darkened my perspective, that's all. Don't worry. I'll work through it and get on with some lighter work. You'll see." Mina found relief in the sensuous dance of language, working late hours at the kitchen table, shaping a series of verses dealing with the diversity of the human experience. One night she read some of them to Chana, who shook her head.

"Why do you write about such morbid things? Life isn't all that sad, you know." Chana kissed her cheek and whispered, "Come to bed now and let me change your mood."

She got up and followed Chana, leaving two verses still in the typewriter:

Searching the endless stars
gives no answer.
All that is said about it
Is not what it is.
The heart is a well of fire
Hollow and hot
swallowed by time
all turns to cinder and ash.

Lying naked in the dark
Arms empty
comes the insatiable hunger
to know who I am
and what makes us what we are.

∿ ∿ ∿

Tinka, Joan, and a number of others in the Group threw a spaghetti bash at No. 12 the night before Chana's departure for Vermont. Everyone had a hilarious time with many bottles of red wine and lots of singing. Joan brought her guitar and they rolled out all the old favorites until dawn found them exhausted and just a little drunk.

The next day Mina went to Grand Central Station with Chana to see her off. They caught a quick lunch at the oyster bar before walking to the lower level where Chana was to catch the Montrealer for Vermont. Joining the line of waiting passengers at Gate 16, neither spoke. Mina felt the weight of the awkward moment. Chana seemed to be reaching for just the right words to say good-bye. With a toss of her head, Mina pushed aside their silence and held

Chana in her arms. Smiling, she chirped, "Take care of yourself, love. I'll be here to meet you on the 20th." Kissing her cheek then, she lost all pretense and whispered in a broken voice, "I miss you terribly already." Chana clung to her for a moment and then without a word disappeared through the gate.

What a sad and tense parting.

Mina realized there had been many such incidents lately. The old familiar fear of loss was closing in on her now, closing in with a terrible vengeance. The thought that she might be losing Chana was almost more than she could bear.

The subway ride alone back to the Village added to her distress, and her eyes filmed with tears as she climbed the stairs to open the door to the empty apartment. Distraught to the point of exhaustion, Mina made straight for the kitchen, splashed cold water on her face and fell limply across the big iron bed.

41

MISSING CHANA

The next few weeks were full of changes for Mina. She heard from the attorney that Gus's house in Jackson Heights had finally been sold. Now with money in the bank, she gave notice at Schrafft's. The girls presented her with a genuine leather briefcase and wished her straight A's in her classes. Laughing, they said she was the first to graduate from Schrafft's and go on to a university.

Over at NYU Joan took Mina under her wing, guided her through registration, and helped to familiarize her with the campus. Mina found readying herself for being a student again exhilarating. It lifted her spirits and made the waiting for Chana's return somewhat less painful.

Tinka took time to critique Mina's poetry. She was helpful and encouraging. "You'll be a fine poet one day," Tinka said. "Your poems are strange but unique. I'll introduce you at the Harlem Writers' next quarterly meeting if you like. Joining that organization couldn't hurt. You'll get some really constructive criticism. Being a member will give you marvelous exposure, and it's just the place to meet established writers. What do you say?"

Mina agreed, and they planned to go together to the next meeting.

The days began to fly by. She joined Tinka and Joan at Coney Island and Ric's Beach when the Village got unbearable and steamy hot. The summer was ending with the usual heat wave so typical of New York.

During the last few weeks before Chana's return, Mina opened No. 12 to the Group. They considered it a second home. A constant stream of young women flowed in and out of the apartment. Most of them, unfortunately, were in varying stages of distress. One in particular, Chablis, a junior at City College, was having a bad time of it at the hands of an abusive lover. She decided to run off to California. Everyone thought it an unusual and bizarre thing for her to do. She hid out at the apartment for a few days until her plane left for the coast. Mina thought her very daring but at the same time very foolish to quit school like that.

When No. 12 wasn't cluttered with people from the Group, Mina wrote. Those nights were filled with the limping clatter of her battered old typewriter.

One dusky September evening Mina found herself walking the familiar streets, talking softly to Chana as if she were there walking beside her. She came back to the apartment and wrote:

> *That night we walked the cobbled streets*
> *and drank at the bar till it closed*
> *I wore a red shirt and jacket*
> *We swallowed red wine*
> *Your lips were stained scarlet*
> *I wanted to place red kisses*
> *In that hollow of your throat*
> *instead I just smiled at you*
> *across the checkered tablecloth*
> *Leaving, I pulled you along*
> *by your scarf tassels,*
> *kept pulling you toward me*

until our lips met
forming the only warmth in the icy air
All my longings were revealed to you
the bar is gone now
but those footprints on the cobblestones
are your tracks through my life
On winter nights I stand where we kissed
and remember.

Mina wrote at the top of the page "To Chana," and pulled the sheet of paper from the machine. Folding it neatly, she tucked it in an envelope. She'd leave it on Chana's desk along with the mail in the morning.

Tomorrow was the day. She'd be meeting Chana's train at noon and the waiting would be over. That night she lay for a long while watching the stars through the dusty skylight. Sleep evaded her mercilessly. The room was hot. She got up and went to the kitchen for a glass of milk. Lighting a cigarette, she climbed back in bed.

Sometime later her dreams were wrapped in strange combinations of hope and despair. Her fitful sleep finally surrendered to the pale light of morning, and she awoke to the day she'd been waiting for so long.

42

FEELING MORE COMFORTABLE

Chana hugged Mina. "Oh, it's so good to be home," she said. She looked rested and tanned, and several rolls of canvas were strapped to her suitcase. Apparently she'd done a lot of work. On the subway ride downtown she gave Mina a running account of her days in Bennington. She was flushed with enthusiasm over the work she'd accomplished.

Mina couldn't help noticing the first thing Chana did when they arrived at No. 12 was check the mailbox. *Is she looking for a letter from Ben?* Mina wondered. It was lucky none had arrived while she was away, because if one had, Mina thought, she might have been tempted to destroy it. Feeling immediately guilty for entertaining such ideas, Mina said, "I picked up all your mail, Chana. You'll find it on the desk by your phone, along with something I wrote for you. Come upstairs when you're ready. I made iced tea and sandwiches." Giving her a quick kiss, Mina fled up the stairs.

❧ ❧ ❧

That golden August of 1941 was filled with excitement and promise for the coming winter. Chana was seeing to the framing of her paintings for her show at the Harris Gallery. Eli had been delighted with the landscapes she brought back from Vermont and promised her a date in late February for a one-woman show. Mina was preparing for her classes at NYU, which would start the week after Labor Day.

Often the four of them—Joan, Tinka, Mina and Chana—made the bar scene at the San Remo for poetry readings. Life had so many new meanings now. At Tinka's urging, Mina sent several of her poems to a magazine for lesbians. Unfortunately, their prompt return was accompanied by a standard rejection slip which crushed her, but Tinka raised her spirits by saying: "All great writers collect dozens of rejection slips before they make their mark in the literary world, Mina. You should frame these as mementos since they're your first."

As the days grew shorter, the Group started descending on No. 12 for Saturday night get-togethers, bringing in Chinese or Italian. There were long discussions about Gertrude Stein's work and the cryptic writings of the literary world's newest darlings, Dorothy Parker and Alexander Woollcott. Much speculation erupted over the meanings of Virginia Woolf's *Orlando* and *To the Lighthouse*. Some evenings, the flow of red wine impassioned arguments over Marxism, which was becoming rather fashionable. Toying with the idea of communism was the latest thing. Experimenting with reefers was limited to the bolder members of the Group. After her first drag, Mina said, "It makes me nauseous, not high." Passing it to Tinka, she took off for the john.

Chana shook her head when they offered her one. "No thanks. The smell makes me sick."

There was a lot of talk about the new word *gay*. Two colored sisters—Danny from Jamaica and Leta from Puerto Rico—preferred the word *dyke* and said it fit them better.

They didn't want to be called *gay girls*. Most were leery of the way the term was used.

Joan pouted. "There's nothing gay about being a lesbian. After all, sex between women is as rough as it gets. For that matter, I don't like *dyke* either. What's wrong with just being *lesbian* and leaving it at that?"

In the intimacy of the big iron bed, Chana and Mina talked endlessly about life. It seemed there was never enough time to share all the pieces of each other that had existed before they met. As the newness of their love became more known to them, Chana marveled at how close they were becoming. The misgivings she'd experienced about loving a woman were now almost nonexistent. For the first time in her life she felt fulfilled and whole. Each day she savored the exquisite reality of being completely devoted to another human being. The realization that it was what she had always wanted, was an endless revelation to her. It seemed that for every secret hurt of Mina's, there was one of her own to match. Discovering this intense similarity was like unearthing buried treasures that each could share.

One night in late September they lay in the big iron bed watching a full moon play hide-and-seek with the clouds. One minute pale light flooded their tiny room; the next, darkness wrapped them in its soft intimacy. Chana felt the comfort of Mina's body, warm and fragrant next to hers. Under the covers she passed her hand over the now familiar places. For a woman who was spare and lean Mina felt ripe and full under her fingers. Tossing the covers aside, Chana bent her lips to the flat, smooth stomach, following down to the dark mystery of the rising mound beneath.

Mina's joy seemed complete. Only now and then did the old fears trace the words across her mind: *Ben's letters.* Chana never mentioned them, and Mina dared not ask for fear of what Chana's answer might reveal.

43

THE TRUTH

A late October sun gave little warmth as Chana hurried down Macdougal Street toward the Alley. It was almost 5 o'clock. She'd have time for a bath before Mina got home from school. The bag of groceries seemed heavier than when she left the corner market on Eighth Street, and a rough wind off the river made her dig her chin deep into the collar of her coat. Turning into the Alley, she noticed a cab parked in front of No. 12. That's odd, she thought. When she got closer her heart almost leaped out of her chest.

Dressed in Marine greens, complete with overseas cap and shiny gold bars, Ben stood at her apartment door, a duffel bag at his feet. He was writing on a small slip of paper and didn't see her. She called out his name in surprise. He turned. The familiar small-boy grin she remembered so well spread across his tanned features.

"Chana! My God, I was just about to leave. Thought I'd missed you. I was writing you a note, but here you are. What luck." He wrapped her in his arms, groceries and all. The cab driver shifted gears immediately. Ben's eyes crinkled. "May I come in?"

Speechless, she nodded.

He paid the cabbie and retrieved a large canvas suitcase from the backseat.

"What are you doing on my doorstep, Ben?" She finally found her voice as she fumbled for her key.

"Here, let me take your groceries," he said, lifting them out of her arms.

The cab pulled away and started up the alley toward Macdougal Street. Chana could feel his tallness behind her as she unlocked the door. Mina would be getting home any minute. How was she going to explain this turn of events? *God!* she thought. *What a mess. Just when all was going so well with us, now he shows up.* Ben and his gear filled her tiny studio. It was a sight she couldn't have possibly imagined even in her wildest dreams. But this wasn't a dream; it was real. She had to deal with it—and quickly.

He took off his overseas cap. "Great place, Chana." He seemed rather ill at ease. Lighting a cigarette, he settled himself awkwardly on the old couch.

She stood facing him. "All right, Ben, what's this all about? Hope you're not thinking of moving in or something." Laughing nervously, she tried to make it sound like a joke, but the truth was she was scared. Suddenly the past was falling in on her and she felt helpless. Too many memories, some good and some bad, were crowding her. Of course, this was her fault. He wouldn't be here but for her foolishness in maintaining correspondence. It was true she had kept her letters light and impersonal, but it would have been wiser not to have written at all.

She had to think. "May I have one of your cigarettes?" she asked nervously.

His eyebrow raised. "So you're all grown-up and smoking now, my Chanala?" His intimate tone and the familiar use of her name put her on guard. She mustn't let him think their relationship was the same as it had been a year ago. Her hand trembled as she reached for the ashtray. She'd have to watch herself.

"You see, it's this way," he continued. "I would have written or called, but there wasn't time. We got immediate orders to report to San Diego. I only have 12 hours before I have to catch a flight out of La Guardia. I'll be reporting for duty aboard the aircraft carrier *Enterprise* with 11 other officers day after tomorrow. We're taking 12 Grumman Wildcats with us, and our destination is a tiny island in the Pacific called Wake." Ben paused and flicked the ash from his cigarette. His eyes seemed to be drinking her in. "No telling when I'll be able to see you again, Chana. That's why you found me on your doorstep. I came directly from the station on the chance I'd find you home, thinking it might give us more time to spend together." He leaned forward, his face a study of sincerity. "If you'll come with me now, I'll call a cab. I only have to check in with my commanding officers at the Edison Hotel, then we'll have the whole night ahead of us. What do you say, Chanala? Will you spend these last few hours with me?"

His earnest appeal was destroying her resolve to send him on his way immediately. She had to think fast. What would Mina do if she caught him here in her studio? Looking into his eyes she knew she couldn't refuse him. After all, he was going overseas, and she may never see him again. But the most important thing now was to leave before Mina got back. She couldn't handle a confrontation like that. It would be best to leave a note and make her explanation later.

"Yes, I'll come with you," she said, "but I'll have to take these groceries upstairs to my friend's apartment. We were planning to have dinner together. While I'm gone you call a cab. There's a number pasted on the phone. The cab stand is only a couple of blocks away. I'll only be a few minutes."

Grabbing the bag of groceries, she dashed upstairs. There wasn't much time. After putting the things in the fridge she scribbled a quick note and left it on Mina's typewriter, then rushed back down the stairs. Taking a dress from her closet, she disappeared into the john to change.

Smoothing lipstick over her lips, she looked in the mirror. *I've really lost my mind. Oh, God, I hope I'm doing the right thing*, she said to herself as she ran a comb through her hair..

The cab honked just as she was putting on her coat. "OK, Ben, I'm all set. Let's go." Her heart was beating wildly as she locked the door. Ben piled his gear into the backseat as she peered anxiously up the alley and scrambled in beside him. Lord! She hoped they'd get away in time.

An uncomfortable silence ensued as the cab headed up Fifth Avenue. Ben sensed Chana was struggling with some inner conflict. Things hadn't been easy between them since he arrived, and he wondered why. He reached for her hand. It felt lifeless, but she didn't pull away, so he held it lightly, deciding it was best to keep silent for the time being.

Her letters hadn't been all he'd hoped for, but he had kept writing, feeling they might become warmer as their correspondence continued. This was decidedly not the same passionate woman he remembered. What had gone wrong? Seeing each other again hadn't rekindled the old magic. He was at a loss to know what his next move should be. Damn it, this might be the last time he'd be with a woman for God knows how long. Somehow he had to make these few hours count. He was beginning to feel rather sorry for himself. *No matter what, this evening had better shape up. I'll do anything to see that it does*, he promised himself.

⁂

Fifteen minutes later, the first thing Mina noticed at No. 12 was that the lights were off in the studio. *Chana must be upstairs,* Mina thought, but when she let herself in, the apartment was strangely quiet and only the kitchen light was on. She called out.

There was no answer.

As she dumped her books on the table, a paper propped up on the carriage of the typewriter caught her eye. Heart thudding in her throat, she snatched it up and read:

Dear Mina,

    Ben arrived unexpectedly on his way overseas and wants me to have dinner with him uptown. I'll explain everything later. Don't worry.

Love,
Chana

    P.S. I did the marketing. Everything's in the fridge.

An infinite series of impressions crowded in on Mina, transfixing the moment to one of terrifying apprehension. She had found CeeCee's note in much the same manner. Was she to be eaten up by abandonment one more time? *Just behind the miracle of love lies the inherent fear of losing that love one day*, she remembered reading somewhere.

She collapsed on the bed, her mind stretched to the utmost by a number of terrifying feelings of rejection. For a long time she lay there, alone in the dark, Chana's note crumpled in her hand. The hurt and disappointment were too much.

She went back to the kitchen. Opening the cupboard

over the sink, she found the bottle of red wine they'd been saving for a special occasion. Filling a jelly glass, she sat at the table and proceeded to down one glassful after another until the sharp edges of her pain began to blur. She had to face the facts straight on. Ben's letters had been a warning she'd turned away from and denied much too long. She knew Chana was torn between Ben's attention and the love they shared, but her leaving with him tonight showed she preferred his company to hers. That could only mean their relationship was in deep trouble. And yet all the while there was still a piece of her that kept insisting this wasn't happening.

Bizarre images of Chana and Ben together fought against the numbing effect of the wine. Psychic discord was ripping her apart. Stumbling in the dark, Mina threw herself back on the big iron bed to wait. Jealousy, cold as dry ice, throbbed behind her eyes. Finally, the wine overtook her, and she let herself be swallowed into the belly of the Beast as everything went dark.

›• ›• ›•

Chana was more than a little concerned by Ben's silence during the ride uptown. The whole scene was getting on her nerves. Confusion muddied her thoughts. How was she to play her role in this strangest of dramas? The disordered closet of her mind was empty of any solution as the cab slowed in midtown traffic. By the time the driver pulled up to the curb in front of the Edison Hotel she was tired of worrying about it. *What in the world am I doing here?* she thought over and over. *I must be going out of my mind.* All she could do now was play it out the best way she could.

The doorman opened the cab door. "Ev'nin', sir.

Welcome to the Edison." He picked up Ben's luggage and followed them to the front desk.

The small lobby was unpretentious. Commercial and moderately priced, the Edison lacked the elegance of the better establishments farther uptown. As Ben was signing the register, Chana faced the problem squarely. It would take some fancy footwork to survive the evening without giving him what he undoubtedly expected. Anxiety gripped her, and once again she asked herself, *What in God's name am I doing here? Lord, I can't believe I got myself into this.*

The desk clerk's bell summoned an elderly bellhop who seemed to appear out of nowhere. He gathered up the duffel and suitcase and led them to the elevator. On the way up the old man grinned and nodded at Ben. "My boy's a marine," he confided. "A sergeant aboard the battleship *Arizona*. Been on sea duty over a year. He says the scuttlebutt has it there's a big Jap buildup in the South Pacific."

"You don't say," Ben answered, watching the floor indicator over the door.

"Yup, there's all kinds of rumors flying around these days," he continued as they walked down the long hall. In the room, after pocketing his tip, he gave Ben the key along with a smart salute. "Thank you, sir. Hope you and the missus enjoy your stay."

Catching Chana's eye, Ben winked. The blood rushed to her cheeks. Turning her head, she deliberately avoided his mischievous smile.

Putting his things by the bed, Ben said, "I have to report to my C.O., but I won't be long. We're all on the same floor here." He took a folder from his suitcase. "I'll be back as soon as I can. Make yourself comfortable." At the door he turned. "I'm so glad you came, Chanala." Flashing her his wistful little-boy look, he closed the door.

Alone in the impersonal and rather shabby room, she tried to fortify herself for what she knew she'd be up against, but prospects for a happy solution looked dim. Rummaging through her purse, she found a squashed pack of Chesterfields. Her fingers trembled as she lit a stale cigarette. Inhaling deeply, she collapsed in the only chair, a gaudily upholstered affair that seemed oddly out of place in the stark little room. Three more cigarettes and about 20 minutes later she heard a key in the lock.

Ben opened the door, and his bigness immediately dominated the room. Unbuckling his Sam Brown belt, he threw it on top of the dresser, then, tossing his blouse to the bed, he came up to her. "Chanala, I can't tell you how much it means to me having you here." Putting his hands on the arms of her chair, he brought his head close to hers. Looking deeply into her eyes, he said, "I'm not kidding myself. If I come back from this tour of duty it may be only as another statistic. Flying these newfangled fighters is risky business, especially off carriers. Aside from that, who knows? The old man may be right; the Japs could be spoiling for a fight." He paused, and his eyes took on a faraway look. "No one can tell how or when their number will come up." He pressed a light kiss on her forehead, cupped her chin in his hands, and whispered, "It hurts like hell leaving you when we're together again after so long. It was a barren year with only letters holding us together."

Caught by all his earnestness, she felt herself slipping into uncharted waters.

"Chanala, we can be like we were before. Remember? *With a love that is more than love*, just as Poe said. To me you'll always be my Chanabel Lee, my beautiful star of the sea." He fastened his eyes to hers and stared at her in silence for what seemed a very long time.

All that had been light years ago, but she remembered—oh, yes, she remembered—the ecstasy and the agony that followed. She didn't know how to answer, and she couldn't tear her eyes away from his.

"Give me this night." His voice dropped so low she could hardly hear. She felt his breath on her cheek. "Chanala, I want to hold you, that's all. I won't do anything you don't want. You can trust me, you know that. I give you my word as an officer and a gentleman. OK?"

Were those tears that made his eyes gleam in the dim light? Her heart was skidding out of control. She was losing her grip on reality and sliding toward dimensions completely unknown. Her head came up. "Ben, please." Her voice faltered miserably. How was she going to get out of this? Or did she really want to? That was the awful question. Which Chana was she anyway? The Chana who loved Mina...or the Chana who had let Ben lead her this far astray? *Oh, God, help me. This can't be happening. It's more than I can handle.* A voice screamed in her head: *I'm drowning.*

Someone knocked at the door. "Room service."

Ben leapt up. A bellhop pushed a cart into the room. Chana straightened in her chair and primly smoothed her skirt over her knees. Did the bellhop know they weren't married? Did she look like a whore? She got up and went to the window. Lights glowed on a theater marquee across the way. The street below was slick with rain. *Great. Even the weather's against me*, she thought. Going out to dinner would have put some space between them, but now she was trapped with him in this awful room with its green-striped wallpaper and worn gray carpet. A Bible on the nightstand and a coin massage machine attached to the head of the bed completed the sordid scene. Ben flicked the radio on. Bing Crosby was crooning about it being June in January.

Turning angrily, she faced him. "Damn it, Ben. I thought you said we'd go out for dinner. Why didn't you ask me before ordering room service?"

He was opening a bottle of champagne. "This is much cozier," he said as the cork popped. "I don't want to share you with a lot of people in some noisy restaurant."

"But Ben, that wasn't fair and you know it."

"Here," he said, handing her a bubbling glass. "Don't be angry with me, my Chanabel."

Increasingly more nervous now, she gulped the wine. It just might help her to cope with what lay ahead. "May I have a cigarette?" She held out her empty glass. "And some more wine?" Keeping him busy and engaged in conversation seemed like the best strategy. "What sort of duty will you have when the squadron leaves the *Enterprise*?" She let the smoke drift languidly from her lips, hoping it made her look sophisticated and more in control. Getting him to talk was paramount, and it just might keep them out of bed. Lord! She was actually thinking they might end up there. "Tell me more about that island called Wake. Just where is it anyway, and why are they sending a squadron of fighters there?"

She sat in the overstuffed chair with one foot tucked under her. He rolled the table between them and perched on the luggage rack across from her. "Wake is a wishbone-shaped atoll made up of three small islands," he began. "They lie due west of Honolulu. It's a refueling stop for the

Pan American Airway clippers on their way to the Orient. There's even a hotel there that accommodates the flying boat's passengers overnight. The First Marine Defense Battalion and a number of civilian workers are constructing an airstrip for us there. We will augment the Marine defenses if the Japs become adventurous and try to take over the island."

He lifted the silver salver and sniffed. "This beef Stroganoff smells delicious." After spooning out two healthy portions, he filled the wineglasses again.

"Do you think they would bother with such a tiny island?" she asked, hungrily digging into the meat and pasta on her plate. The wine was boosting both her appetite and her spirits. "Would they dare provoke the United States?" She managed a trace of a smile. Conversation was the answer, all right. She just had to keep talking and thinking up more questions.

"The Japanese fleet is based in the Mandate Islands. It's pretty certain that Wake would be one of their first targets." Warming to the subject, he lit a cigarette and poured himself more wine. "We'll be training on shipboard off San Diego for a month or so. F-3s are new. No one has flown the Grumman Wildcats off carriers before. Practice along the West Coast will give us time to become familiar with the aircraft before we touch down on the island. Our squadron is VMF 211. We should make landfall on Wake sometime around the first of December."

His enthusiasm wasn't lost on Chana. She could see how much it meant to him to be a Marine flyer. Consumed with boyish excitement, his eyes shone at the prospect of the adventure before him.

Suddenly he got up, pushed the table to one side, and

bent over her. Touching his forehead to hers, his voice lowered and became intimate. "That's enough serious talk, Chanala." Pulling her up from the chair, his arms stole about her waist, then, straining his pelvis against hers, he backed her slowly toward the bed.

"No, please," she gasped, as the mattress caught her behind the knees. His lips devoured her protest, and they both tumbled onto the bed. "I don't want to. I—" her words were smothered by his hungry mouth. "No!" she managed to gasp. He was trying to pull her dress up. Furious now, she wrenched away from him, but he kept fumbling with her dress, trying to get it over her head. "Stop, Ben, I'm tired. Really, I am!" But, persuaded by the wine and not really wanting to make him angry, she ended her words with a whimper. Maybe she should just go along with him for a moment. She wasn't sure she could trust him, but he had promised with such sincerity that he wouldn't go against her wishes. What harm if she let him hold her? Trying to feel that mix of power and powerlessness—which is the amazing contradiction of sex—she decided to relax.

"That's my Chanabel," he murmured huskily, slipping her dress over her head and carefully unhooking her bra. Her bare breasts tumbled into his hands. "Gorgeous," he whispered, running his fingers over her nipples. Kneeling before her, he brought his mouth first to one, then the other as her body said no...well, maybe.

She was getting hot. Jesus! What would Mina think if she could see her now? The thought of Mina sobered her. She pushed Ben away and crawled to the far side of the bed. He followed, and she went limp under his hands.

"Just let me feel your body touching mine," he coaxed.

"You won't do anything I don't want?" She hardly recognized her own voice.

"No, I already promised you."

"I don't want to go all the way, Ben."

"Fine," he answered, sounding tense.

Feeling about as sexy as a damp dishrag, she relaxed and decided to stop fighting. He got up. "I'll be right back." She grabbed the bedspread and dove under the covers. The water was running in the bathroom, then he came back an stood by the bed. After taking off his shirt he stepped out of his trousers, which he folded neatly and placed on top of his suitcase. Chana turned her head, not wanting to look at him. All of a sudden he was climbing under the covers. In one swift movement he slid her panties off and kicked them down to the foot of the bed. Naked beside her, not saying a word, and all to the task driven, his hands started exploring her body. Burying his face between her breasts, his tongue found her nipples and she got hot again in spite of herself. Where she had been cold and resistant, now she was like warm honey under his touch.

Then suddenly she stiffened. His hand had moved to her pubic hair. She didn't want that, and clamped her legs together hard.

"It's OK," he said, pushing her legs apart. "I told you it's OK."

"I don't want to do it, Ben, please." She was crying.

"What's wrong with you, Chana?" He was getting angry.

"There's nothing wrong with me. You promised, that's all."

"Goddamn it. I'm not going to hurt you."

"But you said—"

"I said shit!"

"You did, Ben. You promised." Tears were choking her.

"OK, OK, I don't need a lecture." He was on top of her, kissing her, caressing her breasts, trying to warm her up once more. His pelvis pressed against hers. He was trying to spread her legs with his thighs. As if suddenly awakening from a stupor, Chana sat up, and with a mighty shove, pushed him off of her. Swearing under his breath, he grabbed her hand and forced it between his legs. "I want you to do this," he growled as he clamped her fingers around his penis. "Press hard." He started pumping her hand for all he was worth. The movement assumed its own rhythm. Open-eyed and numb, she turned her head to the wall and hoped it wouldn't take long to satisfy him.

Completely absorbed with himself and consumed by the pursuit of the final climax, he didn't seem to notice her at all. Automatically the movements increased until his body stiffened, then with a moan the semen flowed hot over her hand. Several shuddering breaths escaped him. It was over. He let go of her hand and rolled over on his side. The room was quiet except for the faint sound of traffic on the wet street far below. Not daring to move, Chana waited until Ben's breath slowed to a gentle snore. Then, after carefully searching the covers for her underwear, she left the tumbled bed and tiptoed into the bathroom. Locking the door, she ran the tap slowly so as not to awaken him. Using lots of soap she scrubbed her hands hard under the hot water. She splashed her face and breasts before putting on her underwear.

Back in the room, Ben was dead to the world. She slipped on her dress and gathered up her coat and purse. She had to get out before he woke up. He was breathing evenly now, his mouth slightly open; his dark head on the pillow looked for all the world like a tousled little boy's. She knew she should be furious with him for the whole humiliating evening, but somehow she couldn't bring herself to be angry. She'd come here with him willingly, looking for answers, and secretly hoping something would happen to clear away all her guilt and self-doubts...and it had.

"*Shalom*, Ben Frank," she whispered softly. "Take care of yourself." Slipping out into the hall, she closed the door quietly behind her.

44

BECHERTAH

A stinging rain washed the sidewalks; the gutters ran deep and a cold wind whipped the awning over the hotel entrance. The doorman held an umbrella over Chana as he hailed a cab to the curb. Giving the driver her address, she settled in the seat for the long ride back to the Village.

Right away the old doubts began gnawing away at the edges of her mind. It wasn't the first time she'd wrestled with these particular demons. An overwhelming skepticism over who and what she was had plagued her for many months. The disastrous encounter with Mina's Aunt Willie marked the beginning of these disturbing thoughts, and this evening's rendezvous with Ben had brought her once more face-to-face with the demons. *Am I willing to be what it is I am?* There was a truth lying near the heart of the question, she was sure, and somehow she had to find that truth...but how? Perhaps it was best just to accept the exquisite constancy of Mina's love and stop concerning herself over the label *gay* that came affixed to it. She'd survived the ugliness of anti-Semitism her whole life, so how could being called a lesbian be any worse? Why was one's personal identification so important to society anyway?

The more sophisticated members of the gay community called themselves existentialists. It was a fashionable topic of conversation amongst the Group. Many evenings rhetoric on the subject soared to heroic proportions as long as the wine and reefers held out.

Tinka, in her own direct way, explained, "An existentialist is one who believes in existence as the basis for all truth."

Lately Chana had been thinking of herself in that context, which brought her right back to the basic question: *What is truth*? Didn't *mind* often eclipse *truth* to serve its own agenda? What then? As an artist, she'd learned the maxim *Truth changes color with the light we see it in.*

Caught in the vortex and whirled to the very center of the dilemma, she realized now she must come to grips with her own sexuality once and for all. Mina had long ago ceased to quarrel with who she was; she accepted being gay with a natural ease that Chana envied and wished she could make her own. As far back as her early high school days, Mina admitted she'd been attracted to members of her own sex. So why was it that she, Chana, had never felt the slightest sexual desire for a woman until Mina came into her life? *Was that miraculous event an aberration*? she wondered. Something that had attacked her when she wasn't looking? A happening so random and unwarranted that its chance of reoccurrence was negligible? Or was her love for Mina the only real thing that had ever happened to her? And if that was so, then why did she keep questioning what was the very core and passion of her life?

Staring out the window of the cab with unseeing eyes, she focused on the inner visions of her mind. Then there was the Ben factor. Just over a year ago she'd thought she was in love with him. Their sexual adventure had brought only misery and pain. Looking back, she now realized there had been little erotic satisfaction for her in that union, and it could never be compared to the wonder she found with Mina. To go to bed and awake again day after day next to a woman; to lie with arms wound about each other, drifting in and out of sleep; to be with each other, not as a quick, stolen pleasure or a wild treat, but like sunlight in the regular course of life. Their very souls had merged, and the first time Mina had taken her to bed, she knew she'd found something beyond compare. Before that momentous happening she had no knowledge of what it meant to truly love another human being. She would never be sure whether she'd found love or whether love had found her, but it didn't really matter. Their loving that first night had been like coming home, and there had been no thought of whether it was right or wrong.

Only by her own foolish letters had Ben nudged his way back into her life. But she knew now that was finished. She would never see or contact him again. There was no way to justify her part in what had happened in that miserable hotel room tonight, but putting it behind her was the best way to lay it to rest.

You'd better choose your words carefully, she said soundlessly to herself in the darkness of the taxi. *You'd better have your explanation ready and plausible. And whatever you choose to tell Mina, one thing is certain: You must never bring pain to her again because of your foolishness.*

The cab slowed and the driver slid the glass partition back. "We're at Washington Square, Miss. How far up Macdougal Street is the alley?"

"Continue on Macdougal. I'll tell you when we come to the turn. It's only a few blocks now." To see better, Chana rubbed the steam from the window. The rain was drumming louder on the roof. Leaning forward she rapped on the glass. "The alley's the next turn on your left. Watch out, it's a real narrow street." She had to shout over the whine of the windshield wipers. "This is it. Stop here."

Fishing her mad money out of her wallet, she handed him a $10 bill. It had been a long drive with no possibility of picking up a return fare. "Keep the change," she said, feeling expansive and terribly glad to be home. Stepping out into the downpour, she made a dash for the stairs. When she let herself in, the apartment felt cold. Apparently Mina hadn't turned up the radiator. The kitchen light was on. Checking her watch she noticed it was 3:30 A.M. There was no sound; just the murmur of rain on the roof.

As she took off her coat, she saw a glass and a nearly empty bottle of wine on the kitchen table. Picking it up, she replaced the cork thoughtfully and quietly returned it to its place in the cupboard. Washing the glass at the sink, her mind churned uneasily. It was pretty obvious Mina had had a hard night of it. There were no dishes in the sink. Apparently she hadn't eaten any supper either.

Taking off her shoes, Chana padded to the bedroom curtain and listened. Mina's breathing was labored and heavy. Tiptoeing back to the kitchen, she undressed quickly. After washing her face with cold water, she turned out the light and groped her way back to the big iron bed.

She stood looking down at Mina's red hair tumbled against the pale pillow.

The moment was short, sharp, and incredibly poignant. She could just make out one limp hand resting on the white forehead, looking as if it had just pushed away some painful dream.

Under the power of the vision of her love lying there in the rumpled bed, Chana felt the exquisite pain of a heart breaking open. Carefully, she drew back the comforter and slipped under the covers to enfold the perfect form she found there.

Mina stirred, a muffled cry of half recognition parted her dream.

Chana held her close and breathed, "I'm home. No matter what, I'll always be here for you. I promise you that, my *Bechertah*, my destined one." Without waking, Mina nuzzled the warm curve of Chana's breast as the rain sang soft and steady overhead.

EPILOGUE

On December 7, Japan attacked Pearl Harbor. The next day their naval armada struck Wake Island.

Sixteen days after the initial strike, which destroyed all their planes, the few surviving airmen of VMF 211 took their places as infantry men alongside their fellow marines and continued to fight on foot.

The morning of December 23 they were surrounded, and every man of the one-time squadron was killed or severely wounded. Among the dead airmen was Second Lieutenant Benjamin L. Frank.

ACKNOWLEDGMENTS

With grateful acknowledgment to my friend and passionate mentor, Faith Berlin, without whose help this book would never have come to publication. Also, my deepest thanks to my excellent editor, Angela Brown, whose thoughtful suggestions pointed the way.